WILD APPLAUSE,
SCANDALOUS WHISPERS

The world's most powerful men and beautiful women were gathered in Vienna to celebrate Napoleon's downfall. Never before had one city been the home of such elaborate splendor and such intricate intrigue. And never before had so many illustrious personages been held in thrall by a single young lady.

Night after night the cream of the aristocracy poured into Harry Tyne's gambling house to see and hear his English songbird. Wild and wicked rumors flew about the true identity of this incredibly lovely creature—while the most lascivious lords and handsome gallants of Europe plotted to make her their conquest.

Letty Montressor had the whole world at her feet—except for the maddening man who made her his puppet and held her by her heartstrings. . . .

LETTY

Love . . . mystery . . . blackmail . . . danger . . . all are ingredients in this latest Clare Darcy delight!

Recommended Regency Romances from SIGNET

- [ ] **ALLEGRA by Clare Darcy.** (#E7851—$1.75)
- [ ] **CRESSIDA by Clare Darcy.** (#E8287—$1.75)*
- [ ] **ELYZA by Clare Darcy.** (#E7540—$1.75)
- [ ] **EUGENIA by Clare Darcy.** (#E8081—$1.75)
- [ ] **GWENDOLEN by Clare Darcy.** (#J8847—$1.95)*
- [ ] **LADY PAMELA by Clare Darcy.** (#W7282—$1.50)
- [ ] **LYDIA by Clare Darcy.** (#E8272—$1.75)
- [ ] **REGINA by Clare Darcy.** (#E7878—$1.75)
- [ ] **ROLANDE by Clare Darcy.** (#J8552—$1.95)
- [ ] **VICTOIRE by Clare Darcy.** (#E7845—$1.75)
- [ ] **THE MONTAGUE SCANDAL by Judith Harkness.** (#E8922—$1.75)*
- [ ] **THE ADMIRAL'S DAUGHTER by Judith Harkness.** (#E9161—$1.75)*
- [ ] **MALLY by Sandra Heath.** (#E9342—$1.75)*
- [ ] **THE COUNTERFEIT MARRIAGE by Joan Wolf.** (#E9064—$1.75)*
- [ ] **A KIND OF HONOR by Joan Wolf.** (#E9296—$1.75)*

* Price slightly higher in Canada

Letty

by

CLARE DARCY

Ⓞ

A SIGNET BOOK

NEW AMERICAN LIBRARY

TIMES MIRROR

PUBLISHED BY
THE NEW AMERICAN LIBRARY
OF CANADA LIMITED

Publisher's Note

Chapter 1

❧

MY LORD OF Aubrey's grand Palladian town house in Grosvenor Square was well known in London as the starchiest of the stately mansions in which the members of Society were accustomed to foregather each spring to celebrate the Season. Its entrance hall, where a copy of the Apollo Belvedere standing under a half-dome dominated the large expanse of marble floor, was justly famed as one of the noblest rooms in England; from it the awed visitor passed to a series of impressive reception rooms, designed by Adam for the present lord's father, a noted diplomat of the late King's reign, and given added dignity by the austerely Roman taste of their current elderly owner.

Harry Tyne, however, was not a visitor in the accepted sense of the word. Having in fact passed a great part of his irreverent childhood within these magnificent walls, he was not in the least awed as he ran up the two long shallow flights of the marble staircase to the first floor. On the contrary, he was whistling—an outrage to the splendid decorum surrounding him that apprised Lord Aubrey, even before his great-nephew's entrance into the library, that he was about to receive an unwelcome caller.

"Harry, by heaven!" his lordship rasped out, looking

up from his book while his face purpled with anger. His craggy brows drew together fiercely over his still keen grey eyes. "Nettleship!" he shouted.

It was Harry indeed who moments later strolled into the room, closing the door behind him to prevent his lordship's furious call for his butler from reaching the ears of that dignified functionary below.

"Good-evening, Great-uncle," he said politely, with the smile whose cool impudence had made many men his enemies and won female hearts in several capitals of Europe. "I take it you didn't expect to see me? No, don't call Nettleship up so you can ring a peal over him for letting me in; you had much better let me have the whole of your budget of ill temper—"

"Aye, I daresay it's you who deserve it!" snapped Lord Aubrey as he struggled to rise. A stab of pain from the gouty foot propped upon the footstool caused him to sink back helplessly into his chair again. Harry came over and stood before him, his cool grey eyes softening somewhat as he looked down into his great-uncle's gaunt, fuming face. There was no outward evidence of their blood relationship except in those eyes and in the fact that both were men well above the average in height; for whereas his lordship was of a spare figure and had never been noted for the comeliness of his features, Harry was magnificently built and, until cynicism and half a dozen years of hard living had somewhat marred his face, had been as handsome as a young Apollo. Added to this was a charm of manner that was frequently successful in swaying even those people who initially disliked him into admiring followers.

His great-uncle looked up at him with a frown of contemptuous acknowledgement of that charm. "He has the strictest orders not to admit you! What tale of misfortune did you cozen him with this time to get him to admit you against my express orders?"

"No tale at all, Great-uncle," Harry said, seating himself comfortably in a winged armchair opposite his lordship's. "He is fond of me for old times' sake, you know."

He cast a fleeting glance down over his own figure, elegant in coat, boots, and Inexpressibles of the latest fashion, though a sharp eye might have detected that no valet's expert attention had been applied to blacking Tyne's gleaming Hessians and brushing his Weston-cut coat of Bath superfine. "At any rate, don't I look up to the rig at all points?" he enquired, his mocking smile very much in evidence now. "I flatter myself that, even though I am only just arrived from Constantinople, my attire is in the latest London fashion."

His lordship snorted. "Yes, and so it would be, though it took your last groat to do it!" he said, unappeased. "I've no doubt you'll continue to go to the gallows in good style, if you ever have the ill fortune to come to it! That doesn't signify, so long as you're not up to your ears in the River Tick and have come to me as a last resort to tow you out!"

The faint smile did not fade from Harry's face. "As a last resort—" he repeated softly. "Oh, yes, as a very last resort, Great-uncle! I know you even better than you know me, you see—which is why I am able to sit here calculating the chances of success of this 'last resort' with a certain amount of philosophical detachment. Would you say, perhaps—fifty to one, I wonder?"

"A hundred to one!" his lordship retorted acidly, "Better still—a thousand to one! You've had your last shilling from me, Harry. I told you that when you came to me with that plan of recouping your fortunes in Ireland three years ago, and I say it again tonight. You lived like a young prince once, thanks to my generosity—but that day ended when you disgraced our name! I can't keep you out of the title when I'm gone, worse luck, but I *can* keep you from wasting the Tyne substance."

"The Tyne substance?" Harry's face had darkened slightly, but his smile was as mocking as before. "Shouldn't you say, rather, Great-uncle," he continued, "the substance your esteemed papa was prudent enough to bring into the family when he married a wine-mer-

chant's daughter *en seconde noces?* Oh, a millionaire
wine merchant I'm willing to grant you—but that
scarcely makes his millions Tyne substance, wouldn't
you say?"

His great-uncle glared at him across the candlelit
room. It was late in the autumn night and the streets outside were quiet and deserted; the only sound in the room
as the two men sat regarding each other—the younger
smiling and imperturbable, the older rigid with disapproval and disdain—was the comfortable crackling of the
fire in the grate and the ticking of the French clock
upon the two-storeyed marble mantlepiece.

What Lord Aubrey saw was a heavy-shouldered
young man—young still but no longer in his first youth,
approaching thirty—the well-muscled limbs of an athlete
evident beneath his fashionably tight-fitting coat and
breeches. The keen grey eyes in that splendidly featured
face were a marksmans' eyes, shrewd and cool behind
the arrogant recklessness of the manner which so offended his elderly kinsman, and which led the latter to fling
at him now, in a goading voice, "At all events, it is substance that is under *my* control at present. When I've
stuck my spoon into the wall it will be under your uncle
Marius's—whom I think you'll find no easier to bamboozle into parting with it than you've found me!"

Harry's eyes had narrowed slightly; the indifferent
good humour which, in spite of the acrimony of Lord
Aubrey's reception, had prevailed in his manner up to
this point, disappeared abruptly, though his pose as he
lounged in the deep leather-covered chair was apparently
as relaxed as before.

"Oh, yes!" he agreed easily. "It would be blowing at a
cold coal to try to *bamboozle* my uncle Marius into anything; I'm well assured of that, Great-uncle. He is far
too clever at that sort of game himself."

The faint contempt with which the words were uttered brought the dark angry colour again into Lord
Aubrey's face.

"Your uncle is a man of honour, sir!" he snapped. "It

ill becomes you, of all people, to cast aspersions upon his character."

Harry's black brows lifted. "On the contrary," he said, still with that same air of negligence masking the new grimness in his eyes, "I rather fancy that it *does* become me, of all people, to cast aspersions upon your much-esteemed nephew Marius, Great-uncle! But as we have discussed this subject at rather tedious length on other occasions and—as you have so justly pointed out—I can prove nothing, it may be as well to pass over it now and go on to a topic that may turn out to be more profitable for both of us." His lordship's only reply was an angry shrug, which did not deter Harry from continuing in the same careless manner. "You are aware, of course, of the fact that, for men of my calling, Vienna presents a golden opportunity at present—?"

He got no further, for his great-uncle interrupted him with a scornful repetition of his phrase. "Men of your calling! A common gamester—"

"Oh no—not *common*, Great-uncle!" Harry said softly. "It is a very *un*common gamester, believe me, who can match wits over the green table with the most famous masters of play in Europe and the Levant and come out the winner."

"You were bred for a soldier, sir!" Lord Aubrey's wrath seemed finally to have overmastered the air of disdain with which he had been attempting to cloak it; his voice and his hands shook with fury as he made a gesture as if to rise again. "An honourable profession—not the one I'd have chosen, perhaps, for a young man who would one day inherit the responsibilities of my title and lands, but you were army-mad, it seemed! You should have had a brilliant career there, at any rate. But you threw it away with that curst love of yours for gaming!"

"Any gentleman may have a love for play, Great-uncle—"

"Any gentleman may have a love for *honest* play." Lord Aubrey cut him short fiercely. "He does not stain his own name and that of his family with Greeking transactions fit only for sharpers and black-legs. No, don't attempt to deny it!" he went on violently, as Harry opened his lips to speak. "You have told me your story before, sir, and it doesn't hold water; even that famous charm of yours can't bear down the fact that you had marked cards in your possession, and that you brought young Lord Carlisle to ruin with them! Your own friends and comrades admitted that!" He had succeeded at last in rising, and he faced Harry now, supporting himself on one arm of his chair, his hawkish face suffused with grief and anger. "You were the apple of my eye once, Harry!" he said. "I'd have given you my dearest possession for the asking—but you threw my care and my love for you in my face the day you forgot your honour, and now I've no more use for you than I have for any thieving rogue brought before me to be sentenced to just punishment for his dishonesty. You are a cheat and a scoundrel, sir, and I want you out of my house!"

Harry, too, had risen now. He was paler, it seemed, even in the ruddy firelight that played over his handsome face, but the faint smile still lingered on his lips.

"A most poignant invitation, Great-uncle," he said calmly. "I see I overestimated my chances: even a thousand to one, it seems, would have been too optimistic. You are determined not to hear me—"

"I have heard it all before!" Lord Aubrey said violently. "I am to believe you innocent—against all evidence, against the testimony even of your closest friends—" He made a gesture of dismissal. "No. I'm not such a fool as that! Go to Vienna, sir, go and try your luck at fleecing that horde of golden pagans Metternich has gathered from all over Europe. But don't think to do it on my blunt! I want no part of you—now or ever!"

Harry bowed slightly. There was a light in his grey eyes that men who knew him well could vouch for signifying a contained black fury, but his voice was as ironically civil as ever as he said to his lordship, "Those are plain words, Great-uncle. Not many men would care to speak them to me—"

"Oh, don't brag to me of your exploits on the field of honour—*honour!*" his lordship repeated scornfully. "You don't lack courage; no one ever accused you of that! You've made yourself notorious all over Europe—" He sank down into his armchair again, pain and exhaustion overcoming his anger. "If I were younger—" he gasped.

Harry flung up his hand—a fencer's fatalistic acknowledgement of a hit. "No fear. I shan't outstay my welcome!" he said. "I've tried my luck, and it seems to be out, so I shan't trouble you any further with my company." He stood looking down for a moment into his great-uncle's face, an odd reluctant expression of ironic affection in his own. "You are too ready to think the worst of me, Great-uncle," he said. "Perhaps because once we liked each other so well. "But I forgive you—"

"*You* forgive *me!*"

Lord Aubrey raised himself again furiously in his chair, but Harry was already at the door. His lordship heard light footsteps running down the stairs, the closing of the heavy front door. Outside thunder rolled up sleepily from the south bank of the Thames. There would be a storm, it seemed, before long.

Chapter 2

HARRY TYNE, A moody expression on his face, descended the steps of his great-uncle's house and turned aimlessly out of Grosvenor Square, his air that of a man who has nowhere to go, nothing to do, and unlimited time to do it in. There were no pedestrians in the dark streets where he walked, and only the occasional clatter of hooves and rattle of wheels as a carriage dashed past disturbed the disagreeable tenor of his thoughts. They could scarcely have been anything but disagreeable to a man who had had a run of bad luck that had left him, literally, with no more than a few shillings in his pocket and no idea as to where he might hope to find a roof over his head that night. Harry Tyne, who had lived, as Lord Aubrey had made a point of reminding him, like a young prince when he had been a captain and who had always managed, since the day he had left the army under a cloud, to maintain himself in excellent style by his own wits, had a fixed aversion to publishing his misfortunes by applying to friends for assistance; but even that aversion he had been obliged to overcome that day—without result. A reckless young marquis and a wealthy brewer's sporting son had gone off to Leicestershire to hunt; a famous old politician was taking the waters at Harrowgate; a military nobleman attached to the Russian embassy had departed, like his imperial master, for Vienna to attend the great Congress there.

That was where Harry himself wished of all places to be, for all England, all Europe, and a considerable number of other more exotic foreign capitals had been drained of the cream of their wealthy and powerful by the magnet of Vienna. The leading monarchs of Europe, with their ministers, diplomats, aides, and secretaries by the hundreds, had already arrived in Vienna to settle the fate of the Continent, now that the Corsican upstart who for so long had troubled their kingdoms was safely immured at Elba. In their wake no fewer than a hundred thousand visitors had poured in, led by more than two hundred heads of princely families. Every night, so Harry had heard, forty banquet tables were laid at the Hofburg to accomodate the Emperor's royal guests; every day fourteen hundred horses and hundreds of carriages waited in the palace stables to take them to the balls, the hunts, the festivities, and theatricals and musicales that had been arranged by the Emperor and his beautiful young Empress for their entertainment.

And in the Prater, in the public dance halls, in the little cafés outside the city walls, all Vienna and its guests waltzed, quaffed quantities of heady beer, ate the delicious violet and cinnamon ices that the summerlike warmth of this splendid autumn made so palatable, and waited to pour their gold into the eager hands of the gamesters, the entertainers, the Fashionable (and not so fashionable) Impures who, scenting profit, had swarmed to the city to play their own modest part in this universal revelry.

But how was a man with only a few shillings to jingle in his pockets to join in this lucrative venture? That was the question Harry was asking himself as he turned the corner, a question that was immediately driven from his mind, however, by an abrupt near-collision with a smaller, more slender figure hurrying around that same corner from the opposite direction. A large portmanteau fell with a thump upon the flagway, and what appeared to be a covered birdcage tilted precariously in the figure's grasp.

"Damnation!" said Harry, and at the same moment a feminine voice gasped indignantly, "Oh! *Do* look where you are going!"

Harry, stooping automatically to retrieve the portmanteau, glanced up and found himself gazing into all that was visible of the face of the voice's owner, beneath the shadow of a plain hooded cloak.

"I beg your pardon!" he said shortly, in no mood to do the civil to an impertinent servant. "But why the devil don't you look where *you* are going, my girl?"

He handed her the portmanteau. As he did so, the hood of the cloak fell back and he found himself gazing, astonished, into one of the loveliest feminine countenances it had ever been his fortune to look upon. The features were not classic. The eyes, wide-set and candid, dominated the face, and the lovely generous mouth was no prim cupid's bow. The small head, set proudly on a long slender neck, had the cool perfection of that of a princess in an Egyptian frieze. The figure beneath it, under the falling lines of the cloak, was spare and slender as a boy's; its owner could not, Harry guessed, be more than seventeen. And no servant. The conviction immediately came to him—that was a girl certainly gently bred and as certainly of good blood.

Taking it all in conjunction with the portmanteau, the birdcage, and the muffling cloak, it was not difficult to come to a swift conclusion.

"You," said Harry, stating that conclusion in a tone of interested detachment, "are running away."

A slight shrug confirmed his deduction, without indicating the least discomposure on the young lady's part over her secret having been discovered. "I *can't* see," she said, rather austerely still, as she accepted the portmanteau from him, "that that is any of *your* affair, sir. And I should advise *you* not to walk down the streets of London in a brown study. You are very apt to meet with an accident if you do—or to cause one to an innocent person."

She was about to step past him on the flagway when another thought apparently occurred to her. "If," she offered, "you should wish to make amends for almost running me down, however, you may do so by directing me to the waterfront. I had thought it would be a very simple matter to get there, but it seems that I have lost my way."

The voice, Harry noticed, was the most enchanting he had ever heard, meriting the appellation "silvery," which poets are so fond of using, but which he himself, despite his rather wide experience, had never felt to be applicable before this time. He found the request the girl had made of him so astounding, however, that his own voice was more than a little abrupt as he said in reply, "The waterfront? Why the deuce should you wish to go there—and at this time of night?"

"I know it may seem quite unusual," the young lady acknowledged, her manner still showing a considerable chilly hauteur. The hauteur was assumed, however, with such an inexpert air that Harry found himself thinking with faint amusement of an inexperienced young actress whom he had once seen thrown without warning into the role of a world-weary lady of fashion. "But I *do* think," she continued, "that that, again, is none of your affair—*n'es-ce-pas?* So, if you will kindly give me the necessary directions . . ."

"I shall certainly kindly do nothing of the sort," said Harry. "Good Lord, you'd be robbed, or worse, in a flea's leap if I sent you there! I repeat—why the deuce should you wish to go there at this hour of the night? If you *are* engaging in an elopement, your young man must be short of a sheet to think of charging you to meet him in such a place!"

The slight figure drew itself up. "I am *not*," its owner said coldly, " 'engaging in an elopement,' as you so un-genteelly put it, sir! I am merely on my way to visit friends."

"Friends?" Harry's skepticism was so spparent that he found himself once more the target of a highly disapproving glance from the hazel eyes.

"Friends," the young lady repeated firmly. "Or at least," she went on, suddenly abandoning her air of hauteur as inadequate to the occasion and becoming instantly confidential, "it is my old nurse, you see, who is married now to a bargeman and came to visit me only last week. She was so *very* much put out at my being obliged to marry Mr. Sludge, who is a curate and quite middle-aged, and would not have the least thing to do with me if his promotion did not depend upon it, that I am sure she will be happy to take me in to live with her on the barge until other arrangements can be made. She says it is very clean and neat, at least inside the cabin, and that her husband is a very accommodating sort of man."

Harry, faced with this barrage of information, most of it of a highly thought-provoking nature, seized upon what appeared to him to be the crux of the matter and enquired why she was obliged to marry the unwilling and middle-aged Mr. Sludge."

"Because my great-aunt is dead," the young lady explained, setting the portmanteau down again with the air of one prepared to deal patiently with a slow-witted henchman. "She died last month, and of course I cannot be useful to her niece as I was to her, because she is a great Lady of Fashion and not at all interested in being read to for hours and having her forehead bathed with lavender water, as the old Countess was. And so she says I must be Suitably Settled. But I shouldn't like in the least to be Suitably Settled with Mr. Sludge—fancy going through one's whole life as Mrs. Sludge!—which is why I am running away to Nora. So now will you *please* direct me to the waterfront?"

Harry shook his head. "The answer is still no," he said. "Besides they will come after you, you know."

"They won't. I've left a note saying I was in flat despair and was going to throw myself into the Thames," said the young lady promptly, with an air of having disposed of *that* objection. She looked at him hopefully, and, seeing no appearance of yielding upon his face, once more assumed her austere manner. "Very well, if you intend to be disobliging," she said, "I daresay you are not the only person I shall meet with if I continue on my way."

"If you continue on your way at this hour of night, unattended, you are likely to meet a number of persons, most of them ugly customers," Harry said frankly. "If you had the sense of a pea-goose you'd know that." She drew herself up, offended. "No. Don't poker up at me. Good God! If you've been bred in London—"

"I haven't been! I never set eyes on London in my life until I came here eighteen months ago when Mama died, and I have never been *anywhere* because my great-aunt didn't go out. Except," she added scrupulously, "that I was allowed to go to Astley's Ampitheatre at Christmas time with the children, but in terms of worldly experience that scarcely signifies, don't you think?"

Harry was obliged to agree that it did not. In something of a quandary he stood gazing at the cloaked figure before him. Obviously, he was not going to direct the girl to the waterfront, as she wished, and equally obviously it was out of his power as an unattached bachelor and a penniless one at that, to do anything more helpful for her. It was the devil's own luck, he thought—exactly the sort that had been pursuing him for weeks—that he had been pitchforked into her affairs by a chance collision in the dark, and he had half a mind—he told himself—to wash his hands of the whole matter and go on about his own nonexistent business.

Unfortunately, he knew himself to be temperamentally incapable of doing anything of the kind. If there was an imbroglio to be got into, Harry Tyne, who was entirely reckless, not overburdened with scruples, and always bored with a quiet life, was sure to get himself into it. Probing for a solution to a seemingly insoluble problem, he said to the girl, "This Nora of yours, is she expecting you to come to her?"

"Well, naturally *not!*" the girl said. "After all, matters only came to a head about Mr. Sludge *after* she had come to visit me."

"And this barge of hers," Harry persisted, "are you sure it's still moored here at London?"

"N-no! But it was a week ago—"

"A week ago!"

"You—you don't think it will be here any longer?"

"No, I don't," said Harry roundly. "More than likely it's a hundred miles away. It seems to me that the best thing you can do, my girl, is to scurry off home as fast as you can, destroy that note you left, and marry Mr. Sludge—"

"Well, I shan't!" The small head lifted defiantly. "And I think it is very poor-spirited of you even to suggest such a thing to me! One can always find a position somewhere—"

"In the middle of the night?"

Harry, whose temper was not of the longest, was about to launch into a scathing description of the perils that would be encountered by any young female bird-witted enough to cast herself on the tender mercies of London at that hour, when the sound of coach wheels rattling to an abrupt halt beside him interrupted him.

"Harry!" a soft, quavering, elderly, masculine voice pronounced joyfully as a grey head protruded from the coach window. "Harry, *mon cher!* It *is* you? *Vraiment?*"

The next moment, in answer to a command from the same soft, attractive, elderly voice, the coach steps were let down by one of the two gold-laced footmen perched up behind, and the figure of an old man in fashionable evening dress emerged slowly from the carriage, a beaming smile upon his face.

"Harry, *mon vieux!*" he exclaimed and followed that with a very Continental embrace. "The very man I most wished to see! But I did not know you were here, in London!"

Harry, who had returned the old man's embrace with the greatest cordiality, said he had arrived only two days ago from Constantinople.

"But you!" he said, holding the old man away from himself to survey the *ton*-ish magnificence of his knee-breeches and silk stockings, his silk-lined cloak and the ornately chased gold quizzing-glass slung around his neck. "*You* have changed fortunes since last I saw you, Max! What goldmine have *you* discovered?"

The old man made an apologetic gesture. "No gold mine at all, *mon cher*—only a very foolish set of your English milords, who like deep play but have not the wits for it. Do you remember in Lisbon—?"

Harry grinned. "Do I not? Good Lord, it's been three years! But you haven't lost your skill, it seems."

The old man shook his head. He was so old that all his movements had a deliberate, dreamlike quality, as if he were living in some strange dimension outside the world of everyday affairs. But there was a warmth in his voice and in his still very blue eyes that belied this odd air of separation from ordinary human concerns.

"I am a very old man, *mon enfant*," he said with simplicity, "but this"—he tapped his forehead—"is still as young as ever. But," he added, turning courteously to the unknown young lady who had been following this exchange with a great deal of interest, "you do not make me known to your charming companion, *mon cher*. Will you not present me?"

"So I should—with the best will in the world," Harry said, with a glance at the young lady, "only unfortunately I don't know her name. We are chance-met, you see. She is running away, and wishes me to direct her to the waterfront, where a week ago a barge inhabited by her old nurse was to be found."

The old man's brows went up; he looked sympathetically at the young lady. "I see," he said slowly. "I see, Mademoiselle. I do not know in what way I may be of service to you, but believe me when I say that I am Max von Bergheim and entirely at your command.

Harry, who was well aware that M. von Bergheim, as he was known in every capital in Europe, had the right to a far more prestigious title, which, however, he had abandoned so long ago that even his intimates spoke of him only as "*der alte Baron*," saw with some amusement that the young lady was already falling under his spell. All the young ladies he met confided in the old Baron; it was a legacy, no doubt, of the days when a much younger M. von Bergheim had carried on *affairs du coeur* in a stately and poetic eighteenth-century style with great ladies who even now sighed and smiled (those who were left) over faded letters and old keepsake books full of measured compliments and classical allusions. The legendary charm. Harry saw, was still operative, for the unknown young lady, smiling warmly at the old Baron, said that her name was Letty Montressor. "Lettice, really, only it sounds so much like greengoods!"—and plunged into a far more detailed account of her present predicament than she had seen fit to bestow on Harry.

"And so you see," she concluded at last, "I really *cannot* go home again—not that it *is* my home—and they are all out of London now except the servants, and *they* have orders to convey me to Bournemouth tomorrow so that I may meet Mr. Sludge's mother, who lives there, and stay with her until I am married. And I don't *wish* to be married!" she added passionately. "Not to Mr. Sludge nor to *anyone!*"

The old Baron took her hands comfortably in his. "There, there," he said soothingly. "Of course you need marry no one, *mein kind!* You are like a blossom, a snowdrop, so cool and pure; it would be beyond thinking. We must contrive something—"

She looked at him hopefully. "Oh, I am sure you will!" she said. "I am a very neat seamstress—and I am used to looking after invalids—and even the old Countess said I have a voice that would make my fortune if I were not too genteelly bred to think of performing in public. But I don't care about being genteelly bred; it is no use at all to one in earning one's living! Would you like me to sing for you, perhaps?" she enquired with one of her swift bird-flight changes in manner.

The old Baron, ignoring Harry's blunt query as to whether they wished to bring the watch down upon them, said cordially, "By all means!"

Young Miss Montressor, also ignoring Harry, set the birdcage upon the flagway, clasped her hands before her, and lifted up her voice.

Before the first phrase had died away in the still, thundery night air Harry's objections were forgotten. It was a simple Scottish song of parted lovers that the girl sang, but the voice—magically pure and clear, with the throbbing poignancy of a bird's notes in its artless tones—lifted it from the commonplace to the realm of enchantment. It was as if, standing in the dark London street, that small figure were weaving a spell as potent as any necromancer might cast with all the power of his art. The two men, arrested and silent, listened to the end of her song; the older was moved as he had not been for so many years that he had all but forgotten the emotions those simple thrilling notes called up in him. The very coachman and footmen felt a sudden sting of tears behind their eyelids. Only Harry Tyne stood listening with a gamester's cool jubilation in the impossibly lucky turn of a card that had brought fortune his way, and ejaculated as the soft notes died away in a low mutter, "By God, Max, was I talking of gold mines? What do you say to this one? I thought *Vienna* as soon as I clapped eyes on you tonight; now I *know* we must go there at once! A hundred thousand pigeons for the plucking, *mon vieux*, and this 'tassel-gentle' to lure them into our net!"

Miss Montressor was looking bewildered. The coachman and the footmen, ashamed of their unprofessional behaviour, instantly resumed their masklike expressions.

The old Baron, however, openly wiped his eyes with his handkerchief and turned reproachfully to Harry.

"You have no heart, my boy," he said. "Mademoiselle has sung to us as the angels sing and you think of money—"

"My dear Max," said Harry, with a shrug of his wide shoulders, "when one has no money it is unfortunately impossible to think of anything else! Mademoiselle indeed sings like a linnet—but how am I to enjoy her song when I haven't a feather to fly with myself? But only get the three of us to Vienna, old friend, give me a suitable setting for this linnet of yours, and I'll guarantee you such a golden hoard of guineas and gulden that none of us will ever feel needy again!"

The old Baron shook his head at him. "You have no heart, Harry," he repeated sadly. "But you *have*"—with a resigned twinkle in his blue eyes—"a head. Yes, yes, you have indeed a head! The Catalini herself will be put in the shade when *this* voice is heard in the salons of Europe, just as Art cannot compete with Nature—"

"You see my point, then?" Harry said swiftly. "Good! A singing master, a clever mantua-maker, someone to drill her into manners of an angelic modesty instead of this unseemly pertness—"

"If you are speaking of me," said the outraged Miss Montressor, "I am *not* pert, sir. Or at least," she conceded, "if I am it is because *you* are rude."

"Whether *I* am rude or not is beside the point," Harry said ruthlessly. "It won't bring a groat into any of our pockets. But you, Miss Malapert, will learn the manners of a docile *juene fille* if I have to beat them into you." He turned again to the old Baron. "Where are we to bestow her tonight?" he demanded. "I think for the sake of appearances she had best become your grand-niece, just up from the country. We can make some excuse for her turning up at this odd hour."

The old Baron held up a hand. "Harry, Harry, Wait! You go too fast!" he protested. "We can't abduct this child from her relations, and without asking her consent—"

"Oh, I should like it of all things, if I am to go with *you*, sir!" Letty said earnestly. "And, indeed, I have no relations; they are relations of the old Countess's, not on the maternal side, so that we are actually not related in the least. And I do assure you that they will be only too happy to have me taken off their hands in *any* way."

The old Baron looked at her compassionately. "My poor child!" he said. "If it is so—yes, yes, you are better off with us. A gaming establishment, no matter how elegant, is scarcely the setting from which to launch into Society a *jeune fille* and make for her a proper marriage—but stranger things have been accomplished! You will be *bien gardée* with me, *ma fille*, and who knows? One day you may be a *duchesse*—"

"But not," Harry interrupted, "before she has made our fortunes, Max! By Jupiter, to think how the luck has turned for me in a scant half-hour! That space of time ago, as Mademoiselle Linnet so aptly put it, I was in flat despair, and now—"

But he was interrupted in turn by the old Baron who exclaimed delightedly, "Mademoiselle Linnet! The very name for our songbird! You shall go to Vienna *incognito*, my child, and leave Miss Lettice Montressor to lie, to the wicked relatives' satisfaction, at the bottom of the Thames. James," he addressed one of the gold-laced footmen, "you will take Mademoiselle's portmanteau to a lonely spot on the bank of the river and leave it there. The birdcage, I daresay," he was now looking inquiringly at Letty, "you will wish to keep?"

"Yes, of course! It has Alexander inside it—my pet canary," said Miss Montressor indignantly. "At least, he belonged to the old Countess, but no one else wanted him when she died—"

"You shall change him for a linnet when we reach Vienna," Harry said, already shepherding her, birdcage and all, towards the carriage—to which unfeeling statement, however, Miss Montressor returned such an outraged negative, indicative of an undying loyalty to the hidden Alexander, that he was obliged to retreat to the extent of agreeing to discuss the matter further when they were all comfortably settled at the old Baron's hotel.

Chapter 3

A WEEK LATER—a week crowded with more eventful and bewildering occurrences than Miss Montressor had experienced in the entire previous course of her short life—she found herself seated, with the old Baron and Harry Tyne, in an elegant travelling-chaise drawn by four post-horses which was transporting her, as fast as the execrable state of the roads permitted, down from the low, hilly woods that lay to the west of Vienna into the suburbs of that capital city. Soon the high roof of St. Stephen's Cathedral came into view, its enormous fretted spire dominating the maze of streets below, and then the outline of the city itself, encircled by the huge brick walls that were the legacy of centuries of wars with the Turks. The chaise drove in at the Jozefstadt Gate. It would not be long now, the travel-weary old Baron stated with satisfaction, until they would have the pleasure of alighting at one of Vienna's finest hosteleries, the Kaiserin von Österreich, where, in spite of the highly overcrowded condition of the city, he had been able to procure accommodations for them.

To Letty Montressor, whose previous experience of life in a great metropolis had been confined to the decorous activities glimpsed from the windows of the old Countess's house in Berkeley Square, the narrow, teem-

ing streets of Vienna were full of interest at every turn.
A polyglot throng—Moravian Brothers and Triestine
merchants, Greeks from the Adriatic provinces, Galician
Hebrews, Italian noblemen, and Hungarian magnates—
rubbed shoulders in an exciting mélange of color and ac-
tivity. Many visitors to the ancient city on the Danube
found it disappointing, with its narrow streets and
squares where the towering old houses shut light and air
from the pedestrians and carriages below. But Letty was
fortunate enough to glimpse a column of the famous
Hungarian Hussars dashing by in their red uniforms, tiger-skin mantles, and sable hats topped with white ai-
grettes. She watched with fascination as a prince's state
chariot passed on its way to the Imperial Palace, its six
black horses proudly tossing their cockaded heads, while
before them rode four mounted guards in gold-laced
green uniforms, two running footmen in Turkish dress
carrying silver-tipped batons, and a half-score of liveries
striding sturdily through the muddy streets in their
white silk stockings. Astley's Ampitheatre immediately
lost its place in her mind as the pinnacle of excitement
and glamour, to be replaced on the spot by the streets of
Vienna.

The excellent accommodations in which the party
soon found themselves in the Kaiserin von Österreich had
been made available to them, it immediately transpired,
courtesy of a personage named Sascha, who was shown
up to their apartments shortly after their arrival. He was
greeted as an old friend by both Harry and the old
Baron, and upon being introduced to Letty, bowed to
her with the greatest formality, looked her over frown-
ingly from head to toe—an inspection that included walking completely around her the better to observe her from
all angles—and then briefly pronounced her to be passable.

"Passable! My dear Sascha—!" the old Baron protested,
but the personage named Sascha, who was still examining
Letty closely, his chin propped in his hand, disregarded

him completely. Sascha was a small, dark man of indeterminate age, with a dancer's quick-moving, disciplined body. His face, Letty soon discovered, was as mobile as if it were being covered in quick succession by an endless series of masks, representing, among other emotions, contemplation, contempt, satisfaction, and childlike happiness.

She was also soon to learn who he was—a singing master, a talented dancer, a universal factotum, a man who had sprung from nowhere (or from the slimy back streets of Marseilles, it was whispered) to become the confidant of dukes and generals, since he knew everyone's secrets and had the discretion to reveal them only to those few persons who commanded his loyalty. It was apparent that both Harry and the old Baron were in this latter category. For their part, they had soon made known to him every detail of their plan for reaping a golden harvest from pleasure-mad Vienna—a plan with which he had obviously been acquainted by letter even before their arrival.

There was to be a gaming establishment, Letty learned, of the most elegant, the most private, the most exclusive sort—an establishment to which only the cream of Viennese Society and its guests would have entrée. Here they would find the same amenities in the way of food, drink and décor that they were accustomed to in their own homes. What would draw them to this rather than to any of the rival establishments already thriving in the capital? A singing voice which even the skeptical Sascha pronounced to be a gift from the angels as well as an attraction that would bring all music-mad Vienna to their door.

"But—but—but," he immediately qualified this high praise, "her *tenue*, you see, is deplorable, her figure—ah!—she has no figure! One must send at once for Madame Haussmann. The simplest of white muslin slips but the awkward lines of the body so artfully concealed by Madame's art. White silk sandals, *bien entendu*—the hair—" He frowned over its heavy dark mass, pulled out combs and hairpins ruthlessly, and saw it fall in a rippling dusky mane to her waist, "*Comme ça*," he proclaimed definitely, "and a wreath of flowers, perhaps. A pity she is not a *blonde*."

The old Baron's soft, wavering voice pointed out that in England at least, *brunes* were now in greater favour.

"Ah, the English!" Sascha dismissed them with a gesture of contempt. "Purse-leeches, all of them! It is not with English gold that you will line your pockets, my dear! Do you know that Milady Castlereagh appeared at one of our masked balls in a costume she had stitched together herself? *Mais vraiment!* As a vestal virgin, she came. Do you not believe me?"—as the old Baron waved a protesting hand, a smile upon his wrinkled face. "But I can tell you other stories, too. You would not believe the *folies*, the *singeries*, that go on here—"

Circling Letty all the while and admonishing her in an occasional aside to hold her shoulders more erect, to bend her head slightly forward in a graceful timid curve, or to turn her elbows in and the points of her slippers out, he launched into a series of anecdotes involving the great names in Vienna. Many of his tales were scandalous, most of them were amusing, and all of them, as Harry and the old Baron knew, were meticulously factual.

Did one know, for example, that the middle-aged Crown Prince of Württemberg was attempting to obtain an annulment of his marriage to the Crown Princess so that he might marry the Tsar's snub-nosed, eccentric, widowed sister, the Grand Duchess Catherine? Was one aware that it was rumoured that the Tsar himself required a block of ice to be brought up each morning to his suite in the Hofburg for his toilette? Or that eight thousand candles were lighted in the crystal chandeliers of the Riding Hall every night the Emperor gave a ball there? That Lord Stewart, the English ambassador, had-had his face soundly slapped by a young countess with whose person he had taken a liberty while descending a

crowded staircase at the theatre? And that the Empress
Maria Ludovica herself had been obliged to intervene to
persuade the young Count Wrbna to shave off his cher-
ished Hussar moustache so that he could appear as
Apollo in a *tableau vivant?*

"Also, he went on, now addressing Harry, "do you
know, my dear, that your esteemed uncle, the so proper,
the so correct General Sir Marius Tyne, has succeeded
in becoming the favorite cavalier of the famous cocotte,
Mademoiselle Forel. The lady is to Viennese Society
what I understand your Miss Harriette Wilson is to London Society. And in order to consolidate his victory the
general is joining Lord Castlereagh and his wife in un-
dergoing instruction in the waltz each morning—"

He was interrupted by the old Baron, who said in a
voice for him, of unusual sharpness, "Sir Marius? He is
here?" He cast an anxious glance at Harry. "That is
bad—very bad—"

"So *I* thought," agreed Sascha, nodding wisely and
also regarding Harry, who, however, had shown no signs
of any particular interest in the news. On the contrary, he
was still lounging at his ease in one of the room's elegant
fauteuils, his long legs stretched out before him and his
hands dug deep into his breeches' pockets.

"He is, so they say," Sascha went on informatively,
continuing to cock an inquisitive eyebrow at Harry, "a
bosom intimate of the Imperial family. He plays the
cello, I am reliably informed, in the family quartet when
Prince Metternich, who ordinarily has that honour, is
otherwise engaged, and assists the Emperor in making
lacquer cages in his workshop for the exotic birds His
Majesty raises in his glass-houses."

This last statement was sufficient to raise Harry's eyebrows at least. "You are painting a very odd picture!" he
remarked sardonically. "Music, dancing, mistresses—and
birds! My uncle has *come on* a good deal, apparently,
since I last had the pleasure of meeting him!"

Sascha shrugged expressively. "My dear, you know *ce*

type," he said. "If ambition required him to stand on his head in front of the Kärntnertortheater half an hour before a performance was to take place he would do it—all the while maintaining, of course, an air of the greatest dignity. But what is more to the point for you, my friend, is that he has the Emperor's ear, which means the ear of the police minister as well, which also means that, at a word from him, your faro tables will be closed and you and the old Baron and Mademoiselle Songbird will find yourselves in a closed carriage on the way to the frontier."

He looked for confirmation to the old Baron, who nodded sadly. "Alas, *mon cher*, that is all too true," he said. "And very disagreeable it is—Harry, *nicht wahr?*"

"Disagreeable, but scarcely important," Harry said coolly, his own heavy shoulders lifted in a contemptuous shrug. "My uncle, you see, has taken great pains since that 'unfortunate occurrence in Spain,' as I hear he is fond of referring to it, to make it clear to the world that, far from having had a hand in bringing that *unfortunate occurrence* about, he has only the kindliest of feelings towards me still, in spite of my reprehensible behaviour. It is hardly likely, therefore, that he will care to show any open hostility to me, even at this late date. There *are* people, you know, who might not hesitate to point out that he was the one person who stood to benefit by my downfall."

Sascha nodded sagely. "A point well taken," he said approvingly. "You relieve my mind. *Monsieur le Général* has indeed the reputation for being the most prudent of men. Which is all the more reason why he has taken Vienna by surprise in his conquest of the Forel. She is not a bird—any more than your Miss Wilson—to be lured to the hand by pomposity. One hears, however, that she has taken to flaunting a magnificent diamond parure, which she has no scruples in attributing to the generosity of *Monsieur le Général*. It is scarcely to be wondered at that she finds the blue-velvet-lined barouche and four cream-coloured horses—the best the young Count Balnitz could manage—very small beer indeed, and so has agreed to make her *public* appearance, at least, on Sir Marius's arm."

But at this point Harry, who was as quickly on his guard as the most strait-laced of dowagers where Letty was concerned, stopped any further scandalous remarks in her presence with an imperious word. After ordering Sascha to get on at once with her first singing lesson, he left the room, taking the old Baron with him.

Sascha looked after him, an expression of greatest exasperation upon his face. "No! From Harry, this is too much!" he exclaimed. "Is one to understand, then, that *he* is never guilty of uttering an indelicacy in your presence?"

"Well, yes—one is," Letty said promptly. "That is, when he remembers—and he *does* forget sometimes. But he says it is necessary for me to create an appearance of the greatest innocence, so that I must not learn any improper words or listen to scandalous stories. But that is a great piece of nonsense, as I have tried to tell him, because the old Countess talked nothing but scandal from morning to night, so that I know about all the improper things people do. Is Harry a very improper person himself? He *looks* very improper, but I daresay one can't always tell by appearances."

Sascha agreed with feeling that such was the case, for the greatest scoundrel in all Vienna, he said, which at the present moment abounded in scoundrels from every corner of Europe, was a little man with a face as innocent as a baby's and an appealing whisper for a voice.

"As for Harry," he said austerely, "it would not become me to discuss his affairs with you. Come, Mademoiselle, we shall begin with the breathing."

"That is what the old Baron says," Letty persevered, disregarding the breathing. "But at least *he* has told me all about Harry's career in The Peninsula, before he was obliged to leave the Army, and he says he quite believes that *that*—his having to leave—was a monstrous piece of injustice, brought about by some wicked enemy of his, for no matter how quick-tempered and reckless Harry is, he has never been a schemer or dishonest. The old Baron is very fond of Harry, I think, and even though he shakes his head over him and warns me that he is not at all reliable where females are concerned, so that I am under no circumstances to fall in love with him—!"

"Excellent advice," agreed Sascha. "Now, Mademoiselle, the breathing—"

"Not that I am at all likely to," Letty said severely, "as he is almost always excessively rude to me and never makes the least attempt to make himself agreeable."

Sascha was now looking at her from beneath lowering black brows. *"The breathing, Mademoiselle!"* he said ominously.

"Of course," Letty said generously, "he *is* very handsome—"

"THE BREATHING!"

"Oh, very well!" Letty said, resigning herself to the inevitable.

She found Sascha to be a stern and demanding taskmaster during the days that followed. From morning to night, while—as she was given to understand—Harry and the old Baron occupied themselves with the refurbishing and provisioning of the elegant villa Sascha had hired for them, she was drilled by him more relentlessly than ever any raw recruit in the Emperor's army. Singing lessons were followed by dancing lessons, dancing lessons by hours of fittings for the deceptively simple frocks in which she was to appear before Viennese Society, and in the moments between she memorized the proper forms of address for every Highness, Transparency, and Excellency in Vienna, from the Tsar, the Emperor, and the King of Prussia down to the least of their military aides and secretaries.

His willing assistant in all these endeavours was a tall, bony, acidulous Englishwoman of a certain age rejoicing in the romantic Christian name of Parthenope and the more commonplace surname of Clark, who made her appearance at the Kaiserin von Österreich on the morning after Letty's arrival. She had been hired—also on the ubiquitous Sascha's recommendation, it seemed—to act as Letty's duenna, a post for which she appeared to be admirably suited, for she was the possessor of an excellent education and her ideas of propriety were strict enough to satisfy even Harry. While all Vienna gave itself up to pleasure during the golden days of that splendid autumn, while lilacs pushed forth unseasonable buds in the Prater and the city glowed at night with the flames of a thousand torches as carriages crowded the narrow streets on their way to endless balls and galas, Miss Clark's young ward practised in her bedchamber her French and deportment under the duenna's careful eye. Only by running to the window and peering out at the sound of some unusual commotion in the street below was she able to catch so much as a glimpse of the celebrities whose names were on everyone's tongue—the handsome Tsar Alexander, tall and blond, with a waist like a girl's; the unpretentious, middle-aged Emperor and his beautiful young Empress, Maria Ludovica; Prince Esterhazy, at the head of the Royal Hungarian Guard, in a uniform covered with pearls and diamonds, casqued with feathers, and with pearl pendants on his boots; the suave, supercilious Metternich himself, who was stage manager of this glittering performance that had all Europe for its audience.

"Patience, patience!" the old Baron comforted her when she begged at least to be allowed to join the crowds in the Prater to watch one of the magnificent displays of fireworks—pyrotechnic marvels in which the flags of the nations participating in the Congress, or the principal buildings of Milan, Berlin, and St. Petersburg were painted in great bursts of light against the night sky. "There will be time enough for you to see everything, once you are launched. You will have *un succès eclatant*. Only just wait and see, all the young officers will be vying with one another to gallant you to balls and *fêtes;* you will be presented to the Emperor himself; you will be invited everywhere."

That was all very well, Letty thought rebelliously, only half consoled by all these promises of a brilliant future, but meanwhile there were only Sascha and Miss Clark, who, far from vying with each other to entertain her, seemed intent upon making her life a burden to her. And then there was Harry, with his caustic tongue and indifferent air, making disagreeable comments about her singing, her conduct, or her appearance, and there was the old, old, but kindly Baron.

"You are too hard upon her, *mon cher,*" the old Baron chided Harry more than once, but Harry only shrugged and observed that she would be of no use whatever to them unless she appeared as a diamond of the first water, to which the old Baron could make no rejoinder.

"Which by nature she is not," Sascha, always a ready collaborator in these sessions of criticism, would pronounce. Then Letty, losing her temper in good earnest, would declare her intention of returning to England and seeking out Nora and her bargeman husband, "who at least," she would say resentfully, "will be kind to me."

But even as she made the threat she knew in her heart that she had not the least intention of carrying it out. For, much as it would have distressed the old Baron had she confided her secret to him, much as it horrified her to find her heart turning in such an unlikely direction, she was, she found, falling in love with Harry Tyne. She loved his marred, handsome face and the way he carried himself: more like an emperor, it seemed to her, than any of the Royal Personages she glimpsed from her window. She loved his voice, that resonant instrument of many moods, and his quick grey glance, and his broad shoulders and well-shaped hands. And, most of all, like Desdemona in the play, she "loved him for the dangers he had pass'd," the sense of brilliance, bravery, and resourcefulness in the face of disastrous odds, that ran through the occasional reminiscences the old Baron and

Sascha were unguarded enough to indulge in in her presence. It was—alas!—all too easy to make a romantic hero of Harry Tyne.

As for his loving her in return—she knew better than to expect anything of the sort. She was no more than a necessary encumbrance to him, a stubborn, frequently intractable child with whose tiresome moods he had little sympathy and less patience. She was aware, besides, that already, handsome barques of frailty were calling boldly at the Kaiserin von Österreich to inquire after him. There were even ladies of title, Sascha did not hesitate to inform her, who were willing to brave the scandal-broth they brewed by inviting him into their boxes at the theatre or by being seen driving in the Prater in his high-perch phaeton.

Chief among them, it seemed, was Lady Hester Luddington, a wealthy and slightly scandalous young widow who rivalled the lovely Countess Julia Zichy for the title of the most beautiful woman in Vienna. If one could be said to be the mortal enemy of a person on whom one had never clapped eyes, Letty's feelings toward Lady Hester might be so expressed. Lady Hester, it seemed, was all that Letty was not—an Ornament of Society, a leader of the most fashionable set in Vienna, admired by every gentleman, and the despair of every female seeking to attract male attention where she was present.

How, Letty asked herself dismally, looking at the demure white muslin gown in which she was to appear before Viennese Society, was she to compete with a lady who was apt to present herself in public, when the whim took her, in a gown of all but transparent gauze and a single petticoat, dampened to cling alluringly to every voluptuous curve of her body? Her own spare young figure, she realised sadly, had no voluptuous curves at all, even had she been permitted to display them—and as for being witty and dashingly at ease with the highest personages in Vienna, as Lady Hester was reputed to be, Harry had criticised her more than once for having no more conversation than her canary, Alexander, when

Sascha and Miss Clark perseveringly attempted to rehearse her in the kind of drawing-room small talk she would be expected to carry on with the patrons of the house.

Altogether, she told herself, sighing, it was a hopeless case. But being seventeen and of a highly optimistic nature, she was not prevented from looking forward—blighted love or no blighted love—to her approaching debut.

Chapter 4

❧

LETTY'S DEBUT TOOK place on an evening when winter had at last made its appearance in earnest after that long, lingering autumn; a storm, sweeping down suddenly from the hills beyond the Danube, had laid the old city under a glittering mantle of snow. Many of the guests arrived in sleighs drawn by belled horses, so that the street outside rang with the cheerful jingling of harnesses, lending a mood of holiday gaiety to the warm, candlelit rooms inside. Here, delicate porcelain stoves shaped like inkstands sent out an inviting glow of warmth in every room; at the double windows, heavy crimson draperies under elaborate pelmets shut out the winter night. Great masses of glass-house blooms met their reflections in the bare, polished parquet floors and wafted their fragrance freely through the beautiful high-ceilinged rooms, which, in the current Viennese style, were sparsely furnished with furniture of the light woods—cherry and pearwood and Hungarian ash—that had replaced the more ornate treasure of an earlier day.

Letty, since she had been removed from the seclusion of the room at the Kaiserin von Österreich the day before, had been permitted little leisure to examine the house that was now to be her home, so filled had every moment been with the last-minute preparations for her first appearance in public. A dozen times during those final hectic hours Sascha had flown into a rage with her, declaring that no, and no, and *no!*—if she sang so he would publicly disown having had any part in training her; a dozen times Miss Clark had acidly reminded her that a young lady did not look with frank curiosity into the face of a Great Personage to whom she was being presented, but cast only a brief, timid glance upward at him from under modestly lowered lashes; a dozen times Harry had lost his temper with her and frankly expressed the opinion that they would be better off sending her back to England.

Only the old Baron remained staunch and comforting during all her trials, and it was he who, on the evening of her debut, tapped at the door of her bedchamber, entered to exclaim in unfeigned delight at the picture she presented, and led her gently down the wide, polished staircase to the rooms below, which were already alive with the laughter and conversation of the curious guests who had come to sample this latest addition to the pleasure houses of Vienna.

And, in truth, the old Baron had reason to be delighted. From the top of her flower-wreathed head to the tips of her delicate white silk sandals, this was a dark snow-maiden, an enchanted princess awaiting the awakening kiss, her head poised gently aslant, as if she were listening for the first foot-fall of a rescuing prince, her eyes aloof yet shining with all the expectancy of youth under their fringe of dark lashes.

Undoubtedly, the old Baron thought, Sascha and Miss Clark had done their work well. And a feeling of compassion for this elegant, vulnerable child shook him as he led her into the largest of the *salons*, where a great polished Broadwood pianoforte stood silently waiting. He stared almost angrily at the fashionable crowd idly surveying her through quizzing-glasses and *face-à-mains* as she entered. A lamb before wolves, he thought grimly—and if the wolves included among their number Serene

Highnesses, Royal Personages, titled, play-mad ladies and gentlemen from every country of Europe, a scattering of expensive Cyprians, and the handsomest of young officers in scarlet or blue or dazzling white uniforms, so much the worse, he felt, for the lamb.

He led her to the piano now, where a well-known performer was playing a few preliminary notes to quiet the audience. A hush did not, however, ensue; conversation continued to flourish, and in the far corner of the room, a shrill scream of laughter from one of the expensive Cyprians indicated that a skirmish of quite another sort was taking place there. The pianist, a veteran of these occasions, pursed his lips contemptuously in an angry *moue*, shrugged his shoulders, and launched into the introduction of Letty's first song.

The notes fell upon her ear like a death knell. Her knees were trembling, her heart thudding so uncontrollably that it shook the thin muslin covering her breasts. All she could see was a dazzle of candle-flames, jewels, and uniforms wavering before her eyes in a brilliant haze.

The Cyprian screamed again, struck one of the handsome young officers across the knuckles with her fan, and rushed across the room, creating a commotion.

"Ladies and gentlemen—"

It was Harry's voice, resonant and ironical, cutting through the Babel of conversation. He had the power of commanding attention: the voice, indifferent yet persuasive, seemed to promise something of importance; the very stance of that broad-shouldered figure, imposingly elegant in the long-tailed black coat ornamented by only a single massive fob and the intricate white folds of his cravat, was arresting. Silence fell.

"Ladies and gentlemen," the ironic voice said again, and paused, as if to emphasise its mastery over his audience. "I now present to you the newest sensation of Vienna, a voice from Paradise—Mademoiselle Linnet!"

And with a careless wave of the hand he bade her proceed, while he himself melted back into the audience.

"I will sing for *him*," Letty vowed, aglow at this unex-

pected praise; and as the last chord of the introduction
sounded again her voice rang out, pure and clear, a small
thing but of utter beauty in that hot, crowded room.

She sang no intricate arias by Handel or Gluck; Sascha
had been wise enough to know that this untutored voice
could not hope to compare in dazzling vocal pyrotech-
nics with the trained artistry of a Catalini. The Countess's exquisite, plaintive "Porgi amor" from Mozart's
Marriage of Figaro was as far as she ventured into the
high art of opera; the remainder of the selections were
simple country ballads, or the popular sentimental
drawing-room favourites of the moment.

But the magic of that silver-pure voice was enough to
invest the melodies with a poignancy that entranced even
the motley jaded throng drawn to the villa by the
promise of Harry's faro-tables. Libertines who would
coolly have seduced the innocent village maidens of
whom Letty sang felt a lump in their throats; gamesters
and adventurers who had not set eyes on their mothers
for thirty years saw the scenes of their childhood rising
in silent, unbearable memory before them; titled ladies
and expensive courtesans alike frankly wept. At the conclusion of the first group of songs cheers erupted and by
the time the second group had ended, the room was
crowded almost to suffocation with a new influx of
patrons who had been drawn in from the gaming-rooms
by the sound of that clear, young voice. Ladies climbed
upon chairs the better to see this new songbird, and as
for the gentlemen, they were around her like bees
around clover, clamouring to be presented to her before
the supercilious pianist had so much as sounded the final
chord of her last song.

The old Baron did the honours, beaming proudly at
this fulfillment of his prophesy of *un succès éclatant* for
his young protegée. Letty, dazed and shy, found herself
curtseying to the princes and dukes and counts, heard
compliments showered upon her, but was too much
overcome by the suddenness of it all to savour her triumph to any notable extent. All she desired at the mo-

ment was to flee from the limelight in which she stood, but this was impossible as long as she was the cynosure of every eye and the object of everyone's curiosity.

Fortunately for her self-control, the arrival of a Very Important Personage, indeed one so eminent that he cast all the minor royalties in the shade, presently set the universal attention off in another direction. Before the watchful Miss Clark, who had been in attendance at a distance while awaiting her opportunity to play dragon, could monitor her movements through the shifting crowd, Letty was able to slip through a pair of red velvet curtains into a small and—she hoped—deserted anteroom.

It was not, however, deserted, she found. A very blond young lady in a very décolleté gown of blossom-pink sarcenet was standing before a pier-glass, frowning at her reflection and in vain attempting to secure with a pin the fragile piece of lace that prevented her bodice from slipping down and revealing even more of her rounded white bosom than the gown's artful designer had intended.

She whirled round, a look of satisfaction crossing her pretty face at sight of Letty.

"Good!" she exclaimed joyfully. "*You* will help me, *ma chérie!* Only look what that beast Babnitz has done to my gown! *C'est affreux—n'est-ce pas?* These *gentlemen—!*"

She shrugged her shoulders scornfully, holding out the pin to Letty with a dazzling and expectant smile upon her face. Letty took it doubtfully.

"It is so badly torn," she said, examining the delicate lace. "I doubt I can do it properly—"

"Then we must do it *im*properly—*n'est-ce pas?*" said the young lady buoyantly. "What does it matter, so long as I do not come to pieces entirely? I shall have the price of it out of my fine Count before morning, at any rate—never fear as to *that!*" She looked into Letty's face with open curiosity as she began to pin together the torn bits of lace. "You are Harry's newest girl—*n'est-ce pas?*" she enquired. "He is *tout généreux*—do you not find him so?"

Letty stared at her, letting the pin fall to the floor in her astonishment. For the first time it occurred to her that the young "lady" who had enlisted her assistance was not a lady at all, but what Sascha bluntly referred to as a member of the muslin company, one of the Birds of Paradise who were finding Vienna such a lucrative and enjoyable place to be at the present moment. The shock of this discovery, however, was as nothing in comparison with the disagreeable fact of her companion's having blandly referred to her as "Harry's newest girl," with the clear implication that more than one other ladybird had once claimed that position for herself.

"I am *not* Harry's girl!" she said indignantly, "He is—we are merely business associates!"

Her companion nodded sagely, and, picking up the pin, gave it back to her.

"Exactly as I said to Babnitz," she observed. "You are not at all Harry's type."

For some reason Letty found this remark quite as unpalatable as the one that had preceded it, but as her companion merely waited expectantly for her to resume the task of making her presentable, she swallowed her resentment and went back to the gown, her efforts rather impeded by its wearer's constantly turning about to see in the glass what she was doing.

"You don't know who I am, do you?" the young lady demanded suddenly, as Letty completed her task. "I am Ninette Forel. What is *your* name, *ma chère?*"

"I'm—*Oh!* Ninette Forel!" Letty broke off, as the significance of the name dawned upon her. Her eyes widened as they took in fully for the first time that blooming, rosy face, with its broad Flemish cheekbones and dazzlingly blonde Flemish hair. "Oh!" she repeated breathlessly. "You are the famous—You are General Sir Marius—"

"General Sir Marius Tyne's *chère-amie?* At the moment, yes," agreed Mlle. Forel with a little shrug. "He is *tout distingué, n'est-ce pas?* But so *boring*, my dear! My God, how bor-r-ring. Do you know his notion of entertaining me is to play the cello to me? *Mais vraiment!* That is why I am here tonight with Babnitz, which is most indiscreet of me, but after all, one cannot be discreet all the time!"

Letty, quite out of her depth, said she dared say one could not.

"But, then, why do you—?" she began, most indiscreetly upon her own part, and came to a halt, blushing.

"Why do I allow him to become my lover?" Mademoiselle Forel finished it for her, not at all discomposed. She turned to regard herself once more in the glass, pointing complacently to her diamond necklet, her diamond ear-rings, and the diamonds blazing upon her fingers. "For this—and this—and this—and this!" she declared happily. "They are *merveilleux, n'est-ce pas?* I can scarcely believe they are mine! For these I would stay with the devil himself! And at least," she added, with her ready ripple of laughter, "one would not be bored with *him!*"

Letty, not knowing whether to be more shocked or impressed by this entirely practical approach to the problem of relationships to members of the male sex, was about to ask another indiscreet question when the red velvet curtains abruptly parted behind her and Harry appeared in the aperture.

"Good God," he said in a resigned voice, as his eyes fell upon the two of them, "I might have known it! *Tête-à-tête* with the most notorious courtesan in Vienna! Come out of this, infant, and try to act as innocent and stupid as you are—"

"I am *not* stupid!" Letty broke in hotly, at the same moment Mademoiselle Forel said, with a happy smile that quite belied her words, "What a beast you are, Harry! I am not—how do you say it?—notorious: I am famous! You are having a great success tonight, *n'est-ce-pas?* I shall tell all my friends to come here—even your so r-r-respectable uncle, Sir Marius—"

"Never fear, he won't come," Harry said curtly. "And now listen to me, Ninette. You have never spoken to this young lady—do you understand me?"

"But I *have* spoken to her!" protested Ninette, opening her eyes wide. "I have spoken to her all the while she was mending my gown!"

"*And* she never mended your gown," Harry continued ruthlessly.

Ninette shrugged recalcitrantly. Harry, abandoning English, spoke to her in emphatic, fluent French, of so idiomatic a nature that Letty could not follow it at all. It apparently made the hoped-for impression upon Ninette, however, for she coloured up, bit her lip, and then, regaining her good humour as quickly as she had lost it, gave him another of her brilliant smiles.

"Oh, very well! I shall be good," she promised. "You are *ein guter Kerl,* Harry, and I like you very much. Will you be very *gentil* and let me win tonight?"

"I am never *gentil,*" Harry said. "Ask little Miss Linnet. Come along, my girl," he said to Letty, taking her arm with one masterful hand and holding back the red velvet curtain with the other. "I am going to take you to meet some respectable people."

"I don't think they can be very respectable or they wouldn't come *here,*" Letty said rebelliously. "And I shall speak to Mademoiselle Forel whenever I see her. I think she is very nice!"

"That," said Harry, "is exactly what you would think. If you speak to her, however, I shall beat you."

"That is what you always say, but I do not think you would."

"Don't you? Try me."

Letty gave him a smouldering glance, then tightened her lips and said primly, "No—I shall *not* speak to her because the old Baron would not like it. He says I am to be very respectable and he will arrange a brilliant marriage for me."

"Good luck to you both," Harry said, with complete indifference and a skepticism so marked that Letty's lips tightened once more.

They were in the *salon* again now. The Very Eminent Personage having gone to try his luck at the tables, it was almost empty. As Harry and Letty emerged through the red velvet curtain, however, a young officer in the striking red uniform of the Royal Hungarian Guard came striding purposefully up to them across the parquet floor. He bowed slightly to Harry.

"Monsieur, may I have the honour? Will you present me to Mademoiselle?" he asked.

Letty, looking up, found herself regarding one of the handsomest young men it had every been her fortune to behold. He was tall, fair-skinned and blue-eyed; with features of a classic regularity, and his broad-shouldered, narrow-waisted figure was set off to perfection by the tight-fitting, brilliant uniform with its tiger-skin pelisse falling negligently from one shoulder. If Letty, in her white gown, was a snow-princess awaiting the prince to waken her to life and love, this, a detached observer would have thought, was exactly the young man to fill the part.

This is exactly what Harry, a disinterested observer, thought, except for his natural interest that a young lady in whom he had invested a good deal of time and money not be swept off her feet and out of his ken. But being also highly skeptical regarding the occurrence of fairy-tale events in real life, he thought as well that, for young Miss Montressor's sake as well as his own, this was a young man who would bear watching. Young ladies, no matter how virginally innocent they were, had been known to throw their caps over the windmill for handsome young counts before this time.

"Mademoiselle Linnet—Count Radoczy," he said briefly, and was cut off as the young officer said quickly, raising Letty's gloved hand to his lips, "But that is not your real name, Mademoiselle? May I not have the privi-

lege—? You are Monsieur von Bergheim's niece, I understand—?"

"Y-yes," said Letty, maintaining just enough presence
of mind in the face of this magnificent apparition to cast
a questioning glance at Harry, who, having put the story
about in the first place as the surest means of stopping
the curiosity of busyheads, looked not in the least disapproving of her confirmation of it.

For his part, Radoczy remained quite oblivious to this
bit of by-play, being too intent upon his own ends to be
suspicious of anyone else's. As a member of one of the
first families of the Empire, and the possessor of both a
handsome person and a great fortune, he had found it
easy to embark early upon a series of amorous adventures. They had been carried on too discreetly to do him
a great deal of harm among matchmaking mothers, but
they had given him a considerable reputation among his
peers. In the staid circle of the pre-Congress Imperial
Court he had therefore passed as one of those slightly
dangerous young officers over whom young ladies love
to languish, but in the hectic pace of this new Vienna his
reputation had been so far eclipsed by that of more than
one more dashing visitor that he was determined to do
something to cause it to shine as brightly as before.

The "something" had presented itself to him that evening in the person of Letty. If she was to be Vienna's
newest sensation, it would be a feather in his cap indeed
to walk off with her as *his* conquest; and he was already
planning an attack that would have both amused and an-
gered Harry if he had been able to read his mind. As it
was, he, Harry, was quite shrewd enough to have no intention of leaving his "Mademoiselle Linnet" alone with
the tiger-skinned young Count, and with a lift of his
brows he had the ever-watchful Miss Clark proceeding
across the room from her corner with all dignified haste
to take her young ward promptly in charge.

Miss Parthenope Clark, Harry thought as he went off
to attend to his own pressing affairs, was a female well-
calculated to depress the pretensions even of so deter-

minedly romantic a sprig of Magyar nobility as Count Radoczy—and so, in the event, she proved to be. The count's pressing invitation to "Mademoiselle von Bergheim" to accompany him upon a scenic drive in his sleigh through the winter splendour of the hills beyond Vienna was received by her austere duenna with a contemptuous sniff; indicative, without the necessity of her uttering so much as a word, of the folly of his presuming to consider *her* charge the sort of hurly-burly girl who drove about with young officers unchaperoned; and the greatest concession he received was the promise that if cards of invitation for the young lady were forthcoming to some of the balls being given so incessantly at present among the *haut ton* in Vienna, she would be pleased to stand up with him for a set of country dances upon those occasions. The more daring waltzes, the rage of the moment, were not alluded to; indeed, the Count's well-known verve failed him under Miss Clark's glacial eye when it came to so much as mentioning it.

He did manage, however, to assure "Mademoiselle von Bergheim" in a meaningful undertone of his intention of seeing to it that more than one of these invitations were forthcoming—a prospect which Letty, although perfectly loyal to her unrequited love for Harry, found exceedingly alluring. She was not inclined to be particularly taken by the Count, whose manner she found to be entirely too negligently self-confident, in spite of the well-calculated fervour he had thrown into it. But when one's life has been such that male admiration has been an all but nonexistent quantity, any admirer is better than none. Harry would have been astonished to learn how coolly little Miss Montressor was able to assess this fairy-tale prince who had come to waken her from her virginal slumber—but then Harry did not know that little Miss Montressor was in love with *him*.

The old Baron, with his infinite experience of the female sex, did know, or at least had a shrewd suspicion of it, and was able to view with a good deal of equanimity the attempts of not only Count Radoczy but a number of other young and not-so-young gentlemen to ingratiate themselves with Vienna's newest celebrity. Certainly more equanimity than could Miss Clark, when the Baron came to relieve her gently but firmly of her guard duty over Letty. Now he sat a little distance away and smiled indulgently as Letty, seated upon a small satin sofa, gave audience to her throng of admirers. It was not until a diffident voice at his ear said, "She is very beautiful, Monsieur—and a voice like an angel! May I have the honour to be presented to her?"—that a slight frown crossed his face.

He turned slowly in his chair, confronting—as he had expected—a small man with the face of a dissipated baby, in which a pair of mournful dark eyes stood out like a pair of raisins in a suet pudding.

"Grün," he said, in anything but welcoming tones. "What are *you* doing here?"

"In Vienna?" The little man spread innocently explanatory hands. "But, my dear Baron, like all the world—I have come to see the show! Kings, generals, statesmen—for a poor man like myself, it is a rare opportunity—"

"A rare opportunity for knavery—yes, I make no doubt of *that!*" said the old Baron, regarding him with uncharacteristic grimness. "But I did not mean to enquire what you are doing in Vienna, but what you are doing here, in this house. Who admitted you? You cannot have had a card—"

"No, no, I had not that honour!" Grün hastened to admit, in his eager, plaintive voice. "But when one arrives in the train of an Important Personage, one is not questioned, you see."

The old Baron regarded him with an expression of disgust. "So you have succeeded again in playing the leech," he said. "I should have thought there was no one in Europe who did not know you by this time!"

The little man shrugged, unperturbed. "He is a very small Important Personage, you see," he explained, with his slight, anxious smile. "And he pays very badly, I can

tell you. Monsieur le Baron, I ask you again, will you
not present me to the young lady?"

"I am more likely to show you the door!" the old
Baron said, with unusual energy. "It will save Harry the
trouble—"

"But Harry will not like you to show me the door,"
the little man protested, aggrieved but not offended.
"I have come here particularly to see him—upon a matter of business—"

"Business? Harry will do no business with *you*," said
the old Baron.

"Oh, but he will! It will be so very much to his advantage, you see!" Grün assured him. He leaned over the
old Baron's chair and said in an eager whisper, "I have—"
He added in an even lower undertone, "information—"
while he cast a rapid glance about him to assure himself
that all attention was still concentrated on Letty. "Very,
very valuable information!"

The old Baron continued to regard him with weary
disgust. "Grün," he said after a moment, in his deliberate
way, "I shall give you a piece of advice. Do not go to
Harry with any proposals. You had an opportunity once
to do him a great service—or at least to attempt to do
him one, but God knows your word was worth little
more eight years ago than it is today. You did not take
that opportunity—and now, *now* you wish to go to
Harry and tell him you are ready, *for a certain sum*, to
swear to the world that he is an innocent man falsely accused—! Faugh!" The old Baron made an impatient gesture. "Your word is worth nothing, Grün! Harry knows,
like all the rest of the world, that it is for sale to the
highest bidder!"

The little man began once more to protest, but the old
Baron rose from his chair and walked, oblivious to his
pleas, to the sofa where Letty sat. She glanced up at him
enquiringly, and he looked down affectionately at her
face, flushed and starry-eyed with the excitement of her
triumph.

"Come, *ma chère!*" he said, "it is time for you to say goodnight. There will be other nights—"

A chorus of protests drowned the rest of his words, through which a clear feminine voice abruptly made itself heard.

"Baron! My dearest! You are going to take her away just as I arrive! Let me at least have a look at her! My God, she is an angel, if one can credit half one hears!"

Letty, looking up quickly, saw a tall, dark-haired young woman in white satin, magnificently jewelled, looking as though she had just come from the Imperial box at the Opera—which indeed she had—and carrying what at first sight appeared to be a white fur muff. Only when the silky mass moved and revealed a pair of enquiring dark eyes and a small pink tongue did Letty realise it was a dog.

Lady Hester! some instinct told her—and it was, in fact, the name of Lady Hester Luddington that the old Baron pronounced.

"How do you do?" said Lady Hester, surveying her frankly.

She was not beautiful in the conventional sense of the word, thought Letty as she sank into her curtsey; the features were clear-cut but more boldly defined than the usual standards of feminine comeliness allowed, and the heavy raven hair worn severely swept back from her broad white forehead made no concessions to fashion's current preference for multitudes of curls.

No, "*striking*" rather than "*beautiful*," was the word to describe her, Letty felt; but the sense of defeat and dismay she had always experienced when Lady Hester's name had been mentioned was in no way lessened by this discovery. On the contrary, it was intensified, particularly as she saw that all the gentlemen who a moment before had had eyes only for her were now regarding Lady Hester instead, and with even more animation and admiration than they had bestowed upon her.

"Charming!" Lady Hester was saying meanwhile. She placed a careless forefinger under Letty's chin, the better to examine her face, as Letty rose from her curtsey; "But really charming! And she is your niece? grand-niece, Baron, my dear? Where have you been hiding her all this time? In a convent, I'll swear! She looks entirely too innocent for the likes of this!"

She cast an expressive glance about her at the expensive, wicked-looking room hung in puckered crimson satin, but before the old Baron could answer, her attention was diverted by the sight of Harry, who had just become visible through the doorway at the far end of the room, standing in colloquy with a patron just out of view.

"Harry!" she called out. Harry turned about abruptly. "Harry, my own!" she went on, sweeping down the room towards him in a grand flurry of fluttering draperies, glinting jewels, and yapping lapdog, the latter suddenly roused from passivity by her raised voice. "Where did you find this treasure? Rumours have been flying for days, and, by God, it seems that for once they were true! You will have *un succès fou*, everyone says so. You see I have jeopardised my own reputation to come and view the marvel for myself—".

"Your reputation, Lady Hester?" Harry enquired, coming to meet her, looking grave, but with an ironic glint in his dark eyes. "Is it possible that there is any sort of dangerous situation that it has not already confronted and overcome?"

Lady Hester gave a shout of laughter, and Letty, seizing her opportunity, fled. She did not wish to see any more of that meeting—not, she told herself, her chin in the air, that young Count Radoczy was not far handsomer than was Harry, and *he* had managed to convey to her, in a rapid undertone beneath Miss Clark's very nose, the fact that he considered *her* the most beautiful and desirable creature he had ever met. She cast a sideways glance at her own reflection in a long gilt pier-glass in the empty hallway as she prepared to ascend the stairs, hesitating before it, half doubtful, half enchanged by her own unfamiliar appearance in the gossamer-thin muslin gown with the wreath of flowers in her dark hair.

"Mademoiselle von Bergheim!" a voice suddenly hissed urgently behind her.

She whirled about. A little round man in elegant evening dress, his person strongly scented with Steek's lavender water, was hurrying towards her across the polished floor.

"Mademoiselle von Bergheim! One little moment please! You will allow me to speak with you for one little moment?"

She looked at him enquiringly as he came up beside her, panting slightly from his haste.

"Yes?"

"But one little moment, if you will be so gracious!" The little man paused for a moment to catch his breath. "It is about Harry—Monsieur Tyne," he explained, looking at her out of eager, mournful dark eyes. "You will convey a message to him for me, perhaps?"

"Oh, yes," she said readily. "If you wish me to. But you may just as well speak to him yourself, you know." She pointed towards the room she had just left. "He is in there, talking to Lady Hester Luddington."

"Yes, yes, I know." The little man's eyes became more mournful than ever. "But I am much afraid to speak to him. *Der alte Baron* says he will have me thrown out and that is quite possible, you know. With Harry, one can never tell—"

"No, one can't, can one?" said Letty sympathetically. "He is a *quite* unpredictable sort of person. But why will he have you thrown out? Is it because he doesn't like you?"

The little man said feelingly that that was a great understatement of the situation.

"I will tell you this, however, about Harry," he added earnestly "He has a generous soul—yes! A generous soul! He is not a nip-squeeze, like some I could name! That is the proper English expression—no?—for a man who does not wish to part with his money, even for a deserving purpose?"

Letty sapiently regarded the little man. "Are you the 'deserving purpose'?" she enquired. "I must say, you don't look very deserving to me. Or very needy, either," she added, glancing over his ridiculously elegant person, which was decked with a profusion of fobs, seals, and rings.

The little man looked wounded. "*Gnädiges Fräulein,* I am destitute!" he insisted. "I am the victim of the basest ingratitude! If Harry does not come to my aid, I am ruined!"

"Are you?" said Letty, with great interest. "I have never met anyone who was *really* ruined. Sascha keeps saying that Harry will be if he doesn't stop spending money on this house, but Harry pays no attention to him at all. I don't think Harry has any money, by the bye; it is all the Old Baron's. Why don't you ask *him* to help you?"

The little man brushed this suggestion aside. "Harry will soon have money; he will be floating in it," he said with conviction. "It is you, Mademoiselle, with your angel's voice, who will bring it to him. Is he in love with you?" he asked, suddenly and naïvely.

"With me? No!"

Her companion shook his head sadly. "*C'est dommage,*" he said. "A great pity! If he were in love with you and you were to ask him to help me, then he would certainly do it."

Letty, still somewhat ruffled by having given what she felt was a far too vehement denial when cool indifference would have been far more becoming, said she didn't in the least know why she should ask Harry to help him, whether he, Harry, was in love with her or not.

The little man came closer to her. "Because," he breathed nervously into her ear, "I have information, Mademoiselle. Information of incalculable value to him! And not only information—proof!" He glanced nervously around at the porter, who had just opened the door to admit a fresh bevy of patrons on a gust of cold, wintery night air. "Tell him that, Mademoiselle!" he urged. "Tell him I have proof!"

Letty was burning to ask him, proof of what? but it was quite obvious that the influx of newcomers made the little man even more nervous than he had been before. Fixing an anxious smile upon his face he scuttled to the door, bowing indiscriminately to right and left as he did so—an act of civility that elicited only one response from the entering group, a stare and an exclamation from one young English officer: "Grün! What the devil is *he* doing in Vienna?"

"More than likely what he is always doing—trying to milk pigeons," his companion replied carelessly—a remark that sent Letty up the staircase with a puzzled frown upon her face.

She had a very good idea what the expression "milk pigeons" meant; but the little man must be all about in his head, she thought, if he had any hope in his mind of extracting any milk from Harry Tyne.

Chapter 5

"MR. GRÜN," SHE said conversationally to Harry over breakfast the next morning, "asked me last night to tell you that he had some very valuable information for you."

Harry and the old Baron exchanged glances. They had been deep in a discussion of the success of the establishment's opening night, while Letty interspersed drinking her chocolate and eating the delicious *croissants* prepared by the French chef, with a delightful perusal of the notes accompanying the many bouquets and posies that had arrived for her that morning. The door-knocker had been silent now for some time, and she had had leisure to remember her conversation with the little man and the message with which he had charged her.

The old Baron was the first to speak. "Our friend," he said to Harry in his deliberate, impartial way, "intends to miss no opportunities, it seems. Will you see him?"

"No," said Harry, while at the same moment Letty informed him, "He says he not only has information, he has proof."

Harry merely shrugged and went back to his examination of a long column of figures on a sheet of paper beside his plate. But the old Baron frowned slightly and gave Harry another glance from beneath his grey brows.

"Proof? *That* is something new," he said slowly. "New and—highly dangerous, perhaps—"

"To him, yes—if Marius hears of it," Harry said indifferently. "He will take good care that he does not, I imagine." He glanced up impatiently as the Baron began to speak again, "It is a bag of moonshine, very probably, Max, some faradiddle he has concocted in the forlorn hope I'll be gullible enough to tip over the dibs for it."

The Baron still frowned, though he nodded his head in assent. "Or perhaps," he said musingly after a moment, "it is not you, *mon cher*, but Sir Marius, that he is angling for, after all. That 'proof'—whatever it is—would most assuredly be quite as valuable to your uncle as it would be to you."

Harry, still engrossed in his figures, said that that might well be so, and that if he knew Grün he had at least two strings to his bow and probably several more, each more unscrupulous than the last, all of which, however, still left him, Harry, quite uninterested.

"I am the devil of a lot more interested," he said, turning the subject, "in the reason why we were honoured with the presence of no fewer than three members of the secret police in our rooms last night. They were painfully obvious; that sort of thing can give us a bad name, you know. One doesn't particularly mind secret police if they had the good *ton* to live up to their name and remain secret, but those fellows last night—"

The old Baron shrugged. "*Mon cher*," he said, "this is Vienna. The good Emperor is accustomed to keeping his nose in everyone's affairs. It is all very cosy and *domestique on voit*—so you can scarcely expect such a spectacular establishment as we have set up here to escape his notice. No doubt he is reading a full report this morning of everyone who honoured us with his—or her—presence last night—"

Harry gave a crack of laughter. "Which lands La Forel, for one, in a bumblebath," he said, "for what the Emperor knows, I gather Marius soon knows as well. I can picture the lecture he will read her today!"

The old Baron said indulgently, "She is very indiscreet—but very charming, as well. I doubt that her little escapade will lead to anything serious between them."

"No," agreed Harry, "for once in his life, by what I hear, my cold-livered uncle is thoroughly *épris*. Seriously, though, Max, can't you drop a word in the proper ears that we'd be appreciative of a somewhat higher class of police, if we *must* be kept under surveillance?"

"Oh, yes," said the old Baron, with his weary, kindly smile. "Oh, yes! I will do what I can. The difficulty is, *mon cher*, that Sascha has been too clever in seeing to it that all the servants we have here in this house can be trusted; it makes it so much simpler for the authorities, you see, when they can rely on receiving a report each day from a footman, or a porter, or a coachman—"

"What—a resident spy? No, thank you!" said Harry emphatically. "I'm not such a cod's head as to pay someone to pry into my affairs!"

Letty, who had been waiting with marked impatience for the conversation to come to an end, at this point broke in to enquire what answer she was then to give to Monsieur Grün when next she met him.

"No answer at all," Harry said promptly. "You are not to speak to him again. Is that understood?"

Letty looked rebellious. "First I am not to speak to Mademoiselle Forel," she said, "and now I am not to speak to Monsieur Grün. To whom may I speak, then? To Lady Hester Luddington? Or is she too scandalous for me to know, too?"

Harry, going back to his figures, said not to be impertinent. The old Baron looked at her sympathetically. But Letty, flown with bouquets and compliments, had got the bit between her teeth and said, somewhat gradiloquently, that she would speak to whomever she chose.

Fortunately, at this point a footman entered bearing an impressive-looking billet, which turned out to be a note from no less a personage than one of the Empress Maria Ludovica's ladies-in-waiting, commanding Letty's presence on an excursion that was to be made that very afternoon to Laxenburg, and indicating that she would be expected to sing for the Imperial family and their guests.

The old Baron gave a delighted little crow of laughter. "So soon!" he said. "*Ma chère*, truly, like your Lord Byron, you awake to find yourself made famous over night! One sees for oneself their Imperial Highnesses do not wish to be the last in Vienna to hear this new marvel!"

He beamed upon Letty. She, for her part, had thought herself inured to the splendours of success after the events of the previous evening, but this new evidence of the eminence to which she had suddenly risen almost took her breath away. The only thing she could think of to do, under the circumstances, was to run pell-mell to Miss Clark and discuss with her the burningly important question of what she was to wear for the occasion—a problem which that resourceful lady showed herself to be adept at solving. For the drive to Laxenburg she recommended a costume of royal blue velvet, with a *coureur* jacket faced in white and a white brazeen waistcoat, under her new Polish *witchoura:* a wide, hooded, fur-lined coat worn as a cloak, with the sleeves hanging down behind, which had been purchased with just such a wintry occasion in mind. And, for her evening appearance before the Royal audience, a gown of white tulle with the new shorter, fuller skirt, revealing a decorous glimpse of silk stockings with openwork insets.

The morning passed in a whirl of preparations, a mad scramble of sessions with hairdresser and mantua-maker, rehearsals with Sascha and the bored pianist; and the last-minute instructions from Miss Clark on the fine points of Court etiquette. The result of all this was that by the time she came downstairs, ready for the twelve-mile drive to Laxenburg, she was in such a state of nerves that she would have liked nothing better than to flee to the farthest attic, lock herself in, and throw away the key.

Instead, however, true to her training, she came down the stairs looking as aloof and regal as a princess herself in her long, furred, hooded cloak, only the paleness of her face betraying her terror.

A figure in brilliant uniform awaited her in the hall below, and the joy of recognising a familiar face flooded over her as the figure turned and she saw Count Radoczy.

He hurried towards her. "You see, Mademoiselle, as I told you last night—I have influence and I have used it!" he greeted her, smiling ardently at her as he bowed over her hand. "It does not distress you that I am to have the honour of escorting you to Laxenburg?"

"Distress me? Oh, no!" Letty said in heart-felt tones.

And, indeed, so greatly relieved was she to find she was not to make the drive in company with some austere and elderly State official that the Count might have been pardoned for believing that she was already inclined to respond favourably to his openly expressed admiration.

Not, of course, that the drive was to be made without the proper chaperonage for the young and innocent "Mademoiselle Linnet." Letty found one of the Empress's ladies-in-waiting already ensconced beneath the furs lavishly piled in the gilded, emerald-velvet-lined sleigh that waited outside, its harness joyously decked with silver bells and its six black horses proudly fretting under their tiger-skin caparisons. But thanks, no doubt, to Count Radoczy's influence, she turned out to be a very young and lively *Gräfin*, much inclined to turn an indulgently blind eye and deaf ear to the warm flirtation the Count began as soon as the coachman had given the horses the office to start. Indeed, from what Letty was able to see as they joined the gay cortège of more than thirty sleighs that fell in behind the Imperial equipage for the drive to Laxenburg, flirtation was the rule of the day, and the *Gräfin* herself, as soon as their destination had been reached, was joined by a handsome young officer in the red uniform of the German Guard, who appeared quite oblivious to the fact that there was a gold

wedding ring upon the delicate white hand that now and
again was withdrawn from the shelter of a sable muff to
be raised to the ardent lips of her *cicibeo*.

Letty had never seen Laxenburg, upon which the Emperor had lavished a great deal of money and attention,
having erected a remarkably attractive water castle in
the mediaeval style on an island in the center of an artificial lake, furnishing it with a collection of rare antique
furniture and paintings. She had heard it described by
the old Baron, however, and was therefore prepared to
be charmed and impressed by what she saw, which she
was, to the extent that her exclamations of delight and
awe rudely interrupted the course of the flirtation the
Count was doing his best to carry on with her. Radoczy
was already perfectly familiar with the appearance of the
Laxenburg rising, with its snow-capped spires and bas-
tions, like a fairy-tale castle from the still, frozen waters
of the surrounding lake, and he was scarcely interested
in the raptures into which it cast Letty. He was reduced
to pulling his handsome blond Hussar's moustache in impotent impatience as she then transferred her attention,
with equal ardour to the entertainment provided for the
guests once the sleighs had been drawn up in a half-
circle at the verge of the lake. The young officer's appetite for balls, galas, operas, fire works, *tableaux vivants*,
and sundry theatrical extravaganzas of every conceivable
sort had already been jaded by the ceaseless round of entertainments presented for the Imperial guests. So the
sight of a pair of comely Dutch skaters in milkmaid's
costumes performing terpsichorean evolutions upon the
ice, or a young Englishman tracing with his skates the
monograms of the attendant queens and empresses, was
scarcely a matter for violent enthusiasm, and he became
aware of a distinct sensation of boredom such as what he
felt each December fifth when called upon to take part
in the Krampus Eve festivities held for the benefit of his
elder sister's large brood of small children. "Mademoiselle Linnet," it appeared, was still very much of a
child herself, and, though he shared the fashionable pref-

erence of the day for very young girls, one *did* expect a
female in her position, no matter how young, to be, as
the English expressed it, rather more "up to snuff" than
she seemed.

Meanwhile Letty, quite unconscious of his displeasure,
was enjoying several cups of the hot chocolate brought
to the guests from the gay little tents that had been
erected on the shores of the lake, and would have considered herself in a state of perfect bliss had it not been
for the daunting prospect of being obliged very soon to
perform before an assembly in which kings and queens
were as common as gooseberries. She wished fervently
that the old Baron were there to comfort and encourage
her, or even that Sascha's familiar black-browed, disapprovingly frowning face would suddenly appear beside
her.

But there was no one—once the outdoor entertainment
had ended and the guests had repaired to the castle—but
a prim-faced maidservant to assist her with her toilette in
the splendid bedchamber to which she was shown, and
an equally proper manservant to carry in a supper tray
for her while the Emperor's guests dined in state below.

She felt, however, that it would not do to shame
Harry and disappoint Sascha and the old Baron by giving way to her fears, so she resolutely drank a little soup
and nibbled at the chicken that had been brought to her,
and when a knock fell at the door—the fateful knock
that signalled the moment for her to go downstairs—although she appeared almost as pale as her gauzy white
gown, she was outwardly serene.

To her joy, it was again Count Radoczy, instead of
some formidable Court functionary, who stood outside,
waiting to escort her into the presence of the Emperor
and his illustrious guests.

"Oh, how glad I am that it is you!" she said to him,
quite unwisely, it appeared, for his response was to close
the door behind her in the prim maid-servant's face and,
sweeping her into his arms in the silent, splendid cor-
ridor, implant a fervid kiss upon her lips.

"*Oh!*" gasped Letty. She wriggled free of his embrace and stood looking up at him, an expression of frowning indecision upon her face. "I *don't* think you ought to have done that," she said after a moment. "It is *not* what I have been led to expect of Court etiquette!"

"Didn't you like it?" demanded the Count, a bit non-plussed by this original response to his love-making, but on the whole rather satisfied by the effect he had made.

Letty shook her head definitely. "Your moustache is quite bristly," she said, "and besides I am sure it is all very improper. You must promise me not to do it again."

The Count, twirling the despised moustache, said audaciously that she was entirely too enchanting for him to be able to promise anything of the kind.

"Am I?" asked Letty, pleased by this idea. She considered. "I daresay, from what I have heard and read," she conceded then, "that it *is* difficult for gentlemen not to kiss pretty girls. But you *will* promise to try, won't you?"

The Count assured her that he would, but was again so carried away by his feelings as they descended the stairs together that he was obliged to bend his head and brush the nape of her neck, just where the dark tendrils fell in delicate curls, with his lips.

Once they had entered the presence of the Emperor and his guests, however, he appeared to regain complete control of his feelings, for there were no other demonstrations of an affectionate nature as he led her very properly to the great leather-cased pianoforte. The accompanist, entering unobtrusively behind them, seated himself and ran his fingers over the keys, and Letty heard a rustle of anticipation from the assemblage, so much more brilliant than the one she had faced the preceding evening that she was quite dazzled by the sparkle of priceless jewels, the gleam of lustrous satins and velvets, and the imposing array of orders.

From this brilliant assembly she could distinguish only one face—the pale, beautiful countenance of the Empress Maria Ludovica, with whose portrait she, like everyone else in Vienna, was familiar—though of course the portraits did not show the signs of illness so evident on the face before her. But it showed such an approving smile that Letty took courage to launch into her first song, and soon the perplexing phenomenon that she had noted on the occasion of her debut began to occur: the gentlemen became very red in the face, cleared their throats, and appeared to have difficulty in swallowing, and the ladies—queens and empresses included—drew out their handkerchiefs and frankly wept.

"*Innocente*," "*spirituelle*" were the words that rose from all sides to describe her performance when she had finished; she was "*un petit bijou*," in the Empress's words; and the Emperor himself beckoned her to him and patted her hand in a fatherly fashion. Meanwhile, Count Radoczy, who it was well known had driven this newest sensation out from town, and who had not been averse to dropping a few casual hints as to the inroads he had already made upon her heart, stood by, enjoying her triumph quite as much as she did herself and waiting to be the first to lead her onto the floor, as an orchestra struck up a gay tune for the dancing that was to follow in an adjoining room.

He had the first dance, but not the last, for her hand was sought by so many of the exalted personages present, including an Hereditary Prince and several Highnesses, that she was not permitted to sit down for a single dance. It was like a dream, she thought, one of those splendid, impossible dreams she had made up during the long, tedious hours when she had sat winding yarn for the old Countess or mending linen in the solitude of her own small room. She, Letty Montressor, wearing a beautiful, gossamer-sheer gown, with flowers in her hair and satin slippers on her feet, would dance the night through in a gay whirl of romance and handsome partners, while melting strings played the intoxicating, forbidden strains of a waltz and thousands of candles shone in crystal chandeliers, illuminating her reflection in a hundred mirrors.

The mirrors might be absent now, and her partners, particularly the exalted personages among them, might not all be young and handsome and romantic, but the reality was sufficiently akin to the dream to send her out into the night, when the dancing was over, feeling quite as blissful as Cinderella must have done before the fateful strokes of midnight sounded.

Snow had begun to fall again by that time—great, whirling flakes that settled upon the thick furs wrapped solicitously about her by Radoczy before he took his place in the sleigh beside her and the *Gräfin*, the latter now slightly tipsy and very, very gay.

"What a beautiful night! What thousands and *millions* of stars!" she exclaimed several times, cavalierly rejecting the Count's explanation that they were not stars, but snowflakes—and then she promptly fell asleep.

What better opportunity could a handsome young man have had to press his attentions upon a not entirely unresponsive young lady? Letty was still in her romantic dream; if one shut one's eyes, one might well imagine it was Harry's hand, not the Count's, that clasped hers so warmly under the furs, that it was Harry's lips that brushed her cold cheek—except for the fact, of course, that Harry had no moustache. But then even in a dream one cannot have everything.

"*Mon amour, mon petit chou*," the Count murmured ardently, thinking what a fine story this would make for his cronies over the coffee cups the following morning, and dwelling with particular satisfaction upon the effect his conquest of Vienna's latest sensation would have upon the hitherto unchallenged status of General Sir Marius Tyne, who, by an act of munificent generosity, had quite unfairly managed to cut him out with Vienna's latest sensation but one, Mademoiselle Ninette Forel.

Meanwhile, Letty, still enjoying for her part the heady atmosphere of her romantic dream, was thinking with equal satisfaction that now, most definitely, she was truly grown up and ready to compete even with Lady Hester Luddington for Harry's affections.

Chapter 6

IT WAS A dream from which she was most rudely awak-
ened on her arrival back in town. She found Harry in
what was, for him, a towering rage—that is, he was curt,
bitingly sarcastic, and disinclined to listen to a word she
could say in her own defence. This—alas—was not a great
deal, for it was quite true that the coachman, inspired by
a coin pressed into his hand by Count Radoczy, had
taken a roundabout way back to town; so that she, Radoczy, and the somnolent *Gräfin* had not arrived until
long after the hour at which some of the other guests,
who had decided to finish off the evening by looking in
at Harry's establishment, had alerted him to the fact
that she too ought by that time to have made her appearance. It was, in truth, almost three o'clock in the
morning.

Under the circumstances, Count Radoczy, who was
something of a firebrand himself but not so foolhardy as
to seek a quarrel with so well-known a duellist as Harry
Tyne, was glad to put forth the excuse of being obliged
to escort the *Gräfin* to her home and to disappear
quickly into the snowy night. Letty would have been
happy to do the same, but was obliged to tell Harry,
with what she hoped was a propitiatingly dutiful air, that
she was very sleepy and would go upstairs at once to her

bed. She was, however, at once peremptorily halted by
Harry, who said he had a houseful of people who had
come to hear her, and hear her they should, even though
she were to fall asleep in the middle of a song.

They were standing in the hall, just inside the front
door, when this uncompromising statement was made,
and fortunately (for it had immediately set Letty's back
up and she was about to state categorically that she had
no intention of singing another note that evening) the
door opened at that moment to admit Mademoiselle
Forel on the arm of a tall, austerely handsome gentleman
of middle age, wearing the uniform of a British general
under his cloak. At sight of Harry, he checked slightly
for a moment, then imperturbably removed his gloves
and hat. He then handed them to the porter and allowed
a footman to remove his cloak.

Meanwhile Harry had not moved or spoken, but
Letty, conscious of some unusual tension in the air, cast a
quick glance at his face and saw an odd, mocking smile
upon it that for some reason gave her the instant conviction that if she were the new arrival she would feel very
uncomfortable indeed.

When Harry spoke, however, it was in his usual ironic
drawl. "Well, Marius! Your uniform, I see, is a passport
that opens all doors! You have *not*, however, had a card,
I believe?"

The porter looked abashed; the footman, casting a
glance at Harry's eyes, made haste to escape on the pre-
text of bestowing the newcomer's cloak and hat; but
General Sir Marius Tyne—for of the identity of the
gentleman who stood before her, Letty had not the least
doubt—merely advanced upon Harry with his hand outstretched and a tolerant smile upon his lips.

"Good evening, Harry," he said, and, as Harry ignored the proffered hand, he went on in a tone of faint
reproach, "I had hoped we might meet as friends, my
boy, after the passage of so many years. It can't be that
you are still harbouring the fantastic notion that your

unfortunate difficulties of that time are to be laid at my door!"

"Can't it?" said Harry coolly, but still, a fascinated Letty saw, with that dangerous glint in his eyes. "And what reason can you suggest, my dear Uncle, for me to have changed my opinion?"

A deeper shade of reproach appeared in Sir Marius's fine dark eyes. "Harry, Harry!" he said sadly, "how often must I tell you that no one could have been more cut to the heart than I was to see you fall into those difficulties? Ask your great-uncle. He would be the first to tell you how I urged him not to take any precipitate action against you—"

"Yes, so he informed me at the time," Harry said dryly. "It was easy, I imagine, for you to play a generous role when you were quite sure it would cost you nothing—especially since you took great care to qualify your pleas for mercy with the clear insinuation that I was actually guilty, all under cover of blaming the crime on my youth and inexperience. You played your game very cleverly there, Uncle, I must admit!"

Sir Marius sadly shook his head. "How you misconstrue me, Harry!" he said. "My motives, I assure you, were only to promote your interests with my uncle—"

"Well, you've promoted them so effectively that he has refused to see me since that time," Harry said bluntly, "to say nothing of the fact that he cast me on the world to make my own way in it as best I could—which, as you can see, I've managed to do. But I'm damned if I'll stand here listening to any more of your pious platitudes, Marius. If you came here to play, feel free to go into any of the rooms, but don't expect *my* company when you do!" He turned on his heel, but a new thought caused him to turn again and remark sarcastically, "And, bye the bye, when you've completed your inspection of the house, you might tell your friend the Emperor to call off that battalion of spies he has loosed upon us. What is he expecting to find here? Inter-

national intrigue doesn't interest us; our only concern is
to make money."

To Letty's surprise, an ambiguous expression swiftly
crossed Sir Marius's handsome face as Harry uttered
these words, an expression certainly of agitation, and
perhaps—improbable as it seemed—even of fear. It disappeared almost at once beneath the urbane mask he had
worn until this time, but there was a certain wary eager-
ness behind the elaborately casual tone in which he said,
"My dear boy, of course no one suspects you! These affairs are purely a matter of routine! Although," and here
the elaborate casualness became even more pronounced,
"it *might* help if you were not seen to entertain certain
persons of a—shall we say?—markedly unsavoury character here . . ."

"Such as—" Harry prompted him ironically, his eyebrows high. "I am rather interested in your notion of
'*unsavory characters*,'" Marius; I think you must be a
connoisseur in that field!"

A faint flush tinged Sir Marius's sallow cheeks. "I find
such humour in singularly bad taste, Harry!" he said
coldly. "I was referring, however, if you wish me to be
specific, to Grün. A thoroughly unreliable person, and
one whom I think you would be well advised to see very
little of—"

Harry's brows had gone even higher. "Grün," he repeated. "So that's it, is it? My dear uncle, you must have
the wind up very badly to be frightened of anything
Grün may say! It may be to *my* advantage to believe
him, but you are a lobcock indeed if you think anyone
else will! If *that* is all your spies are up to, I can assure
you that we'll show Grün the door on the next occasion
he puts in an appearance here. Anything, so we are left
in peace!"

And he walked off, leaving Sir Marius looking after
him in icy—but, Letty thought, rather relieved—displeasure.

At this point, Mademoiselle Forel, who with unusual
prudence had remained quite in the background as this

dialogue went forward, remarked to her escort that she wished to make some little adjustments to her dress before she went into the room, and, urging him to go on before her, winked at Letty and walked into the ante-room that had been set aside for that feminine purpose. Letty at once followed her, and saw that she had already seated herself at a charming little dressing table and was regarding her pretty face with great complacency in the gilt mirror above it.

"I look beautiful this evening, *n'est-ce pas?*" she enquired buoyantly, giving a careless pat to one of her flaxen-fair curls. "But, my God, how bor-r-ring these men are, with their plots and their intrigues! Do you know what it is about? All *I* know is that Marius is frightened half out of his skin, and it makes him more tedious than ever!"

Letty, sitting down in a small satinwood armchair near her, asked with interest what it was that Sir Marius was frightened of.

"Grün—Grün—Grün!" said Ninette, still smiling pleasurably at her own reflection in the mirror. "Of course," she added, turning to Letty with a more serious air, "he does not *tell* me that, but I overhear a great deal, you understand. In my position, it pays to know what is going on, *n'est-ce pas?*"

"Yes, I daresay it does," Letty agreed, cavalierly setting aside all her scruples against eavesdropping. "But *why* should he be afraid of Grün? And *what* has it all to do with Harry?"

"Oh, my God, it is about some indiscretion of Harry's that happened years ago, I think, when he was in the army," Ninette replied, without displaying a great deal of interest. "Cheating at cards, or some little something of that sort. Just between you and me, *ma chère*, I have an idea that Marius knows more about that affair than he should, and you know Harry swears he was falsely accused. But then, all men do that. Isn't it tiresome of them? *Moi*, when I make a little mistake, I am always the first to admit it, which makes everything much simpler in the long run—"

"Yes, but Grün," Letty somewhat impatiently brought her back to the matter at hand. "What has *he* to do with all this? And why is Sir Marius afraid of him?"

Ninette shrugged. "God knows! But you know how Grün is—if anyone has a dirty little secret, he is always sure to ferret it out. So perhaps he has ferreted out one of Marius's. Do you like this dress? It cost three hundred guineas. Marius will be furious when he sees the bill."

Letty assured her that her frock—an enchanting creation of lemon-yellow crêpe, its flounced skirt short enough to give a generous view of a pair of slender ankles clad in golden-yellow silk stockings embroidered with red roses—was charming, but Letty went back persistently to *l'affaire Grün*.

"So what you think is, that Sir Marius is afraid that Grün will tell Harry the secret, and then Harry will be rehabilitated in Society and Sir Marius will be disgraced—is that it?" she demanded. "I *wish*," she added impatiently, as Ninette began to show signs of regretting her indiscretion in speaking so freely, and of being reluctant to continue the conversation, "that people would *tell* me things; Sascha is always dropping hints, but he will never tell me what really happened when Harry was in the army, and even the old Baron doesn't like to talk about it."

But Ninette was to be drawn out no further. "*Ma chère*, I will give you a very good piece of advice," she observed, as she cast a last admiring glance at her reflection in the mirror and arose from her seat before the dressing table. "Never, *never* meddle in men's affairs; they are so bor-r-ring, and then one always ends up in the—how do you say it?—in the brairs, because they become so furious when one interferes! Believe me, they are all alike! And now I must go and try my luck at the tables. I feel very lucky tonight, I think. Who knows? I may win a fortune, and then I shall buy a little farm, and keep chickens and ducks, and snap my fingers—" she suited the action to the words—"under Sir Marius Tyne's nose!"

She was out of the room in a whirl of yellow skirts, and Letty was left to ponder with a frown the significance of their conversation. Quite obviously Sir Marius, at least, believed that the information of which Grün had spoken to her was of the greatest importance, no matter how contemptuously Harry had dismissed the matter when she had broached it to him. Sir Marius was equally prepared to go to considerable lengths to make certain that it did not reach Harry's ears. There was not the least doubt in her mind by this time that Harry was innocent of the charges that had caused him to leave the army so abruptly, and that Sir Marius had somehow been involved in those charges being brought against him; and a beautiful dream began to form in her mind: he would be cleared through her instrumentality, and he would be so grateful to her, and so astounded by her perspicacity, that he would immediately fall in love with her and forget all about Lady Hester Luddington.

At the moment, however, *she* was not going to forget that she was very angry with him for being so rude to her when she had returned with Count Radoczy, and that she was quite determined not to give in to his orders that she was to sing again that night. So she presently arose with the intention of slipping out of the room and up the stairs to her bedchamber before he could lay hold of her again—only to find herself brought up short, the moment she stepped outside the door, by the sight of Grün himself standing not three feet away in the hall, with the patient air of a man prepared to go on standing there all night, if necessary.

His mournful dark eyes lit up as soon as he saw her emerge from the anteroom.

"Mademoiselle!" he exclaimed, hastening towards her eagerly. "You will spare me one little minute? Only one little minute of your time?"

Letty, delighted by her good fortune in coming across

him so promptly, said graciously that he might have as much of her time as he liked.

"What would you like to talk to me about?" she asked. "I told Harry that you not only had information, you also had proof, just as you asked me to, but I *don't* think he was very much interested."

"That is because he does not believe me!" the little man said urgently. "It is the curse of having an unreliable reputation, Mademoiselle; one is never believed, no matter how truthful one wishes to be! And I *am* truthful now. *You* do not believe me, either!" he exclaimed with a despairing air. "And Harry will not even talk to me—or the old Baron—They tell me to leave, or they will have me ejected—"

"Well, I *do* think," Letty said candidly, "that you had better leave then, because if Harry says he will do a thing, he always does it. But before you go, I wish you will tell me what sort of proof it is that you have, because then I can tell Harry, and perhaps he will believe you."

Grün looked obstinate for a moment, but all at once, flinging up his hands in a despairing gesture, he stepped closer to her and spoke in a just audible whisper in her ear.

"Mademoiselle!" he said imploringly, "it is my life I am entrusting to you, you understand! If this were to become known—" He cast a nervous glance about him, but a noisy party at the other end of the hall was paying not the slightest heed to him and obviously could not overhear what he was saying. "It is a document, Mademoiselle!" he hissed into her ear then. "A document—a note in Sir Marius's own hand! Tell that to Harry; tell him it is in Sir Marius's own hand! And I am a ruined man, you understand, Mademoiselle? I am desperate; I am willing to let it go for a song! Tell that to Harry," he repeated earnestly, and then abruptly turned and fled, as if aghast at his own indiscretion at having uttered the words.

Letty, her eyes glistening, stood looking after him triumphantly. The pieces were all falling into place in her mind now: Sir Marius, no doubt, had indeed been the man who had contrived Harry's downfall, and in some manner Grün had become possessed of a document that proved this fact. Obviously, all she had to do now, to play her role as the heroine of the little drama she had concocted in her mind, was to inform Harry of this circumstance—which, it seemed, she was to have the opportunity to do immediately, for Grün had scarcely disappeared out the front door when Harry himself came into the hall, searching, it seemed, for her.

"Oh, there you are!" he said. "Come along now; the company is ready to hear you sing."

"Yes—just a moment!" she said eagerly, quite forgetting her previous displeasure with him in her anxiety to communicate her good news to him at once. "I have something to tell you first. I have been talking to Grün, and he says he has a document—a note in your uncle Marius's own hand—that will be of the greatest value to you, and he is ready to sell it to you *quite* cheap—"

She got no further, for Harry, with an expression of cynical exasperation on his face, told her brusquely not to be a gudgeon.

"You are no more fit to deal with Grün than a new-born puppy!" he said. "He has come down in the world indeed if he is approaching infants like you with his schemes! Come along now, and let's hear no more of this Banbury tale."

"How do you know that it is a Banbury tale?" Letty enquired hotly. "He *may* be speaking the truth—"

"Yes, and it *may* snow in July," Harry said impatiently. He turned about as Lady Hester Luddington appeared in the doorway behind him. "We are just coming," he said to her, with a smile that immediately stiffened Letty's resolutions not to sing a note in Lady Hester's hearing that night.

Lady Hester, who was wearing one of her most daring gowns that evening, an exquisite creation of orange silk with its dampened skirt obviously worn over nothing

more substantial than an Invisible Petticoat, so that every
line of her statuesque form was tantalizingly evident to
the beholder, came up to Letty and surveyed her
frankly.

"Again—charming!" she pronounced. "But a bit out of
temper tonight, I think? What a scowl! What in the
world have you been saying to her, Harry, my dearest,
to make her fly up into the boughs?"

"*Is* she in a temper? Well, *that*'s nothing unusual,"
Harry said—a final insult that caused Letty to turn
sharply and fly for the stairs. She heard Harry calling
peremptorily behind her, and Lady Hester's most unfem-
inine shout of laughter; the next moment she was in her
own bedchamber and had slammed the door behind her.
Having turned the key in the lock and tugged a heavy
armchair in front of the door—for she was quite aware
that one could not depend on Harry to observe the pro-
prieties—she waited defiantly for the sound of running
footsteps upon the stairs and a determined onslaught
upon the door.

Neither came. All she heard, indeed, was a low, intimate murmur of voices from below, followed by laughter, which then was silenced also as the two below (she
could see them in her mind's eye) walked off arm-in-arm
into the gaming rooms. She stood there in the center of
the room, her breast heaving with frustrated fury. They
had treated her, she felt, like a naughty child, in whose
tantrums they were no longer interested. She stamped
her foot; this did little to relieve her feelings, and she
hurled a cushion across the room.

A most undignified action, she immediately felt, for a
woman of experience who had become the object of the
amorous attentions of one of the most sought-after
young officers in Vienna. She picked up the cushion, set
the armchair back in its place, and sat down in it, her
chin in the air.

Perhaps, she thought, vengefully, when she had res-
cued Harry from the state of social limbo in which he
now languished and had married the Count, to the envy

of all the other young ladies in Vienna, Harry would sing a different tune.

And at the thought that at least she had carried out her vow not to sing another note that night, and especially none for the entertainment of Lady Hester Luddington, a slight smile erased the scowl Lady Hester had noted upon her face, and she went off to bed quite contentedly.

Chapter 7

UNFORTUNATELY FOR HER dreams of earning his eternal gratitude, Harry showed no greater interest the next morning in the account she attempted to give him of her interview the night before with Grün than when she had first broached the matter. Even the old Baron, disappointingly, appeared to assume that Grün was merely attempting to make use of her for the purpose of extracting money from Harry, and displayed a great deal more concern over the staggering losses Mademoiselle Forel had suffered at the tables the evening before than in anything she, Letty, had to say about Grün.

"*Most* imprudent—*most* indiscreet," he kept repeating, looking as unhappy as if the losses had come out of his own pocket, instead of the other way round. "And Sir Marius has no control over her, you know, *mon cher*—no control at all."

"Yes, I noticed they were having an unholy row last night at the tables," Harry said unsympathetically, "if you can call it a row when one party, at least, manages to look as dignified all the while as if he was presiding over a court of law. But Ninette made up what was wanting in noise and vulgarity."

"He won't make her losses good, you know," the old Baron continued, still worrying over the matter. "What

are we to do, Harry? We can't very well let the matter
go, for the sake of the house."

"There's nothing to concern yourself over; she has
pledged those precious diamonds of hers," Harry said. "I
daresay they will cover the sum, and to spare. *Not*," he
added, with a certain grim satisfaction, "that I fancy it
will sit well with Marius to know they have ended up
in *our* strongbox."

The old Baron smiled faintly. "That, *mon cher*," he
said, "is a great understatement! He will certainly be
most furious over the matter. Still, you relieve my mind.
It grieves me to be obliged to deprive *la petite* Ninette
of the jewels that become her so charmingly, but one
can scarcely make an exception—"

"I had no intention of doing so," Harry said coolly.
"If one plays, one must be prepared to pay; Ninette
knows that as well as anyone. I should never have permitted her to play so deep if she had not, and if those excellent diamonds had not been there all the while in the
back of my mind."

Letty, regarding his unmoved countenance, thought
with some resentment that he had no sympathy at all,
but as the resentment was founded more on his refusal to
take seriously the conversation she had had with Grün
the previous night than on his lack of compassion for
Ninette's loss, it was perhaps not so altruistic as it might
have seemed. She wandered off in search of Sascha, who,
though he was as lacking in sympathy for one's feelings
as Harry was, might at least be prevailed upon to give
her some advice as to how she was to go about rescuing
Harry from obloquy and restoring him to Society.

She found him in the little apartment at the back of
the house that had been fitted up as a music room for
her, standing before one of the long windows and looking out at the snowy landscape with enough fire smouldering in his black eyes to melt it. He turned sharply as
she entered the room.

"Late—late—late again!" he pronounced, bounding over
to the pianoforte and seating himself before it with

the air of a man who had reached the uttermost limits of his patience and was restraining his temper only by the most strenuous efforts of self-control. "You are *im-possible*, Mademoiselle! Now—we shall begin at once—"

"It is not my fault," Letty defended herself, quite unperturbed by the fiery impatient glance that was being turned upon her, for she had long since learned that Sascha's emotions were always expressed in the most violently dramatic form, so that what might have appeared as mild displeasure in another man would come out in him as bloodcurdling fury. "I wanted to talk seriously to Harry at breakfast, only he wouldn't listen to me. Sascha, do you know a man named Grün?"

"Grün? Grün?" Sascha's mobile face took on a portentous frown. "Of course I know Grün. Everyone knows Grün. And *you*, Mademoiselle, are to have nothing to do with him—nothing whatever! He is an insect, a reptile—"

"Yes, I should think he was," Letty said, leaning her elbows comfortably on the pianoforte in preparation for an interesting conversation. "And that is what Harry says, too—that I am to have nothing to do with him. And I shouldn't, if only I could make Harry listen to him."

"Make Harry listen to him? Why should Harry listen to him? I tell you, he is an insect. And *now*, Mademoiselle—"

He ran his fingers over the keys, played a chord with great emphasis, and waited for her to stand erect and begin her vocal exercises. Letty, however, continued to lean upon the pianoforte.

"He ought to listen to him because he—that is, Monsieur Grün—has information of the greatest value to him," she explained. "And not only information—*proof*."

"Proof? Bah!" said Sascha.

Letty gave him a nettled glance. "You can't say, 'Bah!' when you know nothing at all about it," she said. "He *has* proof—"

"Proof of what?" Sascha's skepticism was still quite apparent, and he played the chord again, even more emphatically than before.

"Proof of Harry's innocence," Letty explained patiently. "Of course I don't know the *whole* story, because no one has been civil enough to tell it to me, but I *do* know that Harry had to leave the army because it was said he was cheating at cards—"

"Lies! Cabals!" Sascha said dramatically.

Letty regarded him with interest. "That is exactly what *I* think," she said. "Did you know him then, Sascha?"

"No—but I know he was no different than he is now. He is a very honest man, Harry—disgustingly honest. If I were to tell you of the opportunities he has missed—" Sascha shrugged resignedly and shook his head. "But we are wasting time, Mademoiselle!"

"No, we aren't, because *I* know how Harry can be rehabilitated," Letty insisted. "It is through Monsieur Grün. You see, he says he has a document—a note in Sir Marius Tyne's own handwriting—that will prove that Harry was innocent—"

She looked down hopefully into Sascha's swarthy face, half prepared for it to express disbelief in even more decided terms than Harry's and the old Baron's had done. But it was no disbelief, but interest, that she read there. True, the jet-black brows were drawn together in a frown, but it was a frown of thoughtfulness, not of skepticism.

"How do you know this?" He shot the question at her after a moment.

"Because Monsieur Grün told me so last night. He said Harry and the old Baron wouldn't listen to him, and so I was to tell Harry about the note, and that he—I mean Monsieur Grün—was prepared to let it go quite cheap, because he is a ruined man." Sascha whistled. This seemed to Letty to be, like the frown, an expression of deep thought, not of skepticism. Encouraged, she went on. "But Harry won't listen to *me* either, so I thought that perhaps if *I* could get the money from someone, *I* could buy the document from Monsieur Grün and give it to Harry. He—that is, Monsieur Grün—says he is prepared to let it go *quite* cheap," she repeated, for emphasis. "Have you any money, Sascha?"

"Money? Me?" Sascha's upraised eyes called heaven to witness that he was a poor man, cheated of his just dues by everyone with whom he came into contact. "But for Harry," he continued, coming down to earth again, "I could find it, if the sum were within reason. The point is, with Grün, it won't be. And even if it were, we should find ourselves with a clever forgery on our hands in the end. You won't find Grün parting with a document that is likely to be so useful to him in the future, I can tell you—as I have no doubt it has been useful to him in the past."

"You mean, I daresay," said Letty knowledgeably, "that he has been blackmailing Sir Marius with it. And I expect Sir Marius has tired of paying him at last, and so he thinks he will try selling it to Harry instead. But if he won't give us the real document even though we pay for it, what are we to do, then?"

"Steal it," said Sascha promptly.

"Steal it!" Letty opened her eyes. "But you can't mean that!"

"Of course I mean it," Sascha said impatiently. "What other ways is there to deal with an insect like Grün? You can't do business with him; the only business he knows is how to cheat you. So one must act accordingly—" He played a few notes of a gay waltz tune upon the pianoforte. "Tra-la-la—we dance with him, we lead him this way and that, we spin him round and round till his head is in a whirl, and then, when he is quite bewildered—we steal the document. It is all very simple."

"It doesn't sound simple to me," Letty protested, feeling half shocked, half exhilarated, by Sascha's graphic, but rather sketchy, description of the plot he was obviously improvising in his head with as much facility as his fingers improvised the notes he played upon the pianoforte. "What do you mean, we dance with him? I *don't* think he would be invited anywhere I could—'

"Bah! Do not be so literal-minded!" said Sascha contemptuously. "When I say 'dance with him,' I mean to express a metaphor—"

"Well, you had better tell me plainly, then," Letty said, a little annoyed, "because I *don't* see what good metaphors are to us at a time like this. You said we are to steal the note from him—but how do we know where he has hidden it—?"

Sascha snapped his fingers. "No one, Mademoiselle," he said, with much disdain, "is clever enough to find a place of concealment that *I* cannot discover, if I am given the opportunity to make a proper search. In such matters, one puts oneself into the insect's place and considers: Where, if I were an insect, would I hide a valuable document? Not on my person—my life, I am well aware, would not be worth a *groschen* if I were to walk the dark streets of Vienna with a document so dangerous upon me. A knife thrust, a few moments spent in rummaging through the corpse's clothing—"

"You *don't* think," Letty interrupted, horrified, "that Sir Marius would *murder* him to get the note from him—!"

"Not *murder—have* him murdered," Sascha explained, with an air of pitying tolerance for her naïveté. "You will remember, Mademoiselle, that Sir Marius is a gentleman."

"Well, I *don't* see," said Letty downrightly, "that having someone murdered is one bit better than murdering him yourself. *And* it seems to me that if Sir Marius had had the least degree of sense, he wouldn't have written that note in the first place, so that he wouldn't feel obliged to murder anyone to get it back."

Sascha shrugged. "In that, Mademoiselle, you are precisely correct," he said, "but one cannot expect prudence from amateurs. Sir Marius, you see, was attempting to meddle in a business in which he was not professionally trained: He wished to arrange for his nephew's disgrace, so that *he* might succeed him as the heir to Lord Aubrey's fortune. That is the sort of thing that is always best left to professionals, and, indeed, he obviously had the prudence to employ Grün in the affair instead of attempting to manage it entirely alone. What he apparently did *not* have sufficient prudence to do was to remove himself completely from the matter and leave it wholly in Grün's hands. So he writes him a note, urging some change in plan or emphasising the need for caution—not realising that in doing so he is providing the insect with the perfect weapon with which to bleed him—and bleed him—and bleed him again—"

He emphasised each repetition with a sinister-sounding chord deep in the bass.

"And now," Letty summed up the matter logically for herself, "he is trying to bleed Harry by telling him he will sell him the note—only you are quite sure he has no intention of giving it up, no matter how much he is paid, and so we must try to steal it instead. Very well, then; we shall steal it. But how are we to go about it?"

"You will please to leave all that to me, Mademoiselle," Sascha said superbly. "As I have told you, these are not matters to be placed in the hands of amateurs." Letty looked disappointed. "You may, however," Sascha conceded, "be of some small assistance to me." Letty brightened. "In point of fact," Sascha granted graciously, "you may be my chief confederate. I shall leave it to you, Mademoiselle, to act as the Lure."

"The Lure?"

"Precisely. *You* will lure the insect away from his nest—that is, his house—while I institute a thorough search for the document. I may say that he has provided you with the perfect opening for such a procedure by attempting to enlist your help in reaching Harry—"

Letty said she would love to be the Lure, and enquired if she should write Grün a note, a suggestion that Sascha dismissed with a contemptuous snap of his fingers.

"A note? Bah!" he said. "In that case, he will have ample time to make sure that the document is not left on the premises unguarded. It is a very simple matter, *on voit*, to hire a large, stupid, but very strong person as a watchdog when one has the intention of leaving one's house, and watchdogs can be troublesome even to a man of my talents. *However*"—and he pointed a preceptorial finger at her—"if one is hurried from one's house without a moment's notice, one has no time to fetch a watchdog—"

"I see," said Letty. "But what am I to say to him to hurry him from the house?"

"You will please to leave all that to me, Mademoiselle," Sascha repeated dampeningly. "*I* shall give you your instructions at the proper time."

And brooking no further argument, he launched into the singing lesson, leaving Letty prey to the most romantic speculations as to what her role was to be as the Lure.

It was a subject that was to preoccupy her almost to the exclusion of everything else during the following four-and-twenty hours, full as they were of romantic events on their own account. A masquerade to which she was gallanted by Count Radoczy, and at which she had the satisfaction of appearing as a Snow Princess and of displaying a dazzling costume of white gauze and silver spangles, was the high point of the period; it was held in the great Riding Hall of the Hofburg, which also shimmered in snow-white and silver, the whole scented by dozens of blossoming orange trees. The Count took full advantage of this romantic setting to continue the ardent flirtation he had begun with her on the night of their first meeting and had pursued at Laxenburg.

The old Baron, who, although he was not present, always knew everything that went on, felt obliged to caution her the following morning on placing too much credence in the seriousness of the young nobleman's intentions; but Miss Clark, who had suddenly begun to exhibit unsuspected romantic depths of her own in her spare spinster's bosom, rather counteracted the effect of this warning by relating confidentially to Letty a number of instances she had personally known of young ladies of no particular birth or fortune who had been elevated, by fortunate marriages, into the highest aristocracy of England or the Continent.

She had become, Letty suspected, rather enamoured of the Count herself; and, indeed, as a veteran of many affairs of the heart, Radoczy had long since learned the advantage of having the duenna on his side, an effect he found it exceedingly easy to obtain without the expenditure of so much as a gulden, merely by the bestowal of a small amount of his attention and a few careless compliments. Even the most severe of female dragons, he had found, such as would have spurned a gift of money with righteous disdain, were vulnerable where vanity was concerned.

Chapter 8

EARLY IN THE afternoon of the following day—a day of
brilliant sunshine, which had turned the streets of Vienna
into cheerful quagmires through which wheeled vehicles
instead of sleighs made their laborious way—an elegant
closed carriage drew up before a tiny house perched on
the city walls, near the residence of the famous but eccentric composer Beethoven. The smart footman who
had been perched up behind sprang down to let down
the steps for the passenger who had been riding inside.
This was a slender young lady, her face heavily veiled,
wearing a poppy-red redingote with a muscovy sable
collar and carrying a swansdown muff. She stepped
down lightly from the carriage and followed the footman to the door of the house, upon which he beat an
emphatic tattoo. He then, upon hearing the few words
spoken by the young lady, retreated to the carriage, and
waited there beside the door.

For several moments there was no response to his summons. The street remained bathed in the quiet, placid afternoon sunlight; not even a dog was about. At last,
however, there was a cautious creaking noise from above,
and the young lady, looking up, perceived a window
slowly opening just over her head. Several moments
more passed, while she waited—with some impatience—

and then a small round dark head emerged slowly from the window.

"Who is it? What do you want?" enquired the plaintive voice of Monsieur Grün.

"It's me," the young lady responded, not very informatively, in a silvery voice. "Come down at once! I must speak to you!"

The mournful dark eyes overhead surveyed her suspiciously. "Is it Mademoiselle Linnet?" Grün enquired, half incredulously, it seemed.

Letty—for it was she—flung back her veil. "Of course it is!" she said. "And you must come down at once! There isn't a moment to lose!"

So imperious was her tone that Grün, after a hesitation of no more than a moment, closed and latched the window above; there was the sound of hurrying footsteps on a staircase, and soon the front door of the house was opened and Grün himself appeared in the doorway.

"What is it, Mademoiselle? Why have you come here?" he demanded anxiously. "It is not good—"

"Of course it is not good!" Letty immediately agreed. "I must not be seen here; you must come into the carriage with me at once! *At once!*" she repeated severely, as Grün showed signs of recalcitrance. "Do you wish everyone to guess why I am here? You have told me yourself, it could be extremely dangerous to you!"

An expression of uncertainty appeared in Grün's little dark raisinlike eyes. "But you can't mean, Mademoiselle—" he stammered, "you can't mean that Harry sent you—?"

"Of course he has sent me!" Letty confirmed impatiently. "Why else do you think I am here? He wishes to see you at once—and you must bring the document you have spoken of. But hurry! If we are seen—"

A joyous light suddenly replaced the confusion in the little man's eyes. "You mean he wishes to buy it?" he enquired. "He is ready to do business—?"

"Yes, yes! Only hurry! *He* is obliged to take precautions as well as you, you know; what will Sir Marius do, do you think, if he learns that Harry has the note? That is why Harry has sent *me* to fetch you; Sir Marius may not suspect that *I* may be involved in the matter. *Will* you hurry?" she repeated once more, as the little man, with the caution of years spent in underhanded dealings, stood motionless in the doorway, his mind, no doubt, flitting with ratlike cunning from one speculation to another as he attempted to assess all the advantages and dangers of this unexpected development. "If you do not come at once," Letty went on to warn him in minatory tones, "Harry *may* change his mind and decide not to buy the note, after all, you know. He is not at all certain that he is doing the wisest thing."

Grün appeared to make up his mind. "Very well! One moment, then, only one little moment, Mademoiselle, while I put on my coat—"

"You have the document on you?" Letty demanded.

"I will get it! I will get it at once!"

The little man disappeared abruptly inside the house; a few moments later he came scuttling out, thrusting his sleeves into the arms of a ridiculous multicaped garrick and cramming a hat with a tall tapering crown upon his carefully oiled locks. Letty at once stepped into the carriage, leaving him to follow, and before he had well had time to take his seat beside her in the carriage the footman had put up the steps and jumped up behind, and the coachman had given his horse the office to start.

"Where are we going?" Grün enquired, panting a little from his hurry, and looking out rather wildly through the carriage window as he attempted to see the direction the coachman was taking.

"You will see when we arrive there," Letty said airily. "Harry," she added, as she saw Grün suddenly looking alarmed and suspicious once more, "told me to take the greatest precautions to maintain the utmost secrecy."

"Yes, yes—I can well understand that!" Grün said, still suspicious. "He does not wish this meeting to become known. But *I*, Mademoiselle, will have to know our destination—"

"Well, if you *must* know, it is Jünglings Kaffeehaus," Letty said, apparently with some reluctance.

"Jünglings Kaffeehaus!" The little man's face expressed consternation. "But, Mademoiselle—the whole world will be there—"

"Of course! That is exactly what Harry says. And so you may appear to meet quite by accident, and fall into conversation very casually, and no one will think that anything of importance is occurring—"

The little man looked highly dissatisfied, but as the coachman continued to drive his horses at a rapid pace, there was very little that he could do in the face of Letty's obvious determination not to change her mind about conveying him to the Kaffeehaus. He began to bite his nails in a harassed way, casting a reproachful glance at Letty now and then but otherwise maintaining a thoughtful silence.

When they approached the many-windowed façade of the Kaffeehaus Letty at last spoke again.

"We are to wait for you outside," she said decisively. "Those are Harry's instructions. You will find him sitting at a table near the door; he will get up to leave as you come in, and you will appear to fall into casual conversation with him. *If*," she added impressively, "he feels that it is unsafe to carry out this plan for any reason, I shall receive word of it as I am waiting for you here." The little man was looking at her with a wary expression on his face, much like that of an experienced rat confronted with a new variety of trap and taking the lay of the land before committing itself to further action. "Go *on!*" said Letty impatiently. "Every moment you delay only makes it more dangerous; you, of all people, should know that!"

The footman had again let down the steps of the carriage; the door stood open—and Monsieur Grün, after a last distrustful glance at Letty, clambered out and disappeared across the flagway into the coffee-house. Letty, with a satisfied expression upon her own face, watched him go inside and, folding her hands inside the swansdown muff, settled herself to await his return.

She did not have long to wait. Only a few minutes had elapsed before the door of the coffee-house burst open once more and Grün emerged, hastening towards the carriage. The footman, waiting beside the door, slammed the steps up and sprang back to his perch as soon as Grün had climbed inside, and in moments the carriage was again rolling away through the muddy streets.

"He was not there!" the little man panted, looking accusingly and rather wildly at Letty as he became conscious that the carriage was moving once more. "Where are we going now? I looked everywhere, Mademoiselle, I assure you—and he was not there!"

"Of course he was not," Letty said calmly. "I knew that the moment after you had gone inside. Harry has left word for us, which I have just received from a trusted source: he says it is not safe for him to meet you at the coffee-house. He has named another rendezvous."

"Another rendezvous!" The expression of distrust deepened on the little man's face. "Another—! Mademoiselle, I do not understand this! Who is this 'trusted source'? And why is it not safe?"

Letty looked at him disdainfully. "Naturally, Harry had not time to go into details," she said. "And, after all, what does it matter? *He* must be the judge of what is safe and what is not. It may be," she added, seeing that Grün still looked unconvinced, "that he caught sight of Sir Marius himself in Jünglings, or had word that he was on his way here."

At the mention of Sir Marius, the little man's already sallow face blanched, and he made no further protest when Letty announced to him that their destination was now to be one of the many inns scattered throughout the countryside outside the city, where picnickers gathered during the summer months to sit on wooden benches under the nut-trees and listen to the *Harfenisten* playing the popular music of the day on zither or guitar. This particular inn was on the Gallizinberg, and it went without saying that, owing to the state of the wintry roads, the carriage's progress there would be slow. Letty did her best to mirror Grün's impatience in her own behaviour, but the success of her attempts to keep him away from his dwelling place for a space of time sufficient for Sascha to conduct a thorough search of it filled her with such elation that she found it difficult not to allow Grün to see the true state of her feelings.

The inn—a large wooden structure with a hip roof, its grounds surrounded by wooden palings—looked forlorn and deserted as they drew up before it, and indeed, as Letty was able to perceive from inside the carriage, Grün had difficulty in rousing anyone to answer his repeated onslaughts upon the door. At last, however, it was opened, and a brief colloquy took place, after which Grün turned hastily about and stumbled back along the muddy path to the carriage once more. As he approached, Letty was able to see that his face was white with rage and apprehension. He began shouting at her as soon as he was within hearing distance of the carriage.

"Mademoiselle, it is a trick! You have tricked me! There is no one here! Monsieur Tyne has not been here; he is not expected—"

"Dear me!" said Letty, counterfeiting an expression of dismay which even she, however, felt was far from convincing. "I wonder what can have happened? Are you *sure* he is not here? Perhaps he is only being cautious about showing himself. If I were in your place, I should go back and enquire again—"

"I shall enquire nóthing! Nothing!" shouted the little man, who appeared to be quite beside himself now. He clambered into the carriage, sputtering with wrath. "You will take me back to my house immediately, Mademoiselle! Immediately! Do you understand? You have tricked me! I must reurn at once!"

Letty turned injured eyes upon him. "Certainly we shall return at once, if that is what you wish," she said, "but I *must* say I think you are being quite unwise. I am sure that if Harry is not already here he will come very soon, and if you are gone, you will have missed your opportunity to sell him the document."

"He will not come! No one will come! You have tricked me!" Grün repeated vociferously. "Tell the coachman to drive back to my house! Tell him at once! I demand it!"

"Oh, very well," Letty said, looking resigned, "but I still feel that you are making a great mistake."

She gave the coachman the order to return to town. The slight figure in its top hat refused to sit back against the squabs, remaining bolt upright beside her, his breast heaving with indignation as he peered through the window at the progress of the coach. He was apparently unconvinced that some new deception was not being practised upon him, and that the carriage, instead of returning him to his house, would not instead go off upon a fresh wild goose chase.

The carriage, however, proceeded back to the narrow streets of Vienna, at a pace so deliberate that Grün more than once shouted to the coachman to hurry. Between these objurgations he hissed uncomplimentary epithets at Letty, most of which were fortunately quite unintelligible to her, and all of which she ignored with aplomb. Her task, she felt, had been accomplished with the utmost skill, and if Sascha was to be believed, the document was by this time safely in his possession, and Harry's future was secure.

When they reached the narrow little house in which Grün resided, the little man had the door of the carriage open even before the horses came to a halt, and without waiting for the footman to let down the steps, he sprang down to the flagway and rushed to the door. To Letty's astonishment however—and certainly to that of Grün—it was opened before he could so much as fit his key into the lock, and Sascha, wearing a Polish greatcoat and a hat with a tall, tapering crown set jauntily on his dark locks, and with a malacca cane swinging in his hand, came out into the street.

"Good-day," he said affably to Grün, raising the tall

hat politely, and would have walked past him to the carriage, but Grün, recovering from his astonishment,
grasped him violently by the arm, arresting his progress.

"S-stop!" he stammered. "Th-thief! Scoundrel! Return
to me my possession!"

"Your possession?" Sascha regarded him in courteous
surprise, detaching the little man's hand from his arm
with an ease that would have surprised no one who was
aware of the iron muscles in his slight body. "But you
astound me, Monsieur! Do you accuse me of theft? The
theft of something of value from your house? I should
very much like to know what it is!"

"Housebreaker! Thief!" the little man shouted again,
almost weeping now with rage. "It was all a trick! You
have stolen it—the document—"

Letty, an interested observer of the scene from within
the carriage, put her head out at this juncture and remarked in a reasonable tone, "But he can't have stolen
the document, Monsieur Grün. You have it with you—
don't you remember? You were going to sell it to
Harry—"

Grün turned a distorted face upon her, stamping his
foot upon the flagway. "How can you be so stupid?" he
demanded passionately. "It is not the *real* document that
I have with me; I left it in the house, and he has stolen
it—this thief, this *scelerat*—"

"You would like to go to the authorities and place a
charge against me—*hein?*" Sascha enquired, unperturbed.
"They would be very much interested in the piece of
property you claim I have taken—a document which you
have been using over the years to blackmail a very
prominent person and a friend of the Emperor's—"

The little man glared at him furiously. "I do not care!
I will go!" he screamed. "I shall go and denounce you
and this—this *sorcière!* It shall not be that you can trick
me so! You will be punished! You will both be punished!"

Sascha shook his head tolerantly. "I do not think so,
my friend," he said. "It is you, rather, who will be pun-

ished, and very severely, if you go to the authorities
with such a tale. You have played your cards badly,
Grün; you should have known better than to try such a
risky game. If I were in your shoes, I should leave Vienna at once; it will not go well with you, you know,
once Sir Marius learns that you have disclosed the existence of that document to others."

He stepped into the carriage as he concluded this
speech, and, ordering the coachman to drive on, leaned
back against the squabs with the expression upon his face
of a man who has completed a satisfactory piece of
work. Letty regarded him with mingled apprehension
and jubilation in her own eyes.

"Sascha!" she said. "How splendid! You have it? You
really found it?"

"But of course," said Sascha, lifting his black brows in
faint surprise. "It was child's play, Mademoiselle, I assure
you. It was in an old boot, beneath the sole—really an extremely obvious place to one of my ingenuity."

He took a much creased sheet of fine notepaper from
his pocket and spread it out upon his knee. Letty, leaning
breathlessly over it, read these words, written in a man's
heavy, rather finicking script:

> *Grün: It must be tonight. I will manage the drink,
> and arrange that you will be among those who
> carry him to his bed. You must see to it that it is the
> others, not yourself, who discover the cards in his
> pocket. Do not fail. You may count on your re-
> ward. Tyne.*

Sascha, who had been reading along with her, clicked
his tongue disdainfully as he came to the end.

"Amateurs!" he said disapprovingly. "To sign one's
name—*quelle bêtise!* One would think a child would
have more prudence than to place such a weapon in the
hands of an insect like Grün."

"It will clear Harry; it can't help but do so!" Letty

exclaimed, her jubilation rising. "Oh, Sascha, we've done it, we really *have* done it! *Won't* Harry be pleased!"

"Very pleased indeed," Sascha observed rather dryly, again carefully bestowing the note in his pocket—"that is, if he lives to profit by our discovery. We are dealing with a very dangerous and very powerful man, you must realise, Mademoiselle—"

"Grün?" Letty looked astonished.

Sascha clicked his tongue again, this time in exasperation. "Grün?" he said contemptuously. "No! Grün can do nothing; Grün dares do nothing. I was speaking of Sir Marius. When *he* learns that Harry has the note—"

Letty regarded him in dismay. "But he will not learn it!" she said after a moment. "Why should he learn of it? Grün will not tell him—"

Again she was the target of an exasperated glance. "Mademoiselle!" said Sascha, in the tone of one instructing a nursery child. "Did you not observe the man standing on the other side of the street, pretending a so great interest in the windows of the shop across the way? Was it not obvious to you what he was?"

"N-no!" said Letty, her heart going down with a thud. "Do you mean—the secret police—?"

"The very *un*secret police," Sascha corrected her scathingly. "A bungler, like all the rest—but there in the street, nevertheless. Grün's house is being watched; it has been searched more than once, I can tell you, by those less skilled than myself. This is why I took no pains to conceal my exit from the house; there was no time to play elaborate games as I used to do to prevent them from seeing me enter it, and a housebreaker's exit through a window would have given them the motive to stop and search me before I had had time to dispose of the note. As it is, all they were able to observe was that I am on very bad terms with Grün—hardly a cause for detaining me."

Letty, with an admiring glance, said that he thought of everything, which tribute he received with his customary aplomb; but they both became more thoughtful as the carriage neared the gaming-house and Harry. That Harry would be as pleased as they were over the recovery of the note there could be no doubt; but Sascha's damping words concerning Sir Marius lay heavy on Letty's mind, and the thought of the danger into which they might have plunged him by their daring raid on Grün's house did a great deal to lessen her sense of self-satisfaction over the part she herself had played in the afternoon's work.

Chapter 9

AS IT TURNED out, however, the subject of Sir Marius's note and the difference it must make in the way Harry was at present regarded both by Lord Aubrey and Society in general was not to be brought up immediately upon their return to the house. The porter, upon being questioned as to Harry's whereabouts, indicated that he was in the small morning room that served for the transaction of the house's business, and when further enquiry was made as to who was with him, remarked with a sphinxlike expression that it was Mademoiselle Forel.

"Ninette? What can *she* be doing there?" Letty asked in some surprise.

"A sage question," Sascha remarked. "Mademoiselle's forte is certainly not business. We shall not disturb them, I think—"

"Nonsense! Of course we shall disturb them," Letty said roundly. "I shall simply burst if I have to keep the news to myself, and, besides, Ninette will be as happy as anyone to hear it."

And, disregarding Sascha's disapproving admonition to her to do nothing of the sort, she walked back at once to the morning room, tapped on the door, and walked in.

She was more than a little taken aback to find that she had intruded upon what was evidently a highly emotional scene. Ninette, in a charming bronze-green pelisse, a bronze-green velvet hat trimmed with feathers set upon her burnished curls, and a huge chinchilla muff flung down beside her, was sitting across the desk from Harry, dissolved in tears, while Harry, with a thunderous expression upon his face, sat regarding her in frowning silence. At the sound of the opening door both looked up, and Ninette, jumping up at once, rushed across the room and flung herself into Letty's arms, weeping hysterically.

"*Ma petite*, save me from this *monstre!*" she cried. "He will r-r-ruin me! You must implore him to have pity on me!"

Letty, quite staggered by this application for her protection, nevertheless reacted instinctively to it by putting her arms around the weeping Ninette and embracing her warmly, at the same time looking enquiringly at Harry across Ninette's heaving shoulder.

"Harry! What in the *world* have you done to put her in this state?" she demanded. "What does she think you will do to her?" She patted Ninette's back encouragingly. "Never fear!" she said. "Whatever it is, I shan't let him do it. *Do* stop crying! His bark is a good deal worse than his bite, I can assure you!"

"*Is* it?" said Harry sardonically. He got up from his chair behind the desk and came around to regard the two young women with a highly unsympathetic expression upon his face. "I shouldn't be too sure of that in this case, if I were you," he said. "I don't take kindly to having the change put on me, you know—not even by a very pretty woman."

"But I am not trying to—how do you say it?—put the change on you!" Mademoiselle Forel declared passionately, raising her tear-stained and charmingly flushed face to regard Harry out of swimming blue eyes. "It is not *my* fault that Marius is such a—a *squeeze-crab!* How was I to know that the jewels were paste? I will scratch his eyes out when I see him!" she went on, suddenly dropping several degrees of gentility and speaking in a

French argot that proclaimed her origin. "I will tear him to pieces!"

"Very prettily acted, *chérie*, but hardly convincing," Harry interrupted her, quite unmoved. "You are not such an *innocente* as to be taken in by false jewels; if I know you, you wasted no time, once Marius had bestowed them on you, in having them valued by a competent jeweller—"

"But I did not!" Ninette wailed. "I did not—fool that I was! I th-thought they were so b-beautiful; I only w-wanted to w-wear them—and look at them—"

She burst into tears once more, throwing herself again into Letty's arms. Letty looked indignantly at Harry.

"How can you be such a beast?" she demanded warmly. "Can't you see that she is telling you the truth? But what *is* the matter, then? Are those lovely diamonds that Sir Marius gave her really false?"

"As false as her charming self," Harry said coolly. "And quite worthless as payment for the debt she has incurred to the house." He addressed Ninette. "You will have to think of some more gullible male than myself to play *this* little trick on, love," he said. "Try to fob those diamonds off on one of your many admirers; you may find one who is fool enough to pay you good money for them."

Ninette turned on him, her eyes flashing. "Oh, how I hate you, Harry Tyne!" she said vehemently. "The old Baron is right when he says you have no heart! Besides," she added, drawing herself up with a sudden air of offended pride, "how can you believe that I—I, *la Forel*—would be seen wearing diamonds that I knew were false? It is entirely *beneath* me!"

Harry shrugged. Letty, quite forgetting that she had just spent an afternoon of dangerous adventure in attempting to earn Harry's eternal gratitude, walked up to him and reiterated hotly, "You *are* a beast, Harry! I should like to beat you! You *must* see that she is not lying to you!"

"Little termagant!" said Harry, in not very friendly

fashion, and lifting her off her feet in one powerful movement, he strode across the room with her and deposited her outside the door, which he immediately closed and locked in her face.

Letty recovered her balance, took a deep breath, and began to shout. "Harry! Let me in! Harry! I shall scream!"

She was interrupted by the sound of deliberate footsteps behind her in the hall. It was the old Baron. She rushed up to him.

"Oh! You *must* stop Harry!" she declared. "He *won't* let me in, and he is determined to ruin Ninette!"

The old Baron appeared understandably a trifle surprised by this appeal.

"My dear, this is most extraordinary!" he said, raising his grey eyebrows as he looked down at her. "Are you quite sure of what you are saying?"

"Quite, quite sure!" Letty reiterated, the words tumbling over one another in her anxiety to acquaint him at once with the facts. "The diamonds she has pledged against her debt are false—only I am sure *she* did not know of it, though Harry will not believe her when she tries to tell him so! It is not her fault that Sir Marius is such a—a—*cochon!*"

The old Baron's brows went up another notch. "*Diable!*" he said, a very serious expression now upon his face. "If this is indeed so, *ma chère*—"

"Of course it is so!" Letty declared. "Sir Marius is an odious, odious man, and I am sure it is quite in character for him to have fobbed Ninette off with paste! She says she would never have worn them if she had known they were not real diamonds, because it is quite beneath her to wear false ones—"

A faint smile crossed the old Baron's face. "Yes," he said, "I must believe *that*, my child. Each of us has his pride—and for an expensive courtesan to be seen wearing false jewels—!" He shook his head and made a slight gesture of resignation. "Well, well, I see that I must interfere," he said in his soft weary voice.

He attempted to open the door, and Letty at once explained to him that Harry had locked it to bar her from the room.

"We had a tremendous argument, and he *threw* me out of the room," she informed him, with some slight exaggeration of the facts.

The old Baron, again smiling faintly and shaking his head at her vehemence, knocked gently at the door.

"*C'est moi, mon cher*," he said. "May I enter?"

The door was at once opened, and Letty and the old Baron entered the room to find Ninette once more in tears and Harry looking exceedingly grim.

"Come, come," the old Baron chided him gently, "you must not make the storm in the tea cup, my friend. Letty has been telling me—"

"If this is any of Letty's affair, it is more than I know," Harry said, casting such an unfriendly glance at her that she at once determined never to tell him of the discovery she and Sascha had made that afternoon. "Leave the room, you young idiot—"

"No, no!" wailed Ninette, again casting herself into Letty's arms. "Do not go, *petite*, and leave me with this *monstre!* You will be my saviour—"

"Well, I shall certainly do my best, but I *don't* think he will listen to me," Letty remarked, looking daggers at Harry. "But he can't do anything cruel to you if the old Baron says he may not, and I am sure *he* is on your side."

Harry, giving the old Baron an exasperated and questioning glance, asked him if he knew the facts of the matter.

"We have been gulled—that's the long and short of it," he said. "If *you* believe Ninette's story that she thought the jewels she pledged to us were genuine—"

"But of course I believe it, *mon ami*," the old Baron said placidly. Ninette, in an access of gratitude, then flung herself into *his* arms—an action which he accepted with great equanimity, patting her shoulder reassuringly as he again addressed Harry. "You are angry—*c'est naturel*—but you must see that it is against Sir Marius, not against this charming child, that your anger should be directed," he said, "she has been his dupe as much as you are."

Harry made a wrathful gesture and strode across the room to the window, where he stood with his back to the others, obviously unwilling to continue the controversy any further. Ninette, extricating herself with cautious optimism from the old Baron's fatherly embrace, stared across the room at him, her eyes brightening.

"*C'est fameux*—he will not r-ruin me after all, *hein?*" she enquired in a loud whisper. "You have saved me, my angels, my friends!"

She kissed the old Baron warmly, and then ran over to embrace and kiss Letty. "I shall never-r forget what you have done for me—never-r!" she declared. "You may ask for my heart's blood, both of you, and I will give it to you, to the last drop!"

She then picked up the chinchilla muff that she had flung down, gave a satisfied pat to her modish bonnet, which had become a trifle disarranged by the dramatics in which she had just indulged, and looked brightly over at Harry.

"Harry, *mon cher*, I forgive you!" she declared magnanimously. "*Naturellement*, one does not wish to lose such a very large sum of money—but, after all, it is not *my* fault! And I shall give Marius his own back—never fear of that! I shall have my r-revenge!"

She turned and walked out of the room upon this rather bloodcurdling note, leaving the old Baron smiling indulgently behind her, Letty in triumph, and Harry still standing at the window, obviously having removed himself from the situation. Letty was about to speak when, on the heels of Ninette's departure, Sascha walked into the room.

"So—she has gone!" he said with satisfaction. "Now to business! Harry, what do you think, *mon vieux?* We have had an afternoon's work, I can tell you! *Crois-tu*—the insect Grün was speaking the truth for once—he actually had that so damaging document he spoke of to you! *Had*, I say, because he has it no longer—"

And, walking up to Harry with the proud air of a conjuror producing it by magical means, he took from his pocket the folded piece of note-paper he had removed from Grün's house and opened it with a flourish.

There was complete silence in the room for the space of several moments. The old Baron was looking enquiringly at Sascha and Harry; Letty waited, breathless; and Harry, his face quite immobile except for the grey eyes racing rapidly over the words written upon the paper, stood without moving and without expression.

He raised his eyes at length to glance briefly over at Sascha.

"Genuine, do you think?" he asked.

"*Sans doute*, my friend!" Sascha said promptly. "You need only to have seen the insect's face when he realised he had been diddled and I had the paper to be sure of that. Which is why," he went on more seriously, "you must from this moment be ver-ry careful. Grün is not the only one, you see, who knows that the document is now in your possession; there are also the Emperor's agents, and, since that is so, there is your uncle himself—"

"Yes—I see," Harry said. To Letty's disappointment, there were no signs of elation in his manner; on the contrary, it appeared to her that he looked even grimmer than he had during his controversy with Ninette. There was a kind of cold, contained anger in his eyes that made a shiver run down her spine, and she had a sudden deep conviction that she would not care to be in Sir Marius Tyne's shoes on the next occasion that he came into Harry's presence. It was all very well, she thought, for Sascha to warn Harry that his life might be in danger, now that Sir Marius was aware that the compromising note was in his possession; for her own part, she felt that such a warning might be given, with much more reason, to Sir Marius.

"Well, *mon vieux*," interposed the old Baron finally, when the silence that had followed Harry's last grim remark had stretched out interminably, "what shall you do now? You will send the letter to your uncle, *hein?*"

"No," said Harry trenchantly, his eyes and his thoughts still obviously fixed on the bleak thoughts the reading of the letter had produced.

"*No?*" Sascha exclaimed in astonishment, "but—"

"Harry! Are you mad?" Letty burst in indignantly, "After all we went through to get it!"

"All 'we' went through?" Harry snapped out of his introspection abruptly and swung around on her. "What are you talking about?"

"Sascha and I. We thought—or rather, Sascha thought—of this wonderfully clever scheme. Oh, it was beautiful, we—"

Harry ignored her, turning his cold glance on Sascha. "You involved this child in such a business?"

"Child! Well I like that," Letty protested, stung as always by this appellation.

"Harry, there was no danger, and I could not do it alone. Someone was needed to draw off the insect while I searched his nest," Sascha explained with a shrug.

"No danger? So now the Emperor's secret police and Marius know that she is involved, perhaps even holding the letter. Do you think for one moment that Marius would hesitate to relieve her of it by whatever means necessary? By *whatever* means?" he reiterated flatly.

"He would not be so much a fool as to suppose such an important document would be left in her keeping, Harry," Sascha expostulated.

"Why *must* you be always so odious, Harry? You always cast a blight over everything. Here we concocted this perfectly wonderful plan, carried it through brilliantly, and you refuse to make the least push to be interested, not to speak of grateful. *Not* that I care for *that* of course, for lord knows I have learned by now that such feelings from you are not to be expected. But must you be so—so—stiff-rumped about everything?"

The old Baron clucked disapprovingly at this inelegant

expression, though there was a discernable gleam of amusement to be seen in his eyes.

"My dear Miss Birdwit, if you are waiting for me to express gratitude to you for involving yourself in my affairs I can only hope that you are possessed of the patience of Griselda. Apart from that impertinence, you have created a situation of great danger to yourself for which *I* will be responsible."

"Please do not trouble yourself with any feelings of responsibility for me," Letty responded haughtily.

"Ah—very impressive—*brava!* But I would be much gratified if you would not enact me any Cheltenham tragedies," said Harry gratingly; "we are facing an unpleasant situation of your own devising, and I for one will be able to think much more clearly without any further interference from you."

"Interference? After all the *hours* I spent shut up in that carriage with that—that—*oily* little man! I think I shall have strong convulsions!" she cried, pressing a tiny fist pathetically to her brow.

"Please spare us these dramatic flights, my dear. They'll be much more effective with a larger audience."

"Don't call me 'your dear!' " she raged, stamping her foot impotently. "I won't have you speaking to me in that condescending way!"

"Sascha, please take the child away to have her tantrum in private. I'm sure Miss Clark will know how to deal with it better than any of us," Harry said firmly.

With an apologetic shrug. Sascha took Letty's arm and turned her to the door. She snatched away from his grasp, but then, aware that this childish gesture was undignified, took Sascha's arm, and throwing her chin in the air with a sniff, marched grandly out of the room.

When the door had closed behind them Harry glanced at the old Baron, who was regarding him pensively. Harry quickly looked away.

"Surely it is not necessary to be so rough with her, *mon cher*," the Baron remarked mildly, "I can under-

stand that you are completely *bouleversé* with this most
unexpected development, but still—"

"Oh, she'll take no harm from sparring with me."

"Indeed not," replied the old Baron with a chuckle,
"gives as good as she gets, that one. She is what you English call 'pluck to the backbone'—always rattles back
into the ring no matter how many times she is floored.
As for this other adventure, she will come to no harm
from that either, you may be sure. One of us will always
be with her."

"And if she gives us the slip? Which you know as
well as I she's capable of. I could not live with the
knowledge that something happened to that child when
she was under my protection."

"Oh, it is a matter of defending yourself against a
guilty conscience? I had thought it was more a matter of
defense against her regard for you."

"Really, Baron, such flights of fancy are more worthy
of the child than of you."

"She is not really a child, *mon vieux*. Certainly Count
Radoczy doesn't look upon her in such a light."

"Count Radoczy! Damned over-dressed loose-screw!
Why, the man wears scent! She's to be kept away from
him, do you hear?" said Harry savagely.

"I couldn't agree more. We must all keep a careful
watch over her."

Harry subsided into a chair before the fire and stared
broodingly into the flames. The old Baron watched him
for some time in silence.

"Harry, you will surely send this letter to the Lord
Aubrey will you not?"

"No, I will not," Harry replied shortly.

"But that makes no sense, my boy. It will completely
clear your name and reinstate you with your old uncle."

"He had my *word*. He should have taken it."

"Harry, Harry, what foolishness is this? The plot was
so cleverly executed he could not help but believe you in
the wrong. Think of the heartbreak he must have suffered, loving you as he did. You must believe—"

"This subject begins to bore me. I've said all I intend to on the subject, to you or anyone else, including my great-uncle." Harry sprang from the chair and strode out of the room without a backward glance.

The letter lay on the table where Harry had tossed it after the first reading. The Baron sat staring across the room at it for a few moments, then rose and retrieved it, folding it carefully and tucking it away in the inner pocket of his coat.

Chapter 10

❧

THOSE OBSERVING LETTY that evening as she descended to
the gaily lit rooms below could have been forgiven for
thinking she was the very embodiment of a fairy-tale
princess. The simple white silk gown with silver ribands,
the delicate wand-slim body, the cloud of dark hair
wreathed in silver leaves—all did their part in contribut-
ing to the image.

The old Baron, however, a close observer, noted the
sparks in the heavily fringed hazel eyes, the angry spots
of color on each cheek, and the belligerent thrust of the
sweetly rounded chin. He sighed sympathetically, but he
was not altogether displeased to see her in such a state.
Far better for her to be angry about Harry's unkind
treatment of her than to be dissolved in tears as most
love-sick young girls would be. The Baron was at a loss
to explain Harry's actions regarding Letty, unless, becoming aware of her girlish infatuation with him, he was
discouraging it at every opportunity. However much of
a rakehell he might be in his dealings with women,
Harry was not a despoiler of innocent maidens.

Count Radoczy came forward eagerly to greet her, taking her hand in both of his and kissing it lingeringly,
then straightening up to look ardently into her eyes.

"Ah, *ma petite alouette*, you take my breath away

with your beauty. I cannot believe I am allowed to touch anything so fragile. Ah, but I must," he pressed her hand to his breast, "so soft the little hand—I must kiss it again!"

As he bent again over the hand she looked down on the shining blond head and experienced an overwhelming feeling of gratitude to him. This handsome officer, a scion of one of the greatest Hungarian noble families, friend of royalty, was in love with little Letty Montressor. *He* didn't think her "bird-witted," or accuse her of interfering. The Count would never be so cruel as to be scornful if she tried to help him. He would be gracious and *grateful* and exclaim over her cleverness and courage.

When he stood up she smiled upon him so blindingly that he gasped, "My adorable one! I must have you! Say you will be mine."

"Yours?" she was taken aback by the passionate response she had elicited.

Now, Count Radoczy had been giving the matter of Mademoiselle Linnet and her capture a great deal of thought. Such a proper little English miss was much too innocent to understand any subtle lures he might cast her as an invitation to carry their flirtation a step further. For English girls the next step was a proposal of marriage. Of course there could be no question of a Radoczy marrying a little English nobody. In fact his marriage to the daughter of an immensely wealthy ruler of a small but important principality had been arranged years ago by his parents. This young Princess was exceedingly plain and some few years older than the Count, but would nonetheless be a glittering prize for the Radoczy family, and it would never enter the Count's mind not to go through with the marriage.

But there was a way he could have his cake and eat it, a solution that was dazzling in its perfection. The fact was that no officer in the Emperor's forces could marry without the approval of his commanding officer. If the officer married without this sanction the marriage was considered invalid and was annulled. But it was not possible the little Linnet would know of this, so he would propose an elopement when he felt her properly swooning with love for him, net the delicious little bird for a night of love, and his reputation would once again be secure as the man with the most amorous adventures to his credit in Vienna.

The fact that the delicious little bird's reputation would be ruined by such an event never entered his self-centered calculations. He had spent the past few days in consultation with his brother officers, polishing his plans to the point where they could be put into operation instantly. And unless he was very much mistaken, his moment had arrived. No girl could smile upon a man in such a way unless she was in love with him, he felt, nor look up at him as adoringly as she was doing at this very moment unless she were only waiting his word to fall into his hands.

He pulled her urgently into a window embrasure that gave them some privacy. "Yes, enchantress, mine! My very own bride. *Say* you will marry me, now, tonight!"

Letty gaped at him in stupefaction. Marriage? Then Miss Clark was right, and it did sometimes happen that penniless, untitled girls could make brilliant matches. Here was Count Radoczy actually proposing to her. True, he was proposing an elopement, which she knew no nice girl should even consider, but she was not an ordinary nice English girl, with a family to be outraged. And she would be a Countess, and have for a husband one of the handsomest, most dashing men in Europe. That should prove something to Harry Tyne!

Of course, she did not love Count Radoczy, but she was grateful to him for his love, and she supposed that such devotion and ardour would, with time, raise a like response in her own heart, and obliterate the image of Harry.

Impulsively she held out her hands to the Count, "If you truly mean this, sir—"

"I was never more serious about anything in my life,

adored one!" he responded instantly. "You will come with me tonight?"

"Oh—tonight—yes, certainly."

"Do you love me, *chèrie?*"

"Yes—of course," she said equably, and though he wished there were more evidence of enthusiasm in her voice, he did not press her. All English girls pretended to this coolness in matters of love. "But how shall we be able to leave?" she continued practically; "they will never allow me to go out with you alone."

"Ah, I have the plan, you see. You will go to Miss Clark and tell her I have come for you again at the request of the Empress, that she has sent her carriage and one of her ladies-in-waiting to chaperone you."

Letty went away at once to seek out Miss Clark, glancing about fearfully for Harry. But he and the old Baron were still both supervising at the gambling tables, and wouldn't come out until it was time for her to sing, and Sascha had gone away quite early in the evening on business of his own.

Miss Clark began to twitter nervously when Letty explained to her what she was about to do.

"I must just send for Mr. Tyne, my dear. I'm sure he would—"

"I know he will be very cross if you interrupt him. And after all, what can he do, it's a command performance for the Empress. He can hardly forbid me to go. Now please don't fuss anymore. The carriage is outside, the lady-in-waiting is—er—waiting. I'll be back in time for a performance here, you may reassure Harry of that."

Miss Clark was finally persuaded by the urgency of the Imperial request. She hurried upstairs to fetch Letty's witchoura cloak and in a very short space of time was standing in the doorway waving goodbye to the departing carriage, her heart fluttering romantically as she thought of the gallantry of Count Radoczy. What a perfectly suited couple they made, she sighed.

As soon as the carriage was in motion the Count

reached out to pull Letty into his arms and began kissing her passionately. She struggled, and finally emerged gasping and dishevelled from his arms.

"What are you doing—?"

"But, *mon ange*, I am making love to you," he replied in some surprise.

"No, no, Count Radoczy, you—" she began.

"You must call me Egon now," he murmured, reaching for her again and burying his face against her neck.

"Very well—Egon—but you must not—we are not married yet, you know," she pushed him away again and moved as far into the corner as she could get and she wondered if she might be able to persuade him to shave off his mustache once they were married.

"Ah, enchantress, you wish to drive me mad! But it shall be as you wish. I will wait for tonight, my own."

She shivered and pulled the fur-lined cloak closer. "Er—ah—where are we going, Count—that is—Egon?"

"To a small village I know not too far outside the city. The priest there is the son of a family who have worked on the Radoczy estates for generations. He will marry us and then but a short distance beyond is a hunting lodge owned by my father. We will stay there the night and return to Vienna tomorrow."

She felt her stomach lurch with nerves and swallowed convulsively. What have I done? she wondered, beginning to be aware for the first time that she may have acted a bit hastily. She could not really spend the entire night alone with this man—why, Harry would surely beat her this time! Her imaginings of what the elopement would entail had encompassed so far only the excitement of slipping away and the wonderful moment when she would walk up and announce herself as the new Countess Radoczy to an astonished and then remorseful Harry. The area between these two things had remained murky.

But still, the thought of confounding Harry was bracing, and she concentrated on it gloatingly. An hour later the carriage came to a halt and the Count jumped down, saying he would return for her in a moment, and then hurried away into the darkness. She peered nervously out of the carriage window, but could discern nothing beyond a dark, hulking shape against the night sky, which she assumed was the church. Presently the Count returned and tenderly helped her down from the carriage.

"Come this way, *ma chérie*, it is all arranged. Do not be afraid."

But now not even the thought of Harry served. She *was* afraid and wished very much that she was back in the warm, candlelit rooms with Harry's guests swarming about her, congratulating her on her voice, and Harry glowering at her from across the room.

Harry was glowering at a trembling Miss Clark. Only a few moments after the door closed behind Letty, he had come searching for her to begin her performance. When she couldn't be found he sent for Miss Clark, who excitedly confided in him that the Empress had again summoned Letty.

"The Empress? Impossible! It was announced only today that the doctors had ordered her to cancel all social engagements due to illness. She could not have sent for Letty. Who brought the message?"

"Count Radoczy, Mr. Tyne, and it was an Imperial carriage, for I saw it!"

"Bah, what of that? The Count has the use of those carriages whenever he likes! Good God, Madam, how *could* you have let her go off without asking me for permission?" he roared, furious to think the Count had outwitted them with this pretense, and Letty might be seen alone in a carriage with the Count and her reputation would be in shreds.

The butler, responding to a rap at the door, opened it to admit a figure wrapped from head to foot in a hooded, dark sable cloak. She rushed across the hall to Harry.

"Harry, *mon vieux*, but you must do something! Where is the little one? You must not let her out of your sight!"

"Ninette," he grabbed her shoulders and shook her, "stop babbling and tell me slowly. What do you mean, not let her out of my sight?"

"Oh, it is abominable what he plans, that man. I shall myself tear out his eyes!"

"What does he plan, and how do you know of it?" said Harry softly, but his eyes had narrowed and glittered dangerously.

"I was at the Duchess of Courland's party and all the officers were laughing about how the so pretty new girl of Harry Tyne was to be lured into an elopement by Egon Radoczy. And you know he cannot marry without—"

"Yes, I know all that," he replied grimly. "Do you know where he was taking her? Did he also boast of that?"

"Some village called Leisher or Leiftner, or some name like that."

The butler coughed discreetly. "Sir, forgive me for interrupting, but I could not helping overhearing. I believe the village Madam refers to would be Leipner. About an hour out of Vienna on the North Road."

"Have my horse brought round quickly," Harry ordered and turned to leap up the stairs. In a moment he came back carrying a pistol which he put into the pocket of the cloak the butler held ready for him.

"Ninette, stay with Miss Clark. When Max comes out tell him what has happened and that I've gone to bring her back."

"But I don't *know* what has happened yet—" she called after his departing back.

Letty clung helplessly to the Count's arm as he led her forward in the inky darkness, up some steps and through a heavy doorway that slammed resoundingly behind them. Far ahead in the dimness was a flickering candle, and in a moment another was lit by a shadowy figure she assumed was the priest. When they reached the altar steps he came forward and reached for her hand.

"Mademoiselle von Bergheim? Do not be afraid, my child."

Letty, incapable of speech, hardly capable of coherent thought, didn't realize that the Count still didn't know her real identity. She felt paralyzed, caught in a dream that made no sense to her. She put her hand into the priest's and for a moment felt safe with her icy hand in his large, warm one. Then she was led forward again and gently urged to her knees, Egon kneeling beside her and taking her hand. She was aware of words being spoken, but could not make sense of them because of the curious ringing in her ears.

"Mademoiselle—Mademoiselle—you must answer before we can proceed," the priest was saying insistently.

"Answer?"

"Yes, Mademoiselle. I will repeat it. Do you, Lettice von Bergheim take this man—"

His voice began to fade away again and then the Count nudged her.

"Oh—" she swallowed, "oh—yes—I mean, I do!"

"The devil you do!" came the harsh, ringing voice of Harry from the doorway. He marched down the aisle to the altar, his steps echoing menacingly in the vaulted interior.

Both Letty and the Count sprang to their feet and backed up against the priest as though seeking protection, Letty with a shriek of surprise. All the mists disappeared abruptly from her brain, all the ringing sound from her ears, and she was projected on the instant into full awareness of where she was and what was happening.

The first of the trio at the altar to speak was the priest. "Sir, you are in God's house," he said reproachfully, "what business have you here?"

"The girl is my business, and this unspeakable vermin who would use her for his own pleasure. Come here, Letty, you little idiot," Harry ordered peremptorily.

"How dare you!" the Count shouted, drawing his sword from its scabbard.

"Very easily, I assure you," replied Harry calmly, raising a cynical eyebrow at the sword.

"Sirs, you must not quarrel here, and I must ask you to put away your weapon, My Lord Egon," the priest said apologetically to the Count, centuries of peasant bowing and scraping on Radoczy lands making themselves heard in his voice.

"Yes, Egon, for heaven's sake try not to be so—so—" Letty said crossly.

"Melodramatic? I agree, there is just a tinge of theatricality there, is there not?" said Harry chattily.

"Well, I must say I don't think you have any right to criticise, after the entrance you made," Letty retorted indignantly.

"I got here as quickly as I could," Harry replied, sounding as though she had accused him unjustly of malingering. She shot him a suspicious glance.

"I don't recall anyone requesting you to come here at all," she said loftily, "I wish you will explain to me—"

"Exactly what you are going to have—an explanation, Miss Malapert," he said grimly. His hand shot out, clamped Letty's arm in an iron grip, and yanked her unceremoniously to his side. The Count started forward with an oath, brandishing his sword. Harry stepped back quickly, dragging Letty with him and drawing the pistol from his coat pocket.

"Now we've done with play-acting, sir. Put away that sword before I shoot your hand off. I assure you I won't miss. I'm accounted a crack shot."

The Count stood his ground for a moment, but knew too well the truth of Harry's claim to hold out. With a petulant gesture he shot the sword back into its sheath.

"Sir, I beg you to put away that firearm," pleaded the priest, "and tell me why you have come here to disrupt this sacred ceremony—"

"Yes, and so would I like to know why you are here, yanking me about and being so high-handed. I have a

right to marry whom I choose—and I'll *thank* you to release my arm!"

"I'm here to save you from making a complete fool of
yourself, pea-goose. Of all the caper-witted stunts you've
tried, this is far and away the stupidest."

"Don't you dare speak to me in that way! When I'm
the Countess Radoczy—"

Harry gave a great shout of laughter. "Hah! When
you're the Countess Radoczy pigs will fly!"

"If you hadn't come bursting in here so rudely I
would be so by now!"

"Now, maybe, but what would you be tomorrow?
Tell her, Radoczy—tell her what she'll be tomorrow."

"I'm sure I don't know what you mean," the Count
blustered.

"Tell her, or I will shoot you—first, I think, in the
right knee, and if you take too long about it, in the left,"
said Harry with great deliberation.

The Count turned pale and opened and closed his
mouth several times before managing to say; "Well—
well—I—of course the marriage would need to be approved by—by—"

"Your commanding officer? Is that what you are trying to say?" prompted Harry helpfully.

"Well—yes."

"Actually it needs his approval *before* the ceremony
before it is a valid marriage, does it not?"

"I'm sure he—well, in some cases he—"

"In all cases, sir!" Harry barked, "otherwise the marriage is automatically annulled, am I not right? Answer
immediately." He raised the pistol menacingly.

"Yes, blast you!"

"Thank you for *that* honesty at last. Naturally you
neglected to mention this small detail to your little
bride-to-be. Now, Letty, I'm sure even *you* cannot fail
to grasp the significance of this. Or shall I spell out the
rest of it for you?"

Letty's mouth opened, but no words came out. She
had stopped struggling to free her arm, and stared at the

Count in horror, then turned as though for help to the priest.

He turned to the Count and said, his voice filled with sorrow, "I cannot believe you would trick an innocent child in this way, My Lord Egon."

"Not only would he do so, but he has boasted of it in advance. It's titillating half the drawing rooms of Vienna at this moment. The edifying tale was carried to me by Ninette Forel who tells me his fellow officers are laying wagers on whether he will succeed or not. Letty, go out to the carriage."

"No, I'll stay," she whispered.

"Very well. Now, Count Radoczy, you will put about the rumor that you failed in your assault on the virtues of Mademoiselle Linnet and that will be the end of it. If word ever reaches me that you have spoken of tonight to anyone I will seek you out, you may depend on that, and punish you as I see fit. Come, Letty."

He released her arm and, turning on his heel, walked away up the aisle without a backward glance. She stood there miserably for a moment, wishing the paved floor would open and swallow her, and then turned and plodded after him, rubbing her numb arm.

"Tyne, stop! That carriage is the property of the Emperor," called the Count, suddenly aware that his means of transportation back to Vienna was about to be taken from him.

"I'm sure His Highness would not begrudge Mademoiselle the use of it. If it will help I will, of course, be happy to explain the circumstances to him," offered Harry politely. The Count turned an impossible shade paler. "Perhaps the good Father can find you a horse," Harry added kindly and closed the door firmly.

Harry assisted Letty into the carriage without a word, gave the driver his orders and mounted his horse.

Inside the emerald-velvet-lined coach, wrapped snugly in the thoughtfully provided fur rugs, Letty jolted along in solitary splendour. The hot tears of shame coursed down her cheeks, where the colour came and went as

the full implications of Count Radoczy's scheme passed
relentlessly again and again through her mind.

Not only had she nearly ruined herself completely
owing to ill judgement and hasty temper, she had forever
lost any hope of being regarded by Harry as other than
a paperskull with more hair than wit, who was not fit to
be let out without a keeper. She was forced to face the
melancholy truth that everyone who knew the facts
would agree with him.

Chapter 11

❧

LETTY SPENT THE entire next day in her bedroom, staring bleakly into the fire or out the window, sifting through the rubble of her ruined life, wondering what would become of her now. Heretofore she had faced the disappointments Fate had dealt her with equanimity, even courage. Her parents' deaths, her penniless state, her dependence on the old Countess's charity had all been lived through without complaint. Her relatives' attempt to marry her off to Mr. Sludge she had dealt with with dispatch and great presence of mind, and the ensuing events with hard work, winning great success and acclaim for herself as a result.

How then had she managed to get herself into such a wretched coil? The answer of course was that she had allowed herself to be so foolish as to fall head over ears in love with a cold, heartless creature who regarded her with indifference, except when his precious gaming house was concerned. Her attempts to gain his regard, and the abysmal failure of all her efforts had engendered a need to pay him out, to show him that other men found her desirable. Certainly no very commendable objective.

Her well-deserved reward was to have lost all credit in his eyes, as well as in the eyes of her friends, and doubtless, by this time, all of Vienna! Even now her escapade was probably being tittered over in every drawing room, and bets being paid up in the barracks. She shuddered and paced restlessly across the room.

She had been able to eat nothing all day and had seen no one. She wondered if they would expect her to perform tonight. Surely not even Harry could be so cruel.

But when the hour approached and Miss Clark came to help her dress, it was obvious that Harry *could* be so cruel. She thought wildly that she must pack her box and go away. But when she began to examine in her mind the execution of such a plan she was forced to abandon it as impractical. For one thing, her pitifully few belongings, the things she had when she met Harry, included two rather threadbare gowns and a redingote and bonnet, none of them suited to wear in even so mild a Viennese winter as this one. For another thing, and an even more serious problem, her purse didn't contain even one shilling to enable her to make her way alone in a strange country.

And where to go when she stepped out of the door? Ninette was the only friend she could claim outside the walls of this house, and she didn't even have Ninette's direction, aside from the fact that Ninette might not feel that the ties of friendship between them were so strong that they required her to take in a homeless creature from the streets.

She looked herself squarely in the eye in her mirror and acknowledged that she had no choice but to continue to earn her bread and butter where she was for the moment, however difficult Harry made it for her. She stoically watched a sniffing, red-eyed Miss Clark, who had spent the day crying and castigating herself for having incurred Mr. Tyne's displeasure, brush out the dark hair and adjust the wreath. She pulled back her shoulders and raised her chin. You will march downstairs, smile, and sing as though you were the most carefree creature in the world, and look everyone straight in the eye without cringing, especially Harry, she told herself.

She patted Miss Clark's shoulder and left the room. The old Baron was waiting for her at the bottom of the stairs and watched her descent with admiration. What courage the child has, he thought, smiling at her with warm encouragement. He extended his arm with exaggerated gallantry.

"Mademoiselle, you will allow me the pleasure?"

He saw her glance covertly about the hall and understood she was looking, fearfully, for Harry. Harry had related the whole sorry tale to him when he had returned the evening before with the stricken Letty. The Baron had been horrified at her close escape.

"But I hope you will not berate her, Harry, *mon vieux*. She is so very innocent and young, and the Count is very experienced in persuasion."

"She is very stupid to be taken in by such an obvious loose-screw as that, and I'd swear she was not in love with him, for all his love-making."

"Oh, no, Harry, I'm quite sure you are right about that," replied the old Baron blandly, having every reason to be sure Harry was right, since the Baron knew Letty was very much in love with Harry himself.

"Well, it's all over and as far as I'm concerned there's to be no further discussion of the thing. As for berating her, there'll be no need. I'm sure she's doing all that's necessary in that department herself. And make sure everyone understands that young jackanapes is not to be admitted to this house under any circumstances!"

But the Baron knew that Letty, having refused to leave her room or see anyone all day, would not know of Harry's attitude, so he tried to ease her fears.

"Harry won't be with us this evening. He went to a ball at Lady Hester Luddington's," he informed her kindly.

Letty, who had spent the day dreading this first meeting with Harry and having to face the contempt in his eyes, now felt distinctly let down at the Baron's dismal news. Having screwed her courage up to face Harry, she would have preferred to have it over with. Now she would have another sleepless night to get through. He had probably planned it as a diabolical way to punish her. She began to feel definitely ill used.

She felt a spurt of anger which magically wiped away her melancholy humour. Really, it was too bad of him to leave me to face all these snickering people alone! The least he might have done was give up one ball in order to stay at home and support me in this. Well, he may go to the devil for all of me, I don't need his help!

She flicked open her fan, took the old Baron's arm and tripped daintily across the hall and into the drawing room, dispensing smiles and greetings to everyone. If, here and there in the crowd, she caught a glance of more than usual interested speculation, there were no leering looks, no smiles hidden behind fans. Taking heart, she gave her whole attention to singing better than ever and behaving afterwards amongst her coterie of admirers as though this was an evening much like any other evening.

But when Miss Clark came to fetch her, saying that it was time for her to come to her bed, Letty went with her quite willingly, excessively weary of flirtatious repartee and pretended gaity. Her smile seemed to be frozen into a permanent rictus upon her face and she wondered if she'd be able to stop smiling even when she reached the privacy of her room.

Harry, meanwhile, was propping up the wall of Lady Hester's ballroom with a pair of wide shoulders covered with a corbeau-coloured dress coat over cream kerseymere breeches, and nowhere in the thronged room could a more elegantly-dressed gentleman be seen. Nor a more bored one, if the expression on his face were anything to go by.

When Lady Hester had first invited him he had firmly declined. She had pouted prettily and called him the cruellest thing in nature to be so disobliging.

"I vow, Harry, I cannot think how you could bring yourself to refuse me. When you asked me to come to

your house and bring my friends, I'm sure I didn't hesitate a moment to help you."

"I can't think my presence will do anything to 'help'
you. Your parties are always very successful in any
case."

"But it *will* help me. It will look so odd to my friends
if you are not there—after all we have been to each
other," she added, lowering her eyes demurely and wishing desperately it were possible to produce a maidenly
blush at will.

He raised a cynical eyebrow at her. "I should own
myself astonished if my absence should affect in the least
your friends' opinion as to 'what we have been to each
other.' "

"I'm sure I don't know what you mean by that,
though I suspect from your tone it's something not quite
nice," she replied with a little *moue*, as though humour-
ing a naughty boy.

"Not in the least. What we have been to each other
has been *quite* nice, but I'm sure you are much too—sensible—a woman to expect it to be anything more than
that."

"Oh *là*, Harry, who's to say as to that," she said airily,
and, unwilling to carry the subject further while he was
in such a negative mood, hurried on. "The important
thing is, I *want* you to come to my party and I think
you could give me my way in such a small thing."

So here he was, after leading her out for the first
dance, wondering why he had allowed himself to be
talked into doing something he had so little taste for as
this. He utterly despised Hester's set for the most part,
considering them to be hangers-on, wastrels, and fools
who had nothing useful to do, and generally too much
money to do it with.

His brows drew together in a frown as he watched
Count Radoczy waltz by with a young woman whose
draperies seemed in imminent danger of exposing her
charms in their entirety at any moment. The Count
seemed determined to assist in every possible way by

twirling her vigorously. The girl giggled shrilly, thus capturing every eye not already riveted upon her in anticipation of a wonderful disaster.

Harry wrenched his shoulders away from the wall abruptly and turned on his heel in disgust. He had fulfilled his obligation to Hester who was safely on the other side of the room, flirting outrageously with one of the Emperor's staff officers.

He slipped unobtrusively through the crush of people on the staircase and called for his hat, cloak, and cane. It was a fine, clear night, and not cold in spite of the season. The last snow had melted completely away under a week of sunshine and unseasonable warmth, and altogether, it was a perfect night for a walk. He was happy to stretch his legs and his lungs after the hours spent in the packed ballroom where there seemed to be too many people breathing too little air.

He strode out almost happily, swinging his cane and humming the waltz he had just heard, to keep himself from thinking about anything.

The streets were dark and silent and empty—so much so that a tiny movement in a dark alley as he passed caught his eye. His step didn't falter, but his senses leapt to the alert, and without moving his head he rapidly scanned both sides of the street ahead, while his ears seemed to him to be standing away from his head in an effort to detect a sound. And they were rewarded in less than a minute by the stealthy, but distinct, pad of footsteps following him.

He whirled about and the steps halted for a moment, and in that instance of quiet he heard footsteps behind him on the other side and realised he had an opponent in each direction—and nothing but solid, shuttered house fronts on either side of the narrow roadway.

The footsteps behind him began to quicken, and he forced himself to wait until the very last moment before ducking and throwing himself to one side. A figure, hands outstretched in every expectation of clamping themselves about Harry's throat, shot past, unable to halt the impetuousness of its own rush, and went sprawling on the cobblestones.

Now the attacker Harry had first spotted and whom he had turned to meet moved forward with a growl. His associate clambered to his feet and with an oath turned to face Harry again. They were very ugly specimens and there could be no doubt they had some very ugly business in mind.

They moved apart and then began to advance threateningly on Harry, one with a cudgel raised, the other with large, horny hands extended. Harry could only crouch and raise his cane in readiness. There was a gold knob of some weightiness for a handle and he hoped to bring it down on at least one thick skull before he was overpowered. The throttler made a jump at Harry's throat, causing him to swing the cane at his face, just as the armed fellow brought the cudgel down on Harry's head.

Because of his lunging swing with the cane, the cudgel gave Harry only a glancing blow on the head and landed with its full force on his left shoulder. He felt the numbing pain and knew his left arm to be useless; at the same time a wet warmth flowing down over his ear and a bursting bloom of stars before his eyes told him the man had opened a cut on the side of his head.

Dimly, through the ringing in his ears, he heard the crash of a falling body and had the satisfaction of knowing the throttler was out of action for the moment as a result of the gold knob of Harry's cane making contact with his skull.

He swung around groggily to face the remaining thug and saw him scuttling away without a backward glance for his fallen comrade, obviously unwilling to carry on the fight with one-to-one odds.

Harry staggered over to the wall and leant heavily against it for a few moments to catch his breath and steady his reeling senses. He looked down dispassionately at the still unmoving figure on the cobblestones and wondered if he'd killed the fellow with one blow, and rather hoped that he had.

He speculated grimly on the whereabouts of Marius's spies, who, he was well aware followed him everywhere. Then he laughed mirthlessly; probably these *were* Marius's spies, but with different orders.

By the time he arrived on his own doorstep he had so far recovered himself as to feel only the soreness in his shoulder. The wound over his left ear had stopped bleeding and the dizziness had disappeared.

He was unaware of any singularity in his appearance, and was unprepared, therefore, for the reaction his entrance created, beginning with the butler, who stopped in midsentence to stare at him in astonishment. The Baron, just turning away from the stairs after bidding Letty goodnight, and Letty and Miss Clark, partway up the stairs, all turned and were frozen into a tableau of horrified amazement.

"Well, what the devil is wrong with all of you?" Harry demanded tartly.

"Harry—your collar and neckcloth—the blood!" Letty faltered, clutching the bannister and feeling a most unpleasant swimming sensation in her head.

The old Baron recovered himself and hurried forward. "What happened to you, my dear friend?"

"Two rascals who thought it would be to their benefit to relieve me of my purse. I could not agree with them, and so there was a bit of bother. Nothing serious. One of the fellows had a club and while I attempted to dissuade his friend from strangling me by bashing him on the head with my cane, the club caught me a slight blow. A scratch only."

"A scratch! Good God, Harry, the whole side of your head is covered with blood!" Letty protested.

Miss Clark moved purposefully down the staircase and straight up to Harry. Standing on tiptoe she inspected the wound carefully, then nodded in confirmation.

"You are right, Mr. Tyne. It is not serious in the least. All cuts about the head and face bleed profusely in this

way, Letty. But it must be cleaned and bound up immediately. If you will step up to my sitting room I will take
care of it for you."

She spoke firmly and accompanied her remarks by
taking his arm to lead him away and Harry, unexpect-
edly meek, went along with her.

"Harry, *mon ami*," called the Baron after him, "those
were Marius's men—not common cutpurses! I've been
expecting an attack. Marius would be bound to try to
dispose of you the moment he learned about that letter.
However, I must admit I wasn't expecting him to move
so fast!"

"Of course it could not have been anything of the
kind this soon," said Harry scornfully, with an infinitesi-
mal jerk of his head in Letty's direction to keep the
Baron from pursuing the subject in her presence.

A glance at Letty's stricken face was enough to cause
the Baron to say hastily, "Well, well, no doubt you are
right, Harry, and I'm making a fuss about nothing. Go
along now with Miss Clark, I'll see to everything down
here. Letty, my child, you had best get into your bed as
quickly as possible."

With a gentle smile to all of them he turned away to
go back to the tables where a few unlucky but persistent
players hung on, hoping the cards or dice would change
in their favour if they only tried again.

Miss Clark and Harry proceeded up the stairs and
Letty followed for one step, but had to stop for a moment and clutch the bannister with both hands. As the
other two disappeared from sight she sat down on the
step quite abruptly. Her head was filled with an unpleasant fizzing noise and she knew quite definitely that
she was about to faint, though she had never done so in
her life before and had a great disdain for ladies who
swooned at the least thing.

This, however, was not in any way to be categorized
as "the least thing." At least not to Letty. She was as
convinced as the old Baron that tonight's attack was at
the instigation of Sir Marius. Sir Marius *could* not leave

Harry alive, now that the incriminating letter had sur-
faced and was known to be in Harry's possession.

Letty forced herself to face squarely the fact that in
recovering the evidence she had hoped would enable
Harry to be returned to Society's favour, she had put his
very life in danger. If Sir Marius was successful and
Harry died, the responsibility could fall only on her
shoulders. Because she loved him and hoped to force him
at least to look upon her with gratitude, she had meddled
in his affairs with disastrous results. She could expect
small gratitude from him now! She could not blame him
if he refused ever to speak to her again.

This thought brought a very large lump in her throat
and tears welling up into her eyes, and she put her head
down on her knees and cried heartrendingly.

"*Ma petite pauvre!*" came a warm voice in her ear as
Mademoiselle Forel subsided in a swirl of gold silk and
Brussels lace on the step beside her. She took Letty into
her arms, murmuring endearments and comforting words
while Letty sobbed luxuriously against her powdered
and deliciously perfumed shoulder.

Mademoiselle Forel had agreed to accompany to the
gambling rooms a gentleman friend who was one of
those players who insisted on trying to make a recovery
of his fortune before he left. Since Ninette could not
play herself she had become bored and wandered about
through the nearly deserted drawing rooms before being
drawn into the hall by the sound of crying.

When Letty's sobs had sighed away into hiccoughs,
Ninette supplied her with a handkerchief and assisted
with mopping up the tear-streaked face.

"Now, *ma chère*, you will tell me what has happened
to make you so unhappy. Was it that *monstre* being
beastly to you?"

"No, no, it is Harry—"

"*Exactement*! Just as I thought! I will go speak to him
immediately. He shall not be cruel to you!"

"Oh, please, Ninette, it is not that at all!"

And then, her need to heap the ashes of remorse over

her own head by castigating herself aloud being too great to be denied, she told the entire story to Mademoiselle Forel, not failing to make it quite clear that her own meddling in Harry's affairs had placed him in a position in which his life was forfeit, and of her conviction that he would be killed and that she herself would like to die right at this moment.

"But that would be of small use to Harry, *hein?*" asked Ninette, who might look to be the most bubble-headed charmer in all Vienna, but who actually possessed a very strong strain of stolid Flemish practicality. "That would only make more bother for everyone, is it not so? We must be very calm and think for a moment what would answer. Now it is necessary that Marius act quickly in this matter before Harry can get to his so rich uncle with this letter."

"Yes, and we have all told Harry that he must go immediately to London and expose Marius to Lord Aubrey, but he *will* not. Oh, how can he be so pigheaded? It is all his foolish pride! He only says that he gave his uncle his word and his uncle should have believed him."

"*Tiens, ma petite.* It is the matter of honour with him. Such foolishness! So—be quiet for one moment while I think what it is we must do."

She sat staring off pensively into the middle distance for a few moments, and when Letty impatiently began to speak, she was waved to silence imperiously.

"*Voilá!* I have it!" Ninette said decisively, after a further agonizing moment of contemplation, "I have decided what must be done, and it is I, *la Forel*, who will do it! It will be my revenge on the so miserly Sir Marius who dares make a fool of me with his paste jewels!"

"What—what can you do?" quavered Letty, somewhat doubtfully.

"I shall bring the old uncle here!" Ninette declared dramatically.

"*Bring* him here?" repeated Letty in an awed voice, a picture floating into her mind of Ninette appearing in the hallway below with Lord Aubrey cradled in her arms like a baby.

"Yes! I shall write him this very night and tell him of the incriminating letter and of the stubbornness of Harry in refusing to use it to clear himself, and of the attacks on his life as a result. That will bring the old Lord Aubrey posthaste to Vienna, I think."

Letty was so impressed she couldn't speak for a moment. Why hadn't she thought of such a plan instead of sitting here crying? Much good her tears would do Harry, and surely her motivation to help him was as great as Ninette's to revenge herself on Sir Marius. This last thought brought to a standstill the excited, headlong rush of her mind.

"Oh, Ninette! It is wonderful, of course, that you want to do this thing, but what if Sir Marius learns of it? He will murder *you* then!"

"Bah! I am not afraid of such a one as that. Besides, how is he to learn of it? You may be sure I will take care that he does not see me writing the letter."

"But you know they say the Emperor's people open letters and dispatches sent out of the country. If they should open yours and see Sir Marius's name they would take it to him immediately."

"Ah, but I am not so stupid, me!" replied Ninette triumphantly. "I have many friends who will do whatever I ask with no questions. I know such a one who will be perfect for my plan. He is leaving for England tomorrow and he will carry it personally to Lord Aubrey. Also," she added craftily, "I shall not put my name to the letter so even if something should go wrong it cannot be traced to me."

"Miss Lettice! What on earth are you doing sitting on the stairs in that hoydenish manner at such an hour?" came the scandalised voice of Miss Clark from the landing above them. "You are to come *at once* to your bed."

Letty and Ninette sprang up guiltily. Letty threw her arms around her friend and kissed her fervently.

"Thank you, Ninette, I shall never be able to tell you how grateful—"

"Pooh! It is nothing. Did I not tell you that you were my friend to the last drop of my blood?" Ninette protested, her wonderful eyes flashing, "but you must speak to the old Baron and to Sascha. They must take very great care for the next week that Harry is always accompanied wherever he goes. You understand, *n'est-ce pas?*"

"I will speak to them tonight!" Letty declared.

"Miss Lettice! Must I fetch Mr. Tyne?" Miss Clark asked with a disapproving glance at Ninette.

"At least, I will do so the very first thing in the morning," amended Letty hastily after a glance at Miss Clark's implacable face above told her there was no way in the world she would be allowed to do anything more tonight but climb into her bed.

"Goodnight, *chérie.* I go now to commence my revenge!"

Ninette marched firmly down the stairs as Letty scuttled up them, and presently her voice could be heard from the gambling room demanding that her escort attend her home—"*Instamment!*"

Chapter 12

⁂

IT WOULD HAVE been apparent to the least sensitive observer, had there been one, that General Sir Marius Tyne was seriously displeased. He sat brooding over his desk in the library of the imposing mansion he had taken for his stay in Vienna, and the single lamp on the desk was the only source of light, for the fire had burned down to a few smouldering embers.

The lamp lit only the thin, aristocratic hands clenching the papers he was attempting to study, leaving the other furnishings of the room visible as only dimly perceived shapes. The paintings on the walls, indeed the very walls themselves, had retreated into the gloom that obscured the outer reaches of the room.

Sir Marius impatiently thrust away the papers and threw himself back in the heavy red-velvet-covered chair, and the library seemed to pulsate with his anger. He glared into the dying fire from beneath hooded lids, his mouth stretched into a grim, tight line as though barely containing his rage, and the tightly clenched fists on the arms of the chair pounded their frustration from time to time.

"Come," he rasped when a single light tap sounded on the door, and a thin, beaky head slid around the edge of the door.

"Boris is here."

"Bring him in."

The head withdrew, the door swung open and a large, lumbering figure marched belligerently into the room with a fine show of bravado.

"He got Mischa," Boris announced without preamble, and with a discernable defensiveness. "He had a damned weighted cane and laid Mischa out with one blow."

"And what were you doing while this was going on?" asked Sir Marius, not bothering to conceal his contempt.

"I'd a had him dead at me feet if he hadn't swung at Mischa just then and spoiled my aim. I managed to lay his head open though—bleeding like a stuck pig, he was," Boris paused for a moment of reminiscent satisfaction.

Marius stared at him furiously. Actually, Marius was already in possession of all the facts relating to the abortive attempt by Boris and Mischa to put an end to Harry's life. One of the Emperor's secret policemen was presently augmenting his income by working privately for Sir Marius, and had long since hurried back to report on the thugs' failure.

"Ah, I see. You of course then rushed in to finish him off while he was still groggy from the blow?"

"Well, I did then," Boris declared defiantly, "but he pulled a damned pistol and I was forced to run for my life. You didn't say nothing about no pistol," he added accusingly.

"You lying, cowardly imbecile! There was no pistol and well you know it. D'you think I didn't have you followed? Now get out of here!"

"Here—what about my money?" Boris protested indignantly.

"Money for what? For giving him a scratch on the head and then running at the sight of the blood. Bah! Get out of my sight before I have you arrested!"

Boris stood his ground bullishly for a moment. But, reluctant as he was to forfeit the money, he realized that if he persisted with his claim it was just possible this perishing old pinch-purse would carry out his threat. Boris was very much aware that Sir Marius was capable of it and had enough authority to rig up any sort of charge that could keep Boris mouldering in the Emperor's dungeons for the rest of his life. His shoulders slumping in defeat, he turned and lumbered out of the room without another word.

Sir Marius had picked up the papers on his desk and bent over them seeming to be deeply absorbed, but when the door closed behind the thug, Marius sprang from the chair and flung the papers away furiously. He paced rapidly from the desk to the fireplace and back again before the door opened once more to admit the sleek head, followed this time by the skinny body, of Sir Marius's servant, César.

"Where did you find those monuments of incompetence? I warn you, you'll have to do very much better than this!"

"I can't understand it, M'lord. They've proven satisfactory before."

"No doubt when they could come at their victim from behind. Face-to-face combat doesn't seem to suit them," replied Sir Marius sarcastically. "The next time—"

"Ah—there's to be another attempt," said César, washing his hands together and smirking.

"Of course, you dolt, have I not told you it is absolutely vital that he be disposed of?"

"Then it shall be done, M'lord, have no fear. Of course, to make certain one must hire experts and they will cost more than these other two." He stared hopefully at his master, already, in his mind, putting his commission into his pocket.

Sir Marius, who had recommenced his restless pacing from fireplace to desk didn't answer, still obviously in the throes of his frustrated fury.

"Also there is Grün, M'lord. Shall I have the same person take care of him now?"

Sir Marius paused abruptly and stood staring sightlessly into the darkness of the corner of the room.

"Grün. Grün. Hmmm. Are the men still watching his house?"

"Oh yes, indeed, M'lord. He hasn't stirred all day."

"Good. Put four more men on. I want it to look like an army waiting to attack. I want him frightened out of his wits by the end of the week. We may have to move sooner than that, if my nephew shows any signs of taking action, but I think we'll have a few more days at least."

"And then?"

"Then—ah *then*, César, you'll bring Grün to me. I have thought of the perfect solution to my problem. I won't be troubling you to hire your 'expert.'"

César's face fell in disappointment, and he felt as though Sir Marius had put his hand into his, César's, pocket and removed the commission money.

"Yes, Grün, that scurrilous little sneak!" Marius continued, unaware of the unhappiness he had just caused, "he's the man to do the job, and it won't cost me a penny piece. And when he's done the job I'll see there's enough evidence against him to have him hanged for the murder! He'll regret betraying me before I've finished with him!"

The old Baron and Sascha, unaware of the reprieve allowed them by Sir Marius, had not needed Letty's urging the next morning to set about planning for Harry's protection.

Sascha had departed immediately after breakfast and returned in less than an hour to report that two trustworthy and stalwart men had been hired to take turns shadowing Harry day and night, should he leave the house undetected and on foot.

The Baron meanwhile had been assigned the task of impressing on Harry the importance of going out as little as possible and when it became necessary to do so, to go always in the carriage—the closed carriage with driver and footman, and never under any circumstances in his elegant perch phaeton.

"You'd be a sitting target, *mon cher*, as easy to pick off as a crow on a fence."

"Be damned to that! You're fussing about like an old woman. I have no intentions of skulking about in this house like a rabbit in its hole. As long as Marius sees I'm not attempting to leave Vienna he won't do anything. And as he has access to all outgoing mail he would know immediately if I tried to mail the letter to England."

"And those two cutthroats last night?"

"Pah! They were after my purse. If they'd been hirelings of Marius's they'd never have bungled the job like that. There's nothing to fear, I tell you, he won't do anything as long as I don't."

"I think you're wrong, my friend. He will not stop now, Harry. He dare not, with so much at stake. What puzzles me is why he has not taken steps long ago to recover the paper from Grün, rather than to submit to blackmail."

"Oh, I'm sure he's tried. Sascha said the house looked as though it had been searched before."

"Then not finding it, why has he not eliminated Grün himself?"

"He wouldn't dare before the paper was found. With Grün dead the paper might surface anywhere. Grün might have given it to a friend to hold and use against Marius if anything should ever happen to him. In fact, now I think of it I'm convinced that's what Grün told Marius he had done. Otherwise Marius would never have submitted to his demands in the first place."

The Baron tried to redirect the conversation to the more important subject of protection, but Harry only laughed at him. He sauntered out of the room, called for his cloak and hat and strolled out the door, jauntily swinging his goldheaded cane.

He didn't notice Sascha's hired protector, a very large, nattily attired gentleman who meticulously folded the newspaper he had been reading, stowed it away in an inner pocket, and paced slowly after Harry on the opposite side of the street.

The Emperor's agent who had been posted at the corner since early morning was also unaware that Harry had acquired protection. His orders were to follow Harry Tyne wherever he went. His orders had not included any instructions about protecting the gentleman if he were attacked, so he would not do so, but no doubt the secret policeman's very presence in the street would deter any but the most foolhardy attacker.

So, though Harry was unaware of it, he was well guarded whether he would be or not for the next week, while Grün hid trembling in his house and Sir Marius bided his time, waiting for Grün to reach the absolute apogee of terror.

When he felt this precise state had been reached, he had Grün hauled before him.

Marius sat unspeaking at his desk for several moments surveying the abject figure of Grün, who was visibly shaking and unable to meet Marius's eyes. Grün's unshaven, bedraggled appearance testified to the fact that for the past week, sartorial perfection had been the thing furthest from his mind.

"Well, *cochon*, what have you to say for yourself?" asked Marius, breaking the silence at last in a deceptively quiet voice.

Grün misinterpreted the tone of voice and took heart, thinking possibly Sir Marius intended to come to some financially profitable arrangement with him concerning the stolen letter. He raised his head and began to sputter, "How—how—dare you—per-persecute me in this way?"

"Persecute you? Why, I haven't even begun," Marius replied, spacing the words out slowly and allowing the threat to be clearly heard.

This reply caused Grün to retreat backwards until the backs of his shaking knees found a chair, whereupon he sat down abruptly.

"*Stand up!* You dare to sit down without my permission? Bah! You make me sick to look at you. I'll give you your orders and then you can get out."

"My—my—orders?" quavered Grün, a hopeful gleam coming into his eyes. He had arrived in Sir Marius's presence convinced that his last hour had come.

"You are to kill Harry Tyne. Now. Immediately."

"Kill H-Harry! No—no—I will not! I am not a paid assassin!"

"Paid! Paid! Who spoke of payment. Your payment will be your miserable life which you will be allowed to keep if Harry Tyne is dead by tomorrow."

"But how am I to do such a thing? I know nothing of killing, that has never been a thing I would get mixed up in," whined Grün, his face turning a pasty greenish-white.

"I don't know and I don't want to know. Just do it. Now get out."

Grün stood there, his brain unable to command his legs to move. Finally he began to whimper, "You can't do this—I can't—"

"*Get out!*" thundered Sir Marius, and that command reached Grün's legs, for he shot across the room and out the door without another word or backward glance.

Marius sat there for a moment and then began to laugh, feeling better than he had for days. How easily these things were arranged, he thought, if one is but clever enough to find the answer. In a mood of self-congratulation he rose to go upstairs. He decided he would change and call on Ninette, the little strumpet.

But while he was involved with the intricacies of his neckcloth, César brought him a note, folded and sealed with a seal that caused Marius's eyes nearly to start from their sockets. He broke the wafer and opened the note with trembling fingers.

December 15, 1814
Hotel Kaiserin von Österreich

Marius,

I arrived in Vienna today and you will find me at

the hotel noted above. I hope you will find it con-
venient to call upon me this evening.

Aubrey

Marius stood absolutely immobilized while his brain attempted to assimilate this impossible news. His uncle *here*, in Vienna, unannounced and unexpected? What could have brought him here? And Harry—my God, if Harry found out—not—not *if*—*when* Harry found out he would go straight to him with that letter!

But, he calmed himself, only if Harry were alive to do so. Even now, at this very moment, he might be dead, if the impetus that had carried Grün from the room downstairs—what?—an hour ago?—had sent him scurrying off to do the job immediately.

Yes—Harry might already be dead, and would certainly be so before the night was over. Grün, impelled by the powerful need to save his own skin, would use every bit of that cunning he was notorious for, and find a way.

Marius began to relax. After all, it would surely be a simple task to keep Harry and his great-uncle apart for one night. Marius turned back to the mirror and proceeded with the arrangement of his neckcloth.

I will go immediately, he decided, and persuade him he will be more comfortable in my house and bring him home with me. That will take care of tonight, and just to be safe, I will insist that he remain in his bed all day tomorrow to recover from the rigours of the journey. And after that it won't matter. If the letter should turn up after that I'll simply say Harry wrote it himself and had been attempting to blackmail me with it.

Satisfied with his neckcloth and his plan, he took himself off to the Kaiserin von Österreich to meet his uncle. When he was shown into his uncle's suite, he found the old man standing stiffly beside the fireplace, both hands on the cane planted before him and a solemn expression on his face.

"My dear sir," Marius exclaimed rushing across the room, his face wreathed in smiles, his hand extended, "what a very pleasant surprise. But I must scold you also for not letting me know that you were coming so that I could meet you the moment you arrived and welcome you to Vienna."

Since his uncle didn't seem inclined to take his hand Marius awkwardly patted the old hands clasped on the cane and stepped back.

"There was no time to waste in letters back and forth, Marius. I felt that my own presence here, as speedily as possible, was the only thing that would answer."

"Answer what, sir? Is there a problem? Has the government commissioned—"

"No. This has only to do with you, Marius. You and Harry."

Now Marius felt a bristling on the back of his neck, a warning of danger of some kind. However inconvenient his uncle's visit had seemed to him, he had never thought of it as being in any way dangerous to himself. But the gravity of the old man's voice, his unyielding position and now this last pronouncement all came together and Marius felt as though an icy hand were slowly squeezing his heart.

"Harry, sir?" he asked with an attempt at sympathetic concern blended with a touch of lightness, "not doing anything to bring a glow to the family escutcheon, I fear, but still, we must hand it to the boy, he is working very hard and coining a great deal of money I'm told. And while one can hardly approve of a gambling establishment being operated by a Tyne, still there is honest play there I have heard."

"Honest play? In light of what I have been led to believe about Harry, that seems rather unusual," commented Lord Aubrey drily.

"Ah, but sir, I have always maintained that that little unpleasantness in Spain was all a misunderstanding—"

"Yes, yes, I know what you have always maintained.

And now it has come to my attention that you may very well have been right all along."

"I—I—well, of course nothing could make me happier than to be proven right, sir, but—er—how—?" Marius struggled desperately to maintain his composure, and to ignore the unpleasant sensation of his stomach turning a somersault inside him.

"How have I heard? I had a letter from someone here in Vienna telling me that Harry has in his possession a letter proving his innocence in that card cheating incident."

"May I ask who wrote you this letter, sir?"

"I don't know. It was not signed."

"Ah—well sir, an anonymous letter," Marius said deprecatingly, "someone trying to stir up trouble. Had the unknown correspondent anything else to say?"

"Nothing to your benefit, Marius. The letter in Harry's possession is supposedly written by you to an accomplice, setting the details of the plan to trap Harry and discredit him."

Marius hoped the blood he could feel draining from his face was not apparent to his uncle. He turned away and paced slowly across the room and back.

"Sir—I—I would not ever have told you of this had I not been forced to do so in this way. I—the fact is, you see, I know the letter you speak of."

"You *know* of it!?" cried Lord Aubrey.

"Yes, Uncle. I fear you will be made even more unhappy by what I'm about to reveal to you. Harry himself wrote that letter, you see, cleverly imitating my handwriting, or perhaps employing the services of an expert in the art of forgery. But at any rate, he came to me when he first arrived in Vienna and attempted to—well—to blackmail me with it. I refused to pay him anything, naturally. In fact I begged him not to demean himself in such a way. I told him that if he would promise to burn the letter I would forget the whole incident and never speak of it to anyone."

"Yet here you are telling it to me."

"But he obviously did *not* burn the letter as I thought he had promised. Am I to stand here before you under such an accusation as your anonymous correspondent implied and not defend myself in any way?"

"Very well. I have heard what you have to say. Now we will see what Harry has to say."

"You will see him, Uncle?"

"Certainly I must see him in these circumstances. I have sent for him."

Marius stood quite still, his mind darting about frantically for a way to handle this situation. But then he remembered—Grün. Harry would not come. He smiled involuntarily.

"I see you smile, Marius. I hope you have not found this discussion amusing. For myself, I am not in the least amused."

"Oh no, sir, not at all. It was just—just that I suddenly began to see what has happened here. Our Harry is a very clever young man, I must say that for him. And I have just tumbled to what he has done. I've identified your anonymous writer, sir."

"Oh? And who is it then?"

"Harry himself, Uncle. He is much too busy to be able to leave his business now, so when he couldn't get money from me, he wrote that unsigned letter to you, knowing such a serious matter would bring you to Vienna immediately to investigate."

"All faradiddle! Codswallop, sir! I don't believe a word of that. If Harry wanted me to see that letter he could simply have posted it to me."

Of course, Marius knew very well why Harry would not dare trust the document to the mails, but he had no intention of sharing such knowledge with his uncle.

"I think he must have felt that a face-to-face confrontation would work better for him. You know Harry can be very charming when he likes."

Sir Aubrey stared at his nephew's face for a few moments, then turned away to the fire.

"We shall see," was his only comment. He sat down and motioned Marius to a seat, obviously prepared to wait as long as necessary.

Chapter 13

❧

HARRY RECEIVED HIS summons from his great-uncle with surprise and some amusement.

Dictatorial as ever, he thought, and after throwing me out of his house, he still expects me to come running, wagging my tail. Well, be damned to that! If he wants to see me he'll have to come here.

He tossed the note aside and went on up the stairs to change into evening dress. But he couldn't keep his mind from returning to the note. What was his great-uncle doing in Vienna? Only something of importance could persuade him to undertake such an arduous journey in his present state of health.

A commission from His Majesty to Lord Castlereagh, perhaps? Something too delicate to be committed to paper? It was a fact that Lord Aubrey was intimately acquainted with at least half of the Great Personages now in Vienna. But even so, why should he summon me, Harry worried, whom he has disowned and claimed never to want to see again. Harry thought briefly of Marius's incriminating letter, and of how easily he could regain his great-uncle's love and esteem, but pushed the thought away. Never! I gave him my *word* and he wouldn't take it. Shall I now go whimpering to him with proof?

Still—why does he want to see me now? Could it be the mission he is sent on is dangerous? That it requires physical strength to carry through? It must be so important that he was forced to set aside all personal considerations, such as his distaste for me, in order to carry it out.

"Oh, damn and blast!" Harry yelled aloud, hurling his hairbrush across the room in rage and bewilderment—and at the recurrence of pain in the old wound dealt him by his great-uncle.

Harry stormed out of his room and down the stairs. There was no servant in the hall to hand him his hat and cloak, but Harry had no thoughts of this. He flung open the door and there, providentially, was the old Baron's carriage, a stable boy holding the horses' heads, while the coachman was away in the kitchen having a glass of ale and flirting with the pretty kitchen maid.

"Stand away there," Harry called, jumping into the coachman's seat and grabbing the reins.

The boy barely had time to move before the horses, given the office to start, sprang forward, and the carriage clattered off down the street.

Grün, two blocks away, hugging the sides of the buildings and moving stealthily from shadow to shadow, heard the front door of Harry's house bang open and in the shaft of light from the hall recognized Harry leaping into the carriage. He quickly stepped back into a doorway and drew the pistol from his belt. Was it possible he was to have his chance so soon?

He had wasted no time after leaving Sir Marius to hurry back to his house for his pistol. He knew he must perform this dreadful task immediately, without giving himself time to think, since there was no escape if he wanted to live himself, and if he thought of what he must do he would lose what little courage remained to him.

He had set off on foot for Harry's house, mulling over in his mind how he was to accomplish this thing, but till this moment had received no inspiration. But now, as though the Fates had taken pity on his plight, his victim was being delivered to him, and in the best possible circumstances. The street was narrow here and the carriage would pass within a few feet of him, with Harry clearly silhouetted against the white building opposite, making the chance of missing almost nil. Grün glanced up and down the dark street and found it to be empty except for the rapidly approaching carriage.

He drew a deep breath, steadied the arm holding the pistol with his other hand and—now! He fired, saw Harry's body react to the impact of the bullet, and without waiting a further instant turned and ran.

Harry felt something ram into his shoulder at the same instant he heard the shot. The horses, terrified, reared up wildly. Without a thought for them, or for the bullet in his shoulder, Harry dropped the reins, leapt down from the still moving carriage and set off in pursuit of his assailant, the blood pumping out of the hole in his shoulder. The frightened horses bolted on down the street dragging the empty carriage behind them.

Grün heard Harry coming after him and dodged across the street, looking for an open gate or an alleyway between the buildings. If he could only get into a garden, find some trees for cover, he could surely escape, for Harry had been hit, of that Grün was positive, and might collapse at any moment.

But no opening presented itself and Harry was gaining on him. Grün ran frantically now, whimpering with fear, back to the other side of the street, but it was of no use. He felt an iron grip on his neck, attempted to twist out of it, and then felt an ankle hook around his own, a mighty shove between the shoulder blades, and he fell, his forehead thumping painfully on the cobblestone. He lay there too stunned to move. He felt a foot in his ribs and was helplessly rolled over onto his back.

"Well, well, Grün. Can you never find employment except with my uncle?"

Grün was saved the necessity of replying by the sound

of pounding footsteps, and then they were joined by a large, neatly dressed man.

"Good God, sir, what has happened? I heard a shot—" he gasped.

"This wretch was responsible for the shot, but as you can see, he failed to do the job very well."

The man looked from Grün to Harry. He was one of the men hired by Sascha to follow Harry when he went out on foot. He had been taken very much by surprise to see Harry leap into the carriage and drive off, but since Harry was not on foot, the man considered it no part of his duties to go running after a carriage. The shot, however, had set him in motion.

The other follower, employed by the Emperor, seeing that Harry was safe and the criminal caught, hung back in the shadows of observing.

"Why, he *did* hit you, sir! We must get you into the house at once," exclaimed the large man, noticing the blood running down Harry's coat sleeve and dripping onto the cobblestones.

Harry looked down at his immobilized arm and thought, inconsequentially, why its the same arm at last time, and glanced around in a rather dazed way. Slowly the memory of his errand, whose urgency had driven him so impetuously from the house, returned to his mind. The happenings of the past two or three moments had erased it. He remembered now the horses plunging away down the street and wondered how long it would take to have his own carriage brought around.

"Sir, sir—are you all right? I really think it would be wise to have that wound seen to at once."

"What? Oh—oh yes," Harry replied, looking down again at his red-stained hand. The man was right. Can't very well appear before Great-uncle with blood dripping down my arm, not to speak of the condition of my best evening coat, probably damaged beyond repair.

He shrugged and winced, aware of pain for the first time. Better to go back and have Miss Clark bind up his wounds again, change his coat, and in the meantime his carriage could be got ready.

"Come along then—its only a few steps. Can you bring along the scum?" Harry indicated the still recumbent form of Grün on the pavement between them, who had been lying absolutely quiet, scarcely daring to breathe in the hopes that their concern for Harry's wound would cause them to forget his existence entirely.

The large man reached down and with no visible effort, grasped a handful of Grün's coat front and lifted him to his feet. Deftly twisting one of Grün's arms up between his shoulder blades and offering his other arm courteously to Harry, they proceeded back to the house, where the stream of light still poured from the open front door. By the time they reached the light, however, the old Baron, Sascha, and a worried-looking butler had all appeared in the doorway, at a loss to understand why the front door should stand open to the night.

When the oddly assorted trio were espied, all three in the doorway started forward at once, causing some confusion, from which Sascha emerged first. He rushed forward to support Harry from the other side.

"*Mon dieu*, Harry, what has occurred here? You are bleeding! *Sacre bleu!* It is the insect you are holding, Jacques!" Sascha cried, acknowledging his recognition of the bodyguard and of the stumbling creature he was propelling along.

"Well, I don't know who he is, M'sieur, but the—er—wounded gentleman here has received a bullet in the shoulder and captured the criminal himself. I only came along—er—after." Jacques coughed discreetly, not sure whether he was supposed to reveal his employment or whether Sascha's naming of him had been a slip of the tongue caused by the excitement of the moment.

They had entered the hall by this time and the Baron ordered the butler to send someone for a doctor immediately. The butler hurried away.

"I don't need a doctor, Max," Harry said impatiently, "just send for Miss Clark to come to my room. And

you'd better send the stable boy off to search for your
cattle and your carriage. God knows where they've got
to by this time. The shot frightened them, and when I
jumped out they just kept going."

"Of course, Harry, of course, do not concern yourself. But I must insist that we have the doctor. Competent as she is I feel quite sure Miss Clark has had no
experience at all in removing bullets, and it is clear there
is one to be removed, since I see no exit wound."

The Baron and Sascha had been guiding Harry
towards the staircase as they spoke, but now he halted
the procession. "Where's the child?" he demanded.

"In her room, Harry," replied Sascha.

"Then we'd better not go up there. She'll be sure to
hear us and come out and then—" but before he could
continue, the hallway and the figures of his friends began to recede from his vision and he swayed, his eyes
rolling up into his head.

Sascha stepped behind him and caught him expertly
under the arms; the old Baron picked up his feet, and
they proceeded up the stairs with such an economy of
movement as to give the impression they had been drill-
ing themselves in this routine for weeks.

"Take the insect to the morning room and stay with
him, Jacques. I'll deal with him later," Sascha flung over
his shoulder.

Within moments they had Harry on his bed, and
Sascha was beginning to rip open the sleeve of Harry's
coat, when the butler appeared leading a panting gentleman with a bag, whose dinner napkin was still tucked
into his neckcloth.

The doctor bustled forward, pushing Sascha aside.
"Bring hot water and something for bandaging immedi-
ately," he ordered as he took over the removal of
Harry's coat sleeve.

A half-hour later Sascha emerged from Harry's bedroom bearing a basin of pink-tinted water and some
gruesomely stained clothes over one arm, just as Letty

came out of her room, dressed in one of her usual gauzy white slips for the evening performance.

"Your sash is improperly tied," he said with great presence of mind as he turned smartly away from her and made for the back stairs. Letty automatically turned back to her door and then stopped, stood stock still for an instant, and whirled around again.

"Sascha! What is that? What is all that blood?" she cried.

"Not to concern yourself, Mademoiselle. Go and rearrange your sash and then go down. It is nearly time for your performance."

"Is it Harry? Has something happened to Harry," she shrilled, ignoring his orders.

"*Dieu!* What a *peste* it is. Your sash, Mademoiselle—at once!"

"It *is* Harry! You're trying to hide something from me! I'll find out for myself," cried Letty beginning to run down the hall to Harry's door.

"Stop! Do not—"

But Sascha was too late. Letty flung open the door and stood there, paralyzed by the sight of Harry lying back limp against his pillows, shirtless, his shoulder swathed in bandages. The old Baron was bent over the white face on the pillows in what seemed to be an urgent attitude and to Letty the scene suggested that Harry was in the final moments of life.

The Baron glanced up and frowned when he saw who was there. He opened his mouth to protest, but Letty flew across the room with a soft moan and dropped to her knees beside the bed.

"What the devil—" Harry's lids snapped open as he felt his hand clasped in both of hers and pressed to her cheek. "What to you mean bursting in here without so much as a knock on the door—here—hand me my robe, Max. For God's sake, Letty, *will* you let go of my hand?" he said crossly.

"Oh, Harry—Harry—I thought you were dying! You

looked so—so white," she replied, retaining a firm grip on his hand.

"Dying? I hope I'm not so lily-livered as to die from a shot in the shoulder! Now why are you crying?"

Letty, the relief coming so suddenly after the shock, was not even aware she *was* crying. She could only gaze at him dumbly through her swimming eyes, his hand clasped to her cheek while silent tears filled her eyes and spilled over in a steady stream.

"Max, for heaven's sake, will you take her out of here?" Harry requested plaintively, though the old Baron was interested to note that Harry had ceased trying to tug his hand away from its watery resting place and was watching Letty with a softened expression that did not match the querulous tone of his voice. The Baron, holding the robe Harry had asked for, made no move to interrupt this tableau.

"Letty, you must let go of my hand now," said Harry finally, in an oddly gentle voice. "I must cover myself. It isn't right for you to be in here in any case. I must get up and get dressed."

"No, no, Harry, of course you may not get up," replied Letty soothingly.

"But of course I *may*. I have an appointment and I'm perfectly all right now."

"My boy, it would be most unwise. You have lost a great deal of blood, you know," reproved the Baron.

"I tell you I must get up. Letty, leave the room immediately."

"I won't let you, Harry! I shall call Sascha to take away all your clothes and we'll lock you in if necessary," retorted Letty, feeling very brave with the old Baron on her side.

He wrested his hand away from her rudely. "You're getting above yourself, infant. Now get out of here because I'm getting up immediately."

"I suppose Lady Hester is giving another of her parties and *requires* you to be there?" she flung at him sarcastically.

He glared at her furiously, stung by the implication that he ran to Lady Hester's bidding.

"Where I'm going is my business. Your business is to entertain the customers downstairs. Now go wash your face and get down there at once!"

"Very *well!* Go to her. I'm sure *I* don't care if you're so much in her pocket you'd drag yourself from your deathbed if she crooks her finger!" shouted Letty, the colour pouring back into her pale cheeks. She jumped to her feet and flounced out of the room, slamming the door forcefully behind her.

The old Baron shook his head. "She is right, you know, Harry. You should not leave your bed."

"Now, don't you start," pleaded Harry. "You may rest assured that if I had any doubts about my condition I would never make this call. It's my great-uncle, you see, and it would never do to let him suspect there was anything amiss."

"Your uncle! He is here, the Lord Aubrey? In Vienna? But—but why, Harry?"

"That's what I must find out. I can only believe it's to do with the government. Perhaps some very private negotiation on behalf of His Majesty. In any case, I am sure it must be something very important for him to have sent for *me*."

"Will you take Marius's letter, Harry?"

"The letter? Good God, Max, of course not! I've already said I would never use it. And this is not the time even to think of all that."

The Baron held a very different view on the subject but knew it would be pointless to pursue it now. He went to the door and called Harry's valet in to help him to dress, cautioning them both to be very careful not to start the wound bleeding again.

Finally, with great difficulty, Harry was eased into a fresh evening coat and made his way carefully down the stairs and out, very grateful to be spared any further encounters with Letty.

Letty saw him cross the hall but remained where she

was by the piano. Inside her head the angry dialogue continued as she thought of wonderfully disagreeable things she wished she had thought to say to him while she had had the chance.

The old Baron came in, led her forward, introduced her and retired. Letty curtsied, smiled, sang, acknowledged the applause and found herself back out in the hallway with no real memory of what she had been doing.

"He left," she said to the Baron.

"Yes, *ma p'tite*, but not to Lady Hester, so do not upset yourself."

"Oh, I'm sure it's a matter of complete indifference to me what he chooses to do," she replied airily. He wisely made no reply to this but led her to the stairs.

"Where *did* he go then?" she blurted out in spite of herself.

"It is the old uncle. He is in Vienna and has sent for Harry."

"*What?* Did Harry take the letter?"

"No, child, he would not. You must not concern yourself with this."

"Not concern myself?" she cried, stamping her white satin sandal angrily, "how can you even say such a thing? Where is the letter? I'll take it to him myself!" she declared passionately.

"*Impossible!* To push yourself into his presence with such a story! No, no, my child, it would never do. And Harry would never forgive you for interfering."

Letty contemplated this statement for a moment and finally, grudgingly, was forced to acknowledge that he was right.

"But we must do something!" she persisted, her dark-fringed hazel eyes glittering with zeal.

"*Chérie*, if you will listen to the advice of an old man, you will do nothing. I know how your—ah—affection for Harry compels you. All of us feel the same, but it is not our business. It is a thing Harry feels very strongly to be a private matter to himself. He would not forgive interference."

"Where is the letter?"

"I have it. But I, also, will not interfere."

She stared up into his face, but it was obvious that she did not really see him. He watched the sweet, flower-like face and wondered what her thoughts could be to give her such an abstracted look.

She didn't enlighten him, but only turned away to the stairs murmuring an absentminded "Good night, dear Baron," and climbed slowly up and out of his sight, leaving him to gaze uneasily after her.

Chapter 14

LORD AUBREY STILL sat, with an implacable patience, before the fire in his hotel suite. Opposite him sat Sir Marius, a glass of port in one hand, growing more relaxed as the time passed. He had now been with Lord Aubrey for two hours and had been entertaining him with stories and gossip of Vienna, of which, because of his special position, Sir Marius had a great store—though without any discernible signs of appreciation on Lord Aubrey's part.

He was utterly confident by now that Grün had successfully carried out his assignment and that Harry would never appear before his great-uncle. So confident that when Lord Aubrey's elderly man-servant opened the door and announced, "Mr. Harry, M'lord," the glass of port dropped from Sir Marius's fingers and crashed to bits on the parquet floor.

Harry was equally astonished to see Sir Marius, so completely had he convinced himself that his great-uncle had sent for him on some secret matter of state. He bowed politely and lifted an eyebrow coolly at Sir Marius.

"I see my arrival has shocked you. Now I wonder why that should be?" he said mockingly.

"Nettleship, clean up that mess," snapped Lord Au-

brey, indicating the spilt wine and broken glass. While
this was being done Lord Aubrey studied the two men
before him, both unusually white of face. There could
be no doubt that Sir Marius was shocked to see Harry,
and Lord Aubrey also wondered why this should be so,
since he himself had informed Marius that Harry was expected. As for Harry, Lord Aubrey thought he had
never seen the boy looking worse. His colour was
ghastly, and the old man could have taken his oath he
was swaying somewhat on his feet.

"Are you foxed, Harry?" Lord Aubrey asked suspiciously.

"Certainly not, sir."

"Then you'd better sit down," ordered Lord Aubrey.

Harry was on the point of declaring he would prefer
to conduct the interview on his feet, but realised it might
be better to do as he was told. He sat down rather
abruptly.

Lord Aubrey poured a glass of brandy and brought it
to Harry, who accepted it gratefully. After a few sips,
during which silence reigned in the room, a slight tinge
of colour returned to Harry's cheeks.

"Are you all right?" asked Lord Aubrey gruffly, trying to mask his very real concern.

"Right as a trivet, sir, I thank you," replied Harry
jauntily. "Now, how may I be of service to you?" he
added with the slight smile and careless tone he knew his
great-uncle found irritating. He flicked a glance at Marius and was interested to find that gentleman regarding
him intently. *Probably suspects Grün hit me and won-
ders if the wound is fatal enough to kill me before I can
make any statements,* thought Harry.

"I did not ask you to come here because I required
any services of you—or of Marius either. I have been informed that you have in your possession a letter relating
to the—ah— affair in Spain. I want to see that letter."

"May I inquire how such information came to you?"
countered Harry, carefully *not* glancing at Sir Marius,
who sat frozen, his eyes riveted on Harry.

"It does not signify in the least. I will be much obliged if you will just hand it over to me without any brangling."

"Upon my soul, sir, I would not care for an argument either, but I fear my poor brain has not quite grasped the information as yet—"

"I believe you *are* foxed!" barked Lord Aubrey suspiciously.

"I protest, Great-uncle! Would I be so crack-brained as to appear before you in such a condition?"

"Do not trifle with me, sir!"

"I wouldn't dream of making such a cake of myself as to try it, Great-uncle. You are much too needle-witted for me to think I could get away with it."

"Then we'll have no more of this shilly-shallying. I may look a maggoty creature, but I assure you I am still awake in every suit. Now—do you have this letter?"

"No, sir," replied Harry, quite truthful.

"Do you know where it is?"

"No, sir, I don't," Harry said, again truthfully. He heard a sharp intake of breath from Marius's direction.

Lord Aubrey stood staring at Harry, completely at *non-plus*. He knew Harry too well to think he would lie, and yet there remained an indefinable feeling that something was being withheld.

"Marius admits there is such a letter," stated Lord Aubrey cunningly.

"Sir! I—" Marius protested vehemently.

"Be quiet!" thundered Lord Aubrey. "Well, Harry?"

"Well, what, sir?" asked Harry blandly.

"Harry, you are rapidly putting me out of all patience. If you're playing some devilish deep game with me—"

"No game at all, I assure you, sir."

"Uncle, of course he will deny it," Marius interjected, determined to be heard.

"I will conduct this interview, if you please, Marius. Now Harry, I will know the truth! I have been told there is an incriminating letter—"

"Incriminating to me, sir?" asked Harry, with an assumption of great interest.

"No," replied Lord Aubrey shortly.

"You much relieve my mind, sir. May I ask whom it incriminates then?"

"Marius."

"Marius! Why, bless my soul!" Harry turned now to Marius for the first time, raised his quizzing-glass and inspected his uncle thoroughly. Marius sneered and turned away with an air of indifference.

"Harry, I am not at all entertained by your role of amusing rattle. Marius claims this letter to be a forgery of his handwriting, prepared by you or an accomplice with blackmail in mind. What have you to say to this?"

"Blackmail of whom, sir?"

"Marius, of course!"

"Now let me see if I have this straight. Marius says that I wrote this letter, incriminating to himself, with the intent of blackmailing him. I wonder—was I successful?"

"Harry," said Lord Aubrey through clenched teeth, "I'll have no more of this. I have not come all this way to play games with you."

"Great-uncle, I assure you nothing has surprised me so much as the fact that you have put yourself to such a great deal of bother when your mind was already so comfortably made up on the subject."

"Will you give me a straight answer?"

"I have answered you, many times. I gave you my word. I had thought that would have been enough. Since you chose not to take it, I really see no profit in a discussion of a letter." Harry's voice had lost its tone of bantering amusement and his reply was snapped out with a hard-edged quality that bespoke the soreness the point still caused him.

"I will ask you again. Do you have this letter?"

"No."

"Do you know where it is?"

"No." Harry rose slowly, "And now, with your permission, I will leave you, sir. It has been a most fatiguing

day, and I have still work to do. It would give me great
pleasure to welcome you to my establishment while you
remain in Vienna, if you should feel the inclination for a
few hours of relaxation. Your servant, sir," he bowed,
carefully, and turned away to the door.

"Now look here, Harry," spluttered Lord Aubrey, the
unhealthy purple colour surging into his face at this
cavalier treatment, "I insist that you tell me all you
know of this letter—"

Harry turned back with a careless laugh. "Oh yes, the
letter. Well as to that, I suggest you apply to Marius.
You did say he told you he knew of the letter? Just so.
You may rest assured, sir, that there is very little Marius
doesn't know about that letter," and with an amiable
wave of his hand Harry went out the door, closing it,
very softly, behind him.

"Sascha!" Letty rushed into the music room, the vandyked flounces of her pale blue muslin gown fluttering
like petals about her ankles, "Miss Clark says you want
me to practise this morning, but I can't believe you are
serious! Practise? At a time like this?"

"This is the very time we practise every morning,
Mademoiselle," came Sascha's unruffled reply.

"I have been thinking *all night* of what we must do,"
she exclaimed dramatically, ignoring his remark as the
sort of trivial and prosaic thing older people were given
to making in the face of the most earth-shaking events.

"What we must do is practise the breathing. Now—
begin!" He brought his fingers down emphatically on
the all too familiar chord.

"Miss Clark says Harry is something feverish this
morning and the doctor has ordered him to remain in
bed all day, and the Baron has the letter. I know, for
when I asked what had become of it his hand went up to
pat his pocket, though he said I was not to concern myself about such things, though how he could even say
such a thing—I mean, it's so *silly*—how can one possibly
forbid oneself to think? Anyway, if the Baron has the

letter, that means Lord Aubrey hasn't seen it yet."
Letty's delicate brows drew together in a small frown of
concentration.

"The Baron was right. This does not concern us.
What does concern us is—"

"If you say 'breathing' again I shall scream," Letty
stated in a matter-of-fact tone of voice that carried so
much conviction Sascha's mouth closed with a snap.
"Now—I think what we must do is this: you must ask
the Baron for the letter, as you have a perfect right to
do since if Harry doesn't want it it belongs to you, as
you're the one who stole it from Grün, and then we will
take it to Lord Aubrey ourselves."

"I? Why am I to ask the Baron?"

"Because he will not give it to me since he will suspect
what I plan to do," she replied in sweetly patient tones.

"And when I ask him for it he will suspect what *I* plan
to do. Or rather, what you plan to do, for I will not do
it, Mademoiselle, it is not possible. If the Baron thought
it right to interfere in this matter he would take the letter to the English milord himself. I also think it not right
to push myself into Harry's affairs against his wishes. He
has said he will not use the letter. There's an end to it."

"But he didn't actually forbid anyone else to use it,"
Letty replied cunningly, "and if he must be so mulishly
proud then we must act for him. We cannot stand by
and allow him to be falsely branded a card-cheat and
lose every chance to recover his inheritance."

"Ah—a waste of the most deplorable kind, I agree,
but—"

"Not to speak of another, perhaps successful, attempt
on his life," she interrupted, ruthlessly determined to
force him to act. "You must know the only way to prevent Sir Marius from finally killing Harry is for the old
man to be put into possession of that letter. Once he has
it there would be nothing for Sir Marius to do."

Sascha stared at her for a long moment. "Very well,"
he said finally, "to save Harry's life, I see that I must do
something. But it is of no use to ask the old Baron for

the letter. He will ask what I plan to do with it and I will not lie to my old friend."

"But then—" Letty began in frustration.

"Again, you must leave it to me, Mademoiselle," Sascha commanded masterfully, "I have the plan. I will take the *insect* to the old man and force him to confess."

"Oh, Sascha, how brilliant!" she exclaimed, her eyes sparkling with excitement, "and I will go with you—no! Don't get that forbearing look on your face as though you're dealing with a child. You need me just as much now as you did when you stole the letter from Grün. I shall dress very grand and send up word that I'm the grand-niece of the Countess Dacres. That will get us admitted immediately, you may be sure, where you alone might have a great deal of difficulty," she added with devastating candour.

To his credit, Sascha didn't flinch, being much too practical-minded to be bothered by the inanity of the British caste system. "You are right. Go away and change your costume while I fetch the unspeakable Gürn," he ordered decisively, standing up and closing the lid on the piano keys with a snap.

Thirty minutes later she descended the stairs with as regal a bearing as she could muster, the haughty expression on her face conveying, she hoped, the look of one used to having all doors open before her. Sascha studied her with approval. Her dark green ermine-caped velvet pelisse and matching bonnet were suitably redolent of money and taste. Behind her, dressed with staggering gentility in dove grey, came Miss Clark, only a spot of colour on each cheek betraying her excitement.

When Letty had rushed impetuously into her room and begun hurriedly to remove her morning dress, she had explained that she was going to pay a morning visit on Harry's great-uncle, Lord Aubrey, who was visiting Vienna. Miss Clark had immediately started making preparations to accompany her. Letty's protest died on her lips as she realised how necessary it was that Miss Clark accompany her. No well-brought up young

woman would go unaccompanied to pay a call on a
gentleman in his hotel, no matter how old that gentleman
might be. Sascha and Grün could hardly be put in the
category of acceptable duennas on such an occasion. By
all means Miss Clark must come.

Sascha nodded at Letty, instantly understanding and
approving the necessity for Miss Clark. "It is of the
greatest respectability, Mademoiselle. *Très comme il
faut*. Come along now, let us hurry. I've sent Jacques
ahead with Grün."

The Countess's name had worked its magic, and Letty,
with pounding heart but some semblance of outward
composure, advanced across the drawing room of Lord
Aubrey's suite at the Kaiserin and dropped a deep curtsey to the old man who stood to receive her.

"My dear Miss Montressor, how very delightful. I
knew your dear aunt well—a very great many years ago,
I fear. I was saddened to hear of her death," he took her
hand in both of his and gazed appreciatively at the fresh,
lovely young face before him.

"Thank you, Lord Aubrey. How very good of you to
receive me without warning in this way. I had meant to
write and ask if I might call when I learned you were in
Vienna, but as we were passing I gave in to the impulse
to stop. My great-aunt spoke of you so often," Letty
said artlessly, giving him her most limpidly innocent gaze
and crossing her fingers inside her ermine muff.

"Well, well, did she now?" beamed Lord Aubrey,
much gratified, "beautiful young woman she was. Took
London by storm in her day. Amazing that she should
have remembered me all these years. Well, well, enough
of that. Please be seated, my dear, and tell me what you
are doing here in Vienna."

Letty introduced Miss Clark and allowed the old
gentleman to fuss about seating them and helping them
to remove their wraps without replying to his inquiry
about her presence in Vienna. All the way in the carriage her mind had been wrestling with the problem of

how to introduce the reason for her visit. She had decided to be very brusque and businesslike and lay the whole affair on the table at once, but, now that she was face to face with this awesomely dignified English lord, she found it impossible to say bluntly, "Lord Aubrey, I have proof that your grand-nephew is not a card cheat." But after fidgeting a moment beneath the kindly gaze from the keen old grey eyes, she blurted out just those words. Miss Clark gasped in dismay.

Lord Aubrey went very still and something steely came into his regard of her. "You speak of Harry Tyne, Miss Montressor?"

"Yes," she replied, and then, taking her courage in both hands, she plunged in headlong. "I have never believed it of him and the Baron and Sascha swore it could not be so, and then when we got hold of the letter we *knew* it was all lies, but then Harry would not bring it to you—oh! he is the *most* hard-headed—but then when he was shot—"

"One moment!" commanded Lord Aubrey, rising from his chair opposite her, "Harry was shot? Who—"

"Oh, Sir Marius, of course. At least, not actually Sir Marius who fired the revolver, that was Grün, but of course he was hired to do so by Sir Marius, which is just the same thing," Letty finished breathlessly.

Lord Aubrey sank back down onto his chair, visibly at a loss to comprehend this welter of information. "Young lady," he began rather gropingly, "I can see that you are sincerely convinced of what you say, but—but—this is a most serious accusation—and what—er—proof?"

"Oh, we have Grün. He is outside with Sascha, and he will tell you it is true because Sascha will make him."

"But how can you know this Grün fired a shot at Harry, even if—"

"Because Harry chased him and caught him, in spite of his wound, when Grün tried to run away. And then the other man, the one Sascha had hired to guard Harry after the first attack came running up and—"

Lord Aubrey, the flesh of his face taking on a chalky

hue, waved a pleading hand at her. He sagged against the chair-back and passed a shaky hand over the bald dome of his head.

Miss Clark leapt to her feet and pulled the bell to summon his servant, and Nettleship, who had been hovering just outside the door, keeping his person between the door and the strange trio of men seated together on a bench in the small entrance hall, entered immediately.

"Forgive my presumptiousness, Lord Aubrey, but I think you should have a restorative," said Miss Clark, raising a significant eyebrow at Nettleship, who responded suavely.

"A brandy, M'lord? And perhaps the ladies would take some refreshment also."

"Yes, yes, certainly, very remiss of me," Lord Aubrey quavered.

Nettleship moved to the side of the room and poured and served lemonade to the ladies and a brandy to Lord Aubrey, who sipped it in a determined way, as a man taking a prescribed medicine with every confidence in its power of healing.

"That's right, my lord," said Miss Clark encouragingly, "drink it all up and you'll be feeling right as a trivet in a moment. I'm afraid Miss Montressor has told you all this in an overly melodramatic manner. She is very young and allows her emotions too much expression."

Letty gave her an indignant look which Miss Clark blandly ignored. Nettleship, seeing the situation in capable hands, bowed and slipped out the door to take up guard duty again in the hall.

Letty opened her mouth to speak, but received such a quelling stare from Miss Clark that she subsided with only a tiny *moue* of impatience. Lord Aubrey finished his brandy and set the glass aside. He gazed silently into the fire for several moments, then with a palpable effort he sat up and squared his shoulders.

"I must see Harry," he said gruffly.

"I'm sure he will be happy to wait upon you, sir, at the

irst possible moment. Unfortunately, he is somewhat feverish today—oh, nothing too serious," she added hastily,
seeing his brows drawing together, "only the result of
having a bullet removed from his shoulder and insisting
on coming here to you afterwards. And then there had
been a considerable loss of blood. The doctor assured me
he will be perfectly well, however, if we can keep him
quiet for a few days, and then I'm sure it will be his first
object to come to you again."

"No. I must see him now. I will go to him," said Lord
Aubrey with great decision.

"But, sir, we have Grün here and you haven't heard
his confession," protested Letty. "I will fetch them in
and—"

Lord Aubrey rose. "That will keep. First I must see
Harry. If you will forgive my rudeness in leaving while
you are paying me a call, I will go immediately."

"Well then—if you insist—I suppose we can all go together—you see, all of us live with Harry, so Miss Clark
and I will be happy to take you back with us in our carriage."

"You—*live*—with Harry?" exclaimed Lord Aubrey in
shocked accents.

"Under *my* chaperonage, Lord Aubrey," interposed
Miss Clark challengingly, as though daring him to imagine Parthenope Clark being involved in any situation that
was not of the greatest respectability.

A slight twitch at the corner of his mouth and a meek
bow acknowledged Lord Aubrey's agreement that this
must indeed be so. "No doubt all will become clear to
me in time," he said motioning the ladies to precede him
to the door.

Chapter 15

❧

"HARRY," SAID THE Baron softly, touching the hand lying on top of the white sheet and looking very brown against it. "Harry, *mon vieux*."

The grey eyes opened slowly, "What is it, Max?"

"I regret that I must disturb you, Harry, but I thought I must do so. Your uncle is here."

"Marius *here*—the devil you say!"

"No, no, I have said it wrong. It is your great-uncle, is that the expression? The Lord of Aubrey."

This astounding news brought no response for a moment as Harry's brain, clouded by fever, attempted to find an explanation for it.

"It's that damned letter, I suppose," he said at last, somewhat fretfully. "I should have known he'd come blustering around demanding an explanation."

"Well, I cannot say for sure, of course, but I would not call his manner blustery in any way. He was very calm, asked most courteously to be allowed to speak to you. And I think you must see him, Harry. He—he—looks to be in a very poor way. His colour is bad and his hands—there is a tremor—and—"

"Enough, enough," said Harry weakly, "show him up. Though I don't like to face so formidable an adversary when I'm flat on my back!"

162

"I should imagine you still have the advantage of him—this may help even things out a bit," responded the old Baron wryly as he left the room.

Harry painfully hitched himself up higher on his pillows and ploughed a hand nervously through the fever-dampened curls sticking to his forehead. Damn the hard-headed old codger, he swore silently and helplessly.

And then the door opened and the old codger was before him. Lord Aubrey stumped slowly across to the bedside on his gouty old legs and stood, gnarled hands clasping his cane, looking down at Harry without speaking. But however crippled his body, there was nothing wrong with his eyesight and he saw clearly the flushed cheeks and glassy look of the grey eyes that nevertheless met his own without wavering.

"Well, Harry, it grieves me to find you in such a case. How could you have been so foolish as to come to my hotel immediately after having a ball removed from your shoulder? No, no—don't bother to deny it. I've had the whole story from that young woman. I knew something was wrong at the time."

"Not to worry, Great-uncle, I'll be up to anything by morning. I must say this visit has taken me by surprise. If it's about that damned letter—"

"No!" Lord Aubrey interrupted forcefully. "Forget the letter. I—I—" he came to a full stop and for a time seemed unable to continue. Harry studied the craggy, lined old face above him and felt his heart turn over with love. He thought, "He has come all this long journey in spite of ill health just on a rumour that a letter existed that might clear my name, and the only thanks he gets is evasion from me and lies from Marius. I've been pigheaded and selfish and if this trip kills him I'll never forgive myself."

"Great-uncle, I will tell you—" he began impetuously.

"No, no, my boy. I must speak first. I owe you this—and much more—very much more. You were right. You told me you were innocent and I owed it to you to accept your word no matter what the evidence. You had never lied to me in your life, and yet—"

"Please say no more," Harry pleaded, appalled to hear his great-uncle speaking in such a humble way.

"I must say it all, Harry, now I've begun. I must ask your pardon."

Harry's hot hand came out to grasp the old hands on the cane. "Great-uncle, I beg you to stop. I assure you the evidence seemed indisputable and anyone would have believed—"

"And so they might—anyone—but not I. I had your word it was not so, and it should have been enough for me. As I would have expected mine to be enough for you in like circumstances."

"Sir, won't you please sit down and let us speak of other things?"

"No, dear boy, I will leave you now, for I'm not such a maggoty creature that I cannot see you would benefit by some rest. Perhaps your—er—guardians will allow me to come up to you again this evening."

Harry gave him a tired smile. "Cut up a bit rough with you, did they?"

"Oh no indeed, everything that was courteous, I assure you, but very protective of you. You were always fortunate in your friends, Harry."

He turned abruptly and stumped away across the room and out the door without another word, and Harry watched him go, his eyes drooping shut as the door closed, his face looking very boyish as the harsh lines smoothed away.

But the anxious group below—Letty, Sascha, the old Baron and Miss Clark—were disconcerted by Lord Aubrey's expression. There was a grim set to his mouth that boded ill for someone. There had been much discussion among those waiting concerning the purpose of Lord Aubrey's insistence upon an immediate interview with Harry, about the wisdom of allowing him to have his way when Harry was ill, and about his refusal to interview Grün or discuss the letter the old Baron still held before seeing his grand-nephew.

He didn't enlighten them now, but only requested in a quiet voice, that contrasted oddly with the look on his face and reminded Letty strongly of Harry at his most frightening, if someone would be so kind as to send word to Sir Marius that his uncle would be obliged if Sir Marius could make it convenient to attend him here immediately.

Sascha said he would attend to it personally, *"Instamment!"* and went away. The old Baron then led Lord Aubrey away to the business room, ordering the footman to send in brandy for his lordship.

Letty began to follow them, but the Baron shook his head at her with a sweet, but firm, smile, and though eager to speak further with lord Aubrey about Harry's innocence, she somehow dared not persist. She felt very put upon. How was it that in spite of being the prime mover in all these events, when the *dénouements* came she was firmly pushed out of the room and had the door closed in her face. Not only Harry, but everyone treated her so. Even Lord Aubrey, who, had she not persisted in calling upon him, would not even be here now, had marched past her in the hall as though he had never seen her before. Oh, the unfairness of it! The—the *ingratitude*, she thought, stamping her small foot in its green morocco slipper in frustration. How could even the old Baron join in this conspiracy of exclusion?

Had she but known that the old Baron was very much aware of her feelings! He had seen her look of hurt disbelief when he had signalled her not to accompany himself and Lord Aubrey into the business room, and had understood and sympathised with her. But he had also seen that the old gentleman was in a very bad way and needed a few moments of quiet to recoup his strength and fortify himself for the coming interview with his nephew, an interview that, from the look on his face as he came down the stairs, boded unpleasantness for someone.

Adorable as Letty was, the old Baron did not feel she would be a restful companion for Lord Aubrey at this moment.

He settled the old gentleman into a chair and saw him slump tiredly for a moment, but only for a moment. When the brandy arrived he sat up gamely and began to sip it determinedly.

"Now, sir, if you are feeling somewhat restored I hope you will allow me the honour of presenting myself to you more formally. I fear our dear Letty was too overset with excitement to do it properly when you first arrived. I am Max von Bergheim, Harry's partner in this establishment, at your service."

"Servant, sir," replied Lord Aubrey, sketching a bow from his chair. "I believe I heard the young woman introduce you as the Baron. That is your title?"

The Baron merely bowed in response, and Lord Aubrey seemed contented with it as an answer. He recognised quality and could see the Baron was well supplied with that commodity.

"Perhaps, sir, you would be good enough to explain to me what a young gentlewoman, the niece of Countess Dacres, is doing here? She tells me she lives here—under the chaperonage of Miss Clark, to be sure," he added, his sharp old eyes twinkling.

The Baron put all the facts about Letty before him and Lord Aubrey nodded. "Yes, yes, that sounds just the sort of scrape Harry would get himself into. Well, well, we must see what can be done for the child," he said wearily, and again applied himself to his brandy. Obviously finding strength again, he set the glass aside decisively and addressed himself with resolution to the old Baron.

"Now, sir, I'm going to request your assistance in the matter of this mysterious letter. I received anonymous information in London of the existence of this letter. Sir Marius, when I confronted him with the matter, acknowledged his—er—'awareness' of it, and Miss Montressor mentioned it in a somewhat confusing context.

Harry, however, denied all knowledge of it. If you have anything you can tell me about it I shall be forever in your debt. I hasten to assure you that I do not require the letter any longer as proof of Harry's innocence. I finally realised that this morning when the child told me he had been shot. I knew then what a blind, stupid old curmudgeon I really had been, allowing myself to be swayed in my judgement of Harry's integrity by any evidence to the contrary. Harry's as sound as they make 'em. Always has been, always will be."

"My own thinking exactly, Lord Aubrey. The letter is here," he reached into his pocket and produced it, handing it without comment to Lord Aubrey, who read it through. Angry colour surged up into his face alarmingly, and then, even more alarmingly, drained away. The old Baron started forward with an exclamation of alarm, but Lord Aubrey held up an imperious hand.

"I am perfectly well, I assure you, Baron von Bergheim, you need not be concerned. Even if I were not, I would not allow anything to stand in the way of this interview with Marius. Having accepted that Harry could not have been guilty of such conduct as he was accused of, one needn't seek far for the manufacturer of the evidence that condemned him. I am heartsick that my own brother's son could stoop to such a dastardly trick. I'm only glad poor John is dead these many years and cannot be hurt by it. But even such a despicable plan, terrible as it is, pales to insignificance when compared to *murder!*"

The door opened on the last few words and a puffing Sir Marius appeared in time to hear the horrified accents of his uncle's voice.

" 'Pon my soul, sir! First this urgent summons and now these direful words greet me. I trust you have no dreadful news for me?" gasped Sir Marius. He had obviously wasted not a moment in obeying his uncle's request when he learned his presence was required at Harry's gaming establishment. He felt sure it could only mean that Harry, succumbing to his wound, had died and his frightened associates had sent for Lord Aubrey to come claim the body of his kinsman. Marius fought down his exultation and tried to arrange his face into a suitably grave expression.

"Not the dreadful news I am confident you were expecting, Marius," replied his lordship quietly.

"He's not—" Marius checked abruptly, cursing inwardly at this inexcusable lapse. He tried to recover, warning himself that the old man was very sharp and he, Marius, must be very careful. "That is—Harry's not joining us? Or has he delegated his busines associate to represent him? One knows how busy Harry always seems to be."

"Shall I withdraw, Lord Aubrey?" asked the old Baron softly.

"I would be grateful if you would stay, Baron. It will be unsavoury, I'm sure you will know that, but if you would not mind?"

"With pleasure, My Lord, I do assure you," replied the Baron, an unusual grimness in his voice.

"Uncle, if this is to be a private interview—though I must confess," he laughed deprecatingly, "I find myself somewhat at a loss to understand your choice of venue—still, I would prefer not to have the presence of a man whose reputation as a card-sharp is well known on three continents. I cannot think it fitting—"

"How dare you speak of 'fitting', sir?" demanded Lord Aubrey wrathfully, "you who would stoop to any means to have what is not rightfully yours? I have the letter you wrote to your accomplice and there is not a doubt in my mind as to its authenticity—"

"But I have already explained to you about this forgery, Uncle, surely you remember—" began Marius in the patiently indulgent tones of an adult to a child.

"—and when you were unable to recover the letter from your accomplice," his lordship continued as though his nephew had not spoken, "you did not hesitate to order the man to murder Harry—your own nephew!"

"I?! Who has told you such a monstrous lie? Harry can have no proof of such a thing—"

"I believe your accomplice, this Grün person, is here in the house. We'll have him in now, if you would be so kind as to summon him, Baron?"

The old Baron went to the door and found Sascha waiting there with Grün sagging in his grasp, in readiness for the summons he was sure would come. Sascha jerked Grün upright and hustled him into the room.

Lord Aubrey looked Grün up and down with astonished distaste. How *could* Marius connive with such an unappetising representative of humanity?

Sir Marius managed a creditable imitation of one who has discovered something nasty under a stone and turned away disdainfully, though he very carefully avoided looking anyone in the eye.

"You—*you*—attempted to murder Harry?" Lord Aubrey asked in an incredulous voice.

Indeed, Grün was a pitiful looking specimen as he cringed before the company, his former smartness transformed by a night and day in the same clothing to wrinkled grubbiness. His round, cherubic cheeks were tear-stained and deflated-looking.

"Noble sir!" he exclaimed with a gasp, rushing forward to throw himself to his knees and raise clasped hands imploringly to Lord Aubrey, "please listen for a small moment, but one small moment is all I ask. It was a most foul deed, I admit it freely, but I could not help myself. He made me do it. He said he would kill me if I didn't—" Grün's voice rose shrilly, "it was to save my life, you undersand? To save my *life!*"

"Who ordered you to kill Harry?" demanded Lord Aubrey harshly.

Sir Marius directed an intimidating glare at Grün, but Grün did not see it, he had eyes only for Lord Aubrey, seeming to know instinctively where his best chance for survival lay.

"Sir Marius," he cried. The easy tears brimmed over and rolled unchecked down his cheeks. "Though I told

him I *would* not do it—that I *could* not! But he said that
I must if I wanted to live and kicked me out of his
house."

"Really, Uncle, I must protest. To be made to stand
here and listen to these vile accusations from this—this—
abomination—" Marius began haughtily.

"I will attend to you presently, Marius. For now, be
quiet," answered Lord Aubrey, not bothering to look at
him. He continued to Grün, "You assisted Sir Marius in
Spain in a scheme involving my great-nephew, Harry
Tyne?"

"But only to hide the marked cards on his person,"
babbled Grün eagerly, "it was Sir Marius who put the
drops in his drink, your Highness, I assure you. My part
was very minor—"

"For which you were well paid, no doubt," Lord Aubrey interposed grimly.

"Not as he promised me, My Lord!" cried Grün indignantly, "he promised—"

"Which is why you began to blackmail him, no
doubt?"

The old Baron was somewhat startled by this statement from Lord Aubrey, wondering where he had all
his information. But then he remembered Lord Aubrey's
ride back in the carriage with Letty.

"Never! I would never stoop to such a thing, Sire, I
was only trying to make him pay me what he owed
me—what he promised to give me—"

"And this is the letter you used to try to—ah—extract
the money owing to you?" Lord Aubrey held the letter
under Grün's nose.

"That is *my* property, noble sir, stolen from my own
premises by this—this common thief!" Grün turned accusingly upon Sascha, who merely grinned at him.

"You received this letter from Sir Marius while you
were both in Spain?" demanded Lord Aubrey. Grün
nodded, his eyes fixed greedily on the letter, as though,
in spite of everything that had happened, he still looked

upon it as a legitimate source of income. "Take him
away now, please," requested Lord Aubrey disgustedly.

Grün's head jerked up, his eyes wide with terror.
"You will not have me arrested?! I beg of you, noble sir,
do not—" he halted, a look of cunning narrowing the
baby blue eyes. "I should then be forced to reveal to
them that Sir Marius Tyne ordered me—"

"Say no more. I have said you may go, but I warn you
that it would not be to your advantage if your path
should cross mine or Harry's in the future. I shall notify
the proper authorities immediately upon my return to
England of your undesirability as a visitor, and I can assure you you will never be allowed legal entry there.
Now—leave!" Lord Aubrey turned away and Grün, after
a furtive glance around as though to make sure no one
else would stop him, scuttled rapidly out of the room,
followed by the still grinning Sascha to make sure he left
the premises.

"Uncle, it is inconceivable that you should believe
such a—"

"Yes, Marius, now I will attend to you," interrupted
Lord Aubrey heavily. "There is nothing at all you can
say so you may save your breath. I cannot prevent *you*
from returning to England, though you may believe me
when I tell you that if it were within my power to do so
I would, for I find you not a whit more savoury than
your accomplice. However, I can forbid you ever to set
foot on any property belonging to me. I shall call in a
lawyer here in Vienna before this day is over and have
my will changed in Harry's favour, for I would not trust
you not to set upon *me* to prevent my doing so before I
can get back to London. Other than this, I shall take no
further steps, since it would not suit me to have our
name dragged through the mud by revealing this ugly
tale, Just in case any other nefarious schemes *do* occur to
you, I will warn you now that I shall make it very clear
in my will that under no circumstances are you *ever* to
inherit one penny of my estate. I have nothing further to
say to you—now or ever—nor is there anything I wish to

hear from you beyond the sound of the door closing behind you."

With this Lord Aubrey turned and walked to the window where he stood wtih his back stolidly and formida-
bly turned upon his nephew. Sir Marius, his mouth still
agape with the protests he had not been allowed to
voice, blotches of angry red staining his forehead and
cheeks, tried desperately to form words, but no sound
would come. He was like a fighter who has had the
breath knocked out of him by a sharp blow to the stomach.

The old Baron crossed to the door and held it open
politely. Finally, seeing that Sir Marius did not seem to
understand the invitation, the Baron crossed to him and
taking him by the arm, led him to the door and closed it
gently but firmly behind him.

Chapter 16

❧

WHEN HARRY'S VALET entered his room the next morning he found his master out of bed attempting, one-handedly, to insert himself into a pair of dove-grey Inexpressibles.

"Sir!" the valet exclaimed in horrified accents, "whatever are you doing?"

"What the devil does it look like I'm doing?" asked Harry cheerfully, "Here—give me a hand."

"But you certainly must *not* dream of leaving your bed today. The doctor expressly ordered that you be kept quiet for several days. Whatever will he say?"

"Just what you'd expect an old-womanish fuss-budget like that to say. Hand me my shirt."

The valet dug in his heels. "I'll do no such thing, Mr. Tyne, though I lose my place for saying it. I shall go at once and fetch the Baron and Miss Clark!"

"No need, Crofts, here I am," said the old Baron from the doorway. "Now, what are you doing, Harry, to put Crofts in such a temper?"

"I shall be kicking him down the stairs in a moment if he doesn't do as he's told and help me into my shirt!"

"I will help you with your shirt, *mon cher*, and Crofts will go and bring you something for your breakfast."

"Good! A thick slice of beefsteak, Crofts—I'm famished!" assented Harry.

Crofts departed, allowing himself an unmollified sniff to express his displeasure.

"Now, my friend, I shall help you into a shirt, but I will not help you into a coat. No—don't try that famous charm on me," the old Baron said as Harry gave him an engaging grin and seemed about to speak. He continued, "Nothing you can say could induce me to take the chance of opening that wound again, and you know as well as I that all your coats are so well fitted in the first place it's all Crofts can do to get you into them. To try with that bandaged shoulder would be madness and I will not do it. You can put on your dressing gown, since you won't be going downstairs today in any case."

"Not in a dressing gown, certainly, though I should be glad to hear why I may not go downstairs if I so choose. You know I've never been inclined to be invalidish and I've never felt better."

"*Now* I'm sure you do, but by midday, take my word, you will be very glad to climb into your bed again. The doctor has ordered that you be very quiet today after that fever and losing all that blood, and I'm sure going up and down the stairs will do you no good at all. Do be sensible, my boy."

"I'll be sensible if you'll stop fussing. I dislike being fussed over. How's my uncle this morning?"

"I think very tired after all his exertions yesterday. *Mon dieu*, he was a lion, Harry! First he dissected Grün, then tore Marius into strips, and having disposed of them both, he sent for a lawyer and dictated a new will. After that I insisted he come up to bed. I'd had a room prepared and sent for his man to bring the bags from the Kaiserin. Nettleship—what kind of name is this?—but a remarkable man—had the old gentleman tucked up with a dish of gruel in no time at all."

"Is he keeping to his bed today?"

"Oh, not at all. He's been up for hours. He's in the back drawing room up here with Letty at this moment."

"Good lord!" Harry exclaimed.

"I know—but there was no stopping her. And really, Harry, it's only fair. She went to him in the first place—"

"She went to him! May I know why she should take it upon herself—"

"You may bristle all you like, my friend, but the fact remains if she had not gone you would not now be so felicitously circumstanced with your old uncle. Not to speak of the fact that it was she who persuaded Sascha into the attempt to recover that letter."

Crofts entered at this moment bearing a perilously loaded breakfast tray, saving Harry the need to acknowledge this indisputable truth. He uttered a grumpy "Hmpf!" and turned away. The old Baron smiled blandly.

In the back upstairs drawing room, Letty was prattling away, enthralling Lord Aubrey with a detailed report of the recovery of the letter from Grün's house, generously ascribing all honours to Sascha.

"And then you wrote to me in London?" prompted Lord Aubrey when she paused to draw breath.

"Oh no. I should have, of course, but I didn't think of it. It was Ninette who thought of it. Also, I shouldn't have known how to get information to you without the Emperor's police reading it and reporting it to Sir Marius. But Ninette is very clever and knows ever so many men. She's the most famous courtesan in Vienna."

"The most famous—!" cried his lordship, his grey eyes bulging, "this—this woman—is a friend of *yours?*"

"Oh yes, she said there was nothing she wouldn't do for me—she's very—er—dramatic—but so very nice. You see, when Harry was so angry about the diamonds being paste and no good to pay her gambling debts—I—well, actually, the old Baron and I—protected her against Harry and persuaded him that she would never have worn them if she'd known they were paste and that actually it was Sir Marius he should be angry with—"

"Sir Marius?" gasped his lordship, almost as breathless in the listening as Letty was in the narration of this tale.

"Yes, for he gave them to her so she would become his—his—mistress," Letty faltered only an instant over this indelicacy that she felt would shock him, coming from the lips of a young girl, "I know all about these things from my aunt—she loved gossip and she told me everything," she explained kindly before rushing on, "anyway—so of course Ninette was *very* angry with Sir Marius and swore revenge, so when I was so worried after Harry was attacked the first time and knew it was all my fault for making Sascha steal the letter from Grün, which made it vital to Sir Marius to have Harry killed before he could get the letter to you—though of course then Harry behaved so stupidly and would not agree to send you the letter—well, then Ninette said *she* would send you the information." Letty wound up her story at breakneck speed and was forced to stop again for breath.

A fascinated Lord Aubrey stared at her in silence while he sorted out all this information. Finally he said, "I should like to thank Miss—er—"

"Forel—Mademoiselle Forel."

"Yes—Mademoiselle Forel. You have her direction?"

"Oh, I'm sure that will be no problem."

"I think a nice necklace—diamonds, you said?—yes, a diamond necklace would be an appropriate expression of my gratitude."

"Oh—oh, sir, how absolutely—*splendid*—of you," breathed Letty, clasping his hand in both her own, her huge, black-fringed hazel eyes gazing up at him in adoration. Lord Aubrey thought he had never seen a more beautiful young creature. Why, she's even more beautiful than Amelia Dacres at that age, he thought, awed.

Harry, resplendent in a rich figured India silk robe, entered at this moment to find Letty and his great-uncle gazing into each other's eyes in mutual admiration.

"Very affecting," he commented acidly. "I hope you are not planning another elopement, Letty?"

"Harry! What *are* you doing out of bed?" demanded

Letty, jumping up from her footstool at his lordship's feet and rushing across the room in a swirl of yellow-figured muslin ruffles.

"I was told you were in here with my relative and came at once to rescue him from your brazen clutches. What have you been telling him?"

Letty flushed furiously as the import of Harry's first remark dawned on her.

"You are truly a beast, Harry! I *hate* you!"

"Yes, I know. Now, you run along to Miss Clark and—"

"Why do you *always*—" she began rebelliously, when she herself was interrupted by a loud, feminine voice floating up the stairway.

"Not well? Why, what is wrong? No, never mind, I'll just run up and see for myself." A murmur of protest was drowned out by, "Pooh! Nonsense! Of course I shall go up—no, don't bother to announce me, I'll find my way—"

"Good God!" Harry exclaimed resignedly.

There were running footsteps and then Lady Hester Luddington, breathtaking in wine-red velvet and sables, appeared in the doorway.

"Harry! My darling! They said you were ill! What is wrong?"

"As you can see, not much of anything."

"But you are very pale."

"A touch of indigestion during the night. Great-uncle, you will allow me to present to you Lady Hester Luddington. Hester, my uncle, Lord Aubrey."

Lady Hester smiled brilliantly and dropped a profound curtsey. "*So* charmed, Lord Aubrey. I came as soon as I heard you were here."

"Where the devil did you hear, for God's sake," demanded Harry with great irritation.

"Why, it's all over town, Harry, my love. You know how those hotel servants gossip."

"Yes, very well. But why are *you* here?"

"Don't be rude, my dear, though of course I must forgive you as you are not well," she replied prettily. "And of course you must know why I am here. It is *your* uncle. Of course I felt that *I* must pay my respects immediately." Her delicate implication that some understanding between them made it incumbent upon her to fulfill this duty was too clear to be misunderstood by even the meanest intelligence. Lord Aubrey studied her speculatively and then turned an interested eye on Harry, who was unable to repress a smile in appreciation of her outrageous cleverness. "Oh, and here's the pretty child," she continued, "really, Harry, you must tell her not to scowl so—why *is* she always looking that way when she's not singing? *So* disagreeable." She patted Letty's burning cheek. "We must think of some nice treats for the sweet thing to make her smile," she said in a maddeningly condescending way.

Letty, white to the lips in impotent rage, deliberately turned her back on Lady Hester in the most offensively insulting way possible and stalked stiffly out of the room. She heard Lady Hester's hearty gust of laughter and then, "Such a temper! And no manners to speak of at all. Perhaps a different governess for the child would—" before she reached her bedroom door, which she slammed behind her resoundingly.

Her entire body shook with anger, and the room swam in a red film as Letty walked unhesitatingly across to her washstand in the corner, picked up the ewer and threw it will all her strength across the room. It hit the soft coverlet of her bed and fell harmlessly to the heavily carpeted floor.

Letty stared at it in disbelief, then snatched up the basin and dashed it against the fireplace, where it crashed to bits satisfyingly against the tiles. She sighed, sagged into a chair and burst into tears, her mind a chaotic jumble of imprecations against the detestable Lady Hester Luddington—and Harry! That he could stand there grinning in that revoltingly indulgent way, she raged silently. He seemed positively *besotted* by that dreadful woman! What could he find to admire so much in that

affected manner and that—that overblown figure! It's disgusting! All men are disgusting and I shall never, never
marry! And I'll never even *speak* to Harry Tyne again
as long as I live!

She heard Harry's voice in the hallway and sat up to
listen, childishly rubbing her fists in her eyes. She heard
Lady Hester fluting a good-bye to Lord Aubrey, then
some low, intimate-sounding exchange between Lady
Hester and Harry, a gay, tinkling laugh and Lady Hester's footsteps going down the stairs. She heard Harry
walk back to the drawing room and the door close behind him.

She went to her own door and opened it softly to peer
out. There was no one in sight, and as though pulled by
some force outside herself, she crept down the hall and
shamelessly applied her ear to the panel of the drawing-
room door. Lord Aubrey was speaking.

"—fine-looking woman. I may tell you, Harry, nothing
could please me more than to see you married. I would
like to see you with a son before I turn up my toes.
She'll make you a fine wife, very good family, you
know. She was a Ranceford before she married Luddington. And to my way of thinking, widowed just long
enough to be thinking of the joys of the marriage bed
again."

Letty jerked her ear away from the door panel as
though she had been stung, and, face flaming, turned and
fled back to her room, followed by Harry's shout of delighted laughter. She closed her door and threw herself
across her bed, but this time there were no tears. Her
despair was too deep for tears. What she had heard had
only confirmed her long-held fears, and now not only
was Harry in love with Lady Hester, his great-uncle was
delightedly sanctioning the match! Letty knew she could
not possibly hold any further hope that Harry might
someday come to look upon herself with love. She wondered dismally if the world would forever be this grey
colour?

If she had lingered only a moment more in her dis-

graceful position against the door, she would have heard
words that would have made the world positively rosy.

"Hester!? Marry Hester? You cannot be serious,
Great-uncle. Why, I should have to lock her into the
bedroom to be sure the brats were mine! And I assure
you Hester has not *missed* the joys of the marriage bed.
Not for the past year, at least, to my certain
knowledge."

"Ho! Like that is it? Still, my boy, as you have enjoyed her favours and she seemes to take it for granted
that you *will* marry her, you cannot honourably—"

"Oh, can I not? I beg you will not be taken in by her
performance, sir. I grant you that she would be pleased
to be married again, and would not mind becoming Mrs.
Harry Tyne, but I hope I am not such a moonling as to
fall into so obvious a trap."

His lordship chuckled, "Well, I suppose I must believe
you, Harry. But I am serious about wanting to have you
married and settled. When can I hope to see you in England?"

"As soon as you are there yourself, sir, for it is in my
mind to accompany you back."

"Harry, this is uncommon civil of you, but I cannot
ask—"

"No need to ask, I decided on it last night. There is
nothing to keep me here. I shall sign over my share of
the business to the Baron—it's all his money anyway,—
and see you safely home."

Lord Aubrey turned away and swallowed with a small
convulsion, then took a large kerchief and blew his nose
resoundingly.

"I must own that I shall be glad of your company, my
boy. Very glad," he said gruffly. "Now, what of that
young woman?"

"Letty? Oh, she must return with me, of course. Max
would never be able to control her, and since I brought
her here in the first place, it is my responsibility to see
her reestablished in England. D'you think Aunt Hermione would take her till I can get her married?"

"Perhaps, perhaps. However, a suitable husband won't be easy to find for a girl without a penny to bless herself with. Of course," he added, musing, "there's St. John Champfreys. He's got more money than he knows what to do with and cares nothing for dowry—only an heir."

"You would not suggest that innocent girl be married to that old court card! Why, the man wears stays! Not to mention the bevy of young boys he keeps around him!"

"But she would need only produce a son for him and he'd give her the earth and never bother her again. Or, better still, I will settle a few thousand pounds on her—I'm sure it's no more than she deserves for all she's done on our behalf—why, with her looks and a dowry we can make a brilliant match for her!"

"If you'll forgive me, sir, I find I must return to my bed. Max was right. He told me I'd welcome it in an hour or so, and I do," Harry said, turning away abruptly and heading for the door. "I'm sure I'll be fine by evening. We'll dine up here together. Shall I send Nettleship in to you now?"

"Yes—yes, do so, my boy. You go along," replied Lord Aubrey absently, his mind busy with the problem of what he could have said that Harry found so distasteful that he would not discuss it further. No, he decided finally, it was nothing, only that he was tiring. Should never have been allowed out of his bed today in the first place. I shall have to speak to that man of his—Crofts?—if Harry intends to take him back to London also.

Chapter 17

❧

LORD AUBREY'S CARRIAGE, well sprung though it was, and comfortable with its buff velvet squabs, jolted heavily over a rut in the road. Miss Clark moaned softly, Alexander, the canary, chirped crossly from his covered cage on the floor, and only by a great effort of will was Letty able to keep from expressing her own discomfort. After the long carriage trip through Europe and the misery of the voyage across the heaving Channel, all of them were too weary to sustain the trip up to London with anything but exhausted resignation.

Lord Aubrey's head sagged to his shoulder as he fell into an uncomfortable doze, and Letty allowed herself to relax back onto the swabs and close her own eyes. She had made it her objective throughout the journey to be pleasant and attentive to Lord Aubrey. Not only because he was so unvaryingly kind to her, or even because he was clearly not enjoying the best of health, but because she had determined from the day she had eavesdropped on his conversation with Harry that no one should ever discover that her heart had irrevocably broken when she heard his words and knew that Harry was lost to her. She might be a birdwit, as Harry so scathingly called her, but she was too proud to go about with a long face and a mopish air so that everyone should feel sorry for her. She was a Montressor, after all, which was a family as fine and old as any in England.

The only tears she'd allowed anyone to see were those she shed, along with Miss Clark, when they bid goodbye to Sascha and the old Baron. But those tears were allowable, being from sorrow at parting from friends who had become like family to her. Both Sascha and the old Baron had promised to visit her in England in the Spring, which promise she kept reminding herself of when her private sorrow showed signs of swamping her resolution. *They are my friends now, quite apart from Harry, and I'll never need to feel entirely alone again, no matter where I find myself in the future.*

Her future was a matter she had spent a great deal of the journey brooding upon. What was to become of her? Why would Harry not allow her to stay in Vienna with the old Baron who loved her and said he would happily keep her, though qualifying it by saying gently that he thought it would be better for her to return to her homeland.

"But there is nothing for me to return to there—except Mr. Sludge, of course, though I doubt even he would be available to me now!" she cried wildly.

"Please try to show more conduct, if you please, and try not to be ridiculous. Of course you must return to England, and I don't care to discuss it further," Harry replied, not even looking up from his ledgers.

"But *I* care to discuss it further! I'm not your—your—*chattel*—to be dragged from continent to continent at *your* whim. I suppose I have a perfect right to have a say as to what's to become of me, and I prefer to remain here where I may support myself!"

"Doing what?" he enquired acidly.

"Well, I suppose I may be paid a salary. I think even you must admit that people come here to hear me sing, and I needn't sing *only* for my supper if I attract some business to the establishment," she retorted angrily.

"Don't be absurd," he said witheringly, "you are about as fitted to take care of yourself as Hester's lap dog. The

moment Max turned his back you'd be into some scrape
or other—or having your head turned by some handsome
officer again," he added, flicking a grin at her, "but it is
pointless to discuss it. There is no question of my leaving
you here in Vienna."

"But what will I *do* in England?"

"You will live with my Aunt Hermione and become a
respectable young English girl again."

She had had to be content with that answer for she
could get no other from him or from anyone else. The
old Baron, Sascha, and Miss Clark all repeated Harry's
words as a litany that needed no further explanation. Miss
Clark, indeed, went about in a daze of happiness to be
returning to England in company with the great Lord
Aubrey, to be allowed to remain with Letty, whom she
had grown very fond of, and to see her beloved London
again.

Until today she had reacted to every phase of the
journey with unflagging enthusiasm, but now even she
was unable to exclaim cheerfully any longer over the
beauties of the chill, wintry English countryside. Although every foot of the way Lord Aubrey had com-
mandeered the finest, and in most cases, the most
luxurious, accommodations, the fact was Miss Clark
looked forward to Miss Hermione Tyne's establishment
in Belgrave Square, London, with all the ardent fervour
of a devout Moslem approaching Mecca. She swore,
silently of course, as it would have been unthinkably dis-
courteous to voice any complaint in Lord Aubrey's hearing, that she would not set foot in a moving vehicle for
at least two weeks.

Letty's feelings on the subject were quite different.
She felt that she was being hurriedly disposed of, buried
away in the no doubt gloomy mansion of an elderly female relative, and thus conveniently, for Harry, forgotten. She brooded darkly upon Harry's motives in not
allowing her to stay in Lord Aubrey's London house.
After all, she would be attended by Miss Clark, so there
could be no eyebrows raised by it. But all her brooding

only succeeded in making it clearer to her that Harry was about to embark on the reestablishment of himself as a respectable member of the *ton* before announcing his engagement to Lady Hester Luddington, *née* Ranceford!—a fine old family, indeed! A family of profligate libertines, as she'd heard her great-aunt, the Countess, say many times.

Letty very definitely did *not* want to arrive at Miss Tyne's, in spite of being tired to death of bumping about in this carriage. She sighed irritably and opened her eyes to see Harry cantering along just ahead of the carriage. He, after the first day, had chosen to ride rather than be driven and was obnoxiously cheerful, even boisterous, at every stop, further exacerbating her feelings. However firm her resolve to conceal her emotions from everyone, she could not manage to speak to Harry in any other than cold mono-syllables and was never able to initiate any conversation with him, only answering him briefly if he addressed her directly. He affected not to notice this behaviour, grinning hatefully at her most glacial responses.

This silent battle, together with her efforts at a cheerfulness she did not feel, had begun to exhaust even *her* youthful energies. Her natural personality was open and outspoken, indefatigably curious, and ready for adventure. But she had never given her heart before, and a love that must be hidden was like a weight on her usual elasticity, dragging down her natural high spirits and this was the reason for the artificiality of her present behaviour. Her pride was attempting to assuage her lacerated feelings and arm her defenseless heart.

After what seemed an eternity, they were finally bidding Lord Aubrey good-bye as he was set down first at his doorstep. He promised them they would all dine together before the week was out and bade Letty enjoy herself, then Harry escorted Miss Clark and Letty to Aunt Hermione Tyne's.

Miss Tyne was a tiny, cheerful wren of a woman

who, despite her advanced years, flitted spryly before them into her drawing room, twittering and hopping about the room pushing forward chairs and plumping up cushions exactly like a bird moving amongst the tree branches.

"Dear child," she said, leading Letty to a chair, "what dreadful shadows under those lovely eyes! Really, Harry, an astonishing beauty. She'll have a great success from the moment she—Sills, if you could take the—er—cage?—why, bless me, it *is* a wee birdie—it's quite all right, my dear, Sills will take very good care of it—do sit here by the fire and warm yourself, and you here on the other side, Miss Clark—you must be perished—and Sills shall bring you some nice hot tea—Oh, Harry! Dearest boy!" she cried, turning to throw her tiny body against her nephew's and hugging him fiercely about the waist, it being patently impossible for her to reach his neck, even by standing on tiptoe. "I cannot *tell* you how happy I—I've never believed any of that terrible story from the start and never understood how Augustus could be so cozened by Marius. Why, even as a small boy he was sly and—and—twisty! I could never like him! But there now, it's all resolved so happily and I—I—oh dear!" She burst into tears.

Harry laughed and, prying her wet face away from his shirt front, held her at arm's length. "Dear Aunt, how can you claim to be happy and cry so?"

"H-h-happy tears, dear boy, happy tears," she said, groping ineffectually about her person for a handkerchief. Miss Clark rose and efficiently provided her with one.

"Oh, thank you, dear Miss Clark—how kind you are! I know we shall be great friends and you will tell me all about Vienna. I long to hear all about Metternich and the Duchess of Sagan—is it true they—Ah! here is Sills at last. Now Harry, will you have tea or would you prefer something stronger?"

"Neither, though I thank you. I won't even sit down

in all my dirt. Besides, I'm most anxious to return and make sure Great-uncle has taken no harm from the trip."

"But my dear boy! After all these long months—and we've hardly had a chance to speak—" Miss Tyne protested.

"I'll call in tomorrow morning and we shall speak as long as you like. We must discuss Miss Montressor's future at greater length in any case."

Letty, lethargically sipping her hot tea and staring blindly into the fire, was unable to rouse herself enough to give him a resentful glare at this presumptuous statement. She only wished for him to take his disturbing presence elsewhere and allow her to surrender completely to the motherly ministrations of Miss Tyne.

After he had gone Miss Tyne bustled her up to her room and, seeming to understand Letty's inability to respond, addressed all her remarks to Miss Clark, as that seemingly indefatigable woman helped Letty out of her travelling costume and into a bedgown. Letty climbed beneath the bedcovers and dropped abruptly into sleep even before the door had closed behind the two older women.

Miss Clark dutifully allowed herself to be taken back downstairs for more refreshments and "a good coze" about the scandalous doings of Society in Vienna.

When Letty finally swam to the surface of consciousness the next morning the day was well advanced. This was apparent though her drapes were still tightly drawn and the room in darkness. The bustle of carriage traffic in the streets outside made it clear to her that she had been allowed to sleep well beyond the usual hour for rising. She stretched luxuriously, feeling wonderfully refreshed, and then sprang from the bed to pull open the drapes.

Miss Clark entered at that moment bearing a steaming cup of chocolate.

"Well, child, I was just coming to wake you. I'm happy to see you looking so well after your good sleep. Jump back under the covers now and have your chocolate and I'll ring for the maid to make up the fire. I wouldn't let her do so before for fear she would wake you."

"Dear Miss Clark—thank you! I hope *you* feel better?"

"Indeed I do. Miss Tyne has given me a wonderfully comfortable room. Oh, I do assure you, Letty, she is everything that is kind!"

Miss Clark had not commented on it for she was too reticent to force a confidence, but she was not unaware that her charge was unhappy. Fearing that she might be worried over her reception by Miss Tyne, Miss Clark wanted to assure her that she need have no fears.

"Oh, I knew at once that I should like her excessively—too much for my own good," Letty added after a moment, then seeing Miss Clark's puzzled look changed the subject abruptly. "What time is Harry expected?"

"Oh, Mr. Tyne was here and left some time ago. He sat down to breakfast with us at half past eight!"

"What had he to say? More orders?"

"Why—only pleasantries. He enquired very kindly of me about how I'd slept, said he was glad that you were still resting, reported that Lord Aubrey, though suffering somewhat from an attack of the gout, seemed not to have sustained any more serious harm to his health—"

"Yes, yes, I'm sure he was all charm and civility! I *meant*—what had he to say about what was to happen to me?"

"Why, I don't suppose there can be anything to add to what he has already said. You are to live here with his aunt and become a respectable—"

"—young English girl! Yes, I know that! But I mean—oh, for heaven's sake, Miss Clark, must you be so blindly slavish. He is not God, you know!"

"Letty! You must not blaspheme! And I must say you are uncommon cross this morning. I'm afraid you are monstrously ungrateful for all Mr. Tyne is doing for you."

"I have not asked him to do anything for me! He knocked me down in the street, refused to give me directions when I asked politely, and then took me away to Vienna without so much as a by-your-leave," Letty ranted with reckless exaggeration, "and now he wants only to dispose of me tidily and be rid of me, as though I were a piece of property! I tell you I will not be treated in such a fashion any longer. I'm not a child!"

"You force me to point out that you are behaving in a most *childish* manner. This hysteria is unbecoming in a well-brought-up young woman," replied Miss Clark severely.

The maid entered at that moment with a large pail of coal and set about building the fire to a blaze. Letty subsided mutinously, while Miss Clark calmly pulled open the wardrobe doors and took out a dark green merino wool gown with long sleeves and a guimp of white lawn filling in the wide neckline and pulled up to stand in a ruffle about the throat.

"Best dress warmly, for the day is chilly, though I must say Miss Tyne keeps fires going in every room from early morning!"

After this remark silence spread through the room as Letty sipped moodily at her chocolate and Miss Clark continued to assemble Letty's costume for the day. When the maid departed, after a frankly curious stare at Letty, Miss Clark spoke again.

"Miss Tyne is very eager to see you, so please don't dawdle too long. I'll send someone to help you dress—oh, I must speak to Mr. Tyne about an abigail for you."

"Why is she so eager to see me?"

"I imagine Mr. Tyne gave her instructions regarding you when they were closeted together after breakfast and she wishes to convey them to you," replied Miss Clark, and with this parting shot she exited, closing the door firmly behind her.

Letty sat up indignantly, spilling the last of the chocolate down the front of her bedgown. Instructions! *Instructions!*

Her fury had not abated one whit; indeed, she had deliberately fanned the flames to a white heat by the time she stomped downstairs, dressed in the green merino. Hearing her unladylike tread on the stairs, Miss Tyne came fluttering out of the drawing room to greet her.

"Darling child! Here you are at last—how well you are looking—now, will you have a breakfast—or perhaps a nuncheon—oh dear!—such a difficult time of day—"

"I apologise for causing this inconvenience—" Letty began stiffly.

"Oh, Miss Montressor—may I call you Letty as Harry does?—you are not to think such a thing for the world. I am only worried about what would tempt your appetite at this hour? I mean, is one still inclined towards one's usual breakfast fare regardless of the house—so difficult, you see," fretted Miss Tyne, wringing her tiny hands.

Letty relented immediately, "Dear Miss Tyne, please do not concern yourself. I'm so famished, my appetite could be tempted by the napkin! And of course you must call me Letty."

"What a pretty thing you are—I can see we shall go along very comfortably together. Now come along," she said happily, leading the way into the breakfast room, calling out to a hovering Sills to serve Miss Montressor with just whatever would be quickest and to send word to Miss Clark in case she might like to join them. "How fortunate that Harry was able to procure the services of someone of that calibre in Vienna. Oh! Here you are, Miss Clark!" Miss Tyne halted in surprise to find Miss Clark seated at the table buttering toast for Letty. "I had just asked Sills to bring something for Letty and to ask you—but you are well before me in everything!"

Letty sat down to a large plate of cold sliced beef and coddled eggs, which she polished off rapidly. Miss Tyne watched her with wide-eyed astonishment. "Letty, I fear you will suffer from bolting your food in that fashion," reprimanded Miss Clark in some embarrassment.

"Oh, young people don't seem to have problems with their digestion as we do, don't you find, Miss Clark? It is really wonderful to see the child with such a hearty appetite, and she will need to eat well, for Harry is anxious that she should make a regular come-out in London and meet young people and enjoy herself, so we shall be very busy. I cannot tell you how excited I am by the prospect. I do adore parties and balls, but I've not accepted invitations in ever so long—I dislike going alone—and at my age the gentlemen are no longer clamouring to dance with me," she laughed gaily, but there was something of wistful longing in her voice that touched Letty and softened her instantly reflexive antipathy to falling in with any plans proposed by Harry. "We must go over your wardrobe, Letty. Harry said I was to do as I thought necessary, though he felt you had a great many evening gowns."

"Well, if I'm to appear at every ball in a plain white gown and a wreath of flowers I daresay he's right, though I must say, in my opinion it would appear an affectation to dress in such a theatrical way," snapped Letty.

"Oh, I couldn't agree more, my dear. It would never do for people to think you eccentric. We'll just have Mademoiselle Berthe come in as soon as possible. She's all the rage now and very dear, but Harry said money was no object—"

"Dressing the sacrificial lamb," Letty muttered bitterly.

"I beg your pardon?" said a bewildered Miss Tyne.

"I see that I am to be decked out and put on the block for the highest bidder—or at least for the *first* bidder would be more to Harry's liking, I imagine!"

"Letty, you are distressing Miss Tyne with these unseemly remarks. I must say I find your mood this morning unpleasant. What can you mean—?"

"I mean that Harry is eager to get me married and off his hands, though I cannot think why he feels it is his responsibility to arrange my life for me. I'm sure *I* never gave him permission to do so!"

Miss Clark's lips tightened in prim disapproval at this outburst, but before she could speak, Miss Tyne, in great agitation, jumped up and flew around the table to Letty's side.

"Oh, darling child, you must not think—oh, I do assure you Harry did not mean—there was nothing—he only—" she gasped, her eyes brimming with tears as she held out her hands imploringly to Letty.

Filled with compunction, Letty pushed back her chair and impulsively hugged Miss Tyne. "Oh, what a beast I am to make you cry—and you've been so kind. I'm an ungrateful wretch and you must try to forgive me!"

Miss Tyne promptly raised herself on tiptoe and kissed Letty's cheek, "There is no question of that—I want only for you to be happy—such a dreadful childhood—Harry has told me—it must be made up to you. We shall have lovely times together—there's so much to see and Harry said I was to take you all about London—we'll go to West's Gallery of Waxworks, and Miss Linwood's Gallery of Needlework, and then there's Chunee, the elephant at Exeter 'Change—he can count, you know."

"Miss Tyne," interrupted Letty gently, "did Harry suggest that you take me to these children's entertainments?"

"Well, he said he thought you would enjoy such things, never having—"

"He is much mistaken," Letty said firmly, ignoring the fact that had not Harry suggested such entertainments, she would have been delighted to attend them. "My tastes are quite different," she declared, "I should like—" she hesitated, really at something of a loss to state exactly what she would like. Then in a flash of inspiration it came to her, "I should like to be taken to some musical events."

"Musical events? Well—I—" faltered Miss Tyne.

"Yes! I should like to hear some singers in concerts or on the stage—or—or—in opera!" she concluded, a grandiose vision of herself being pelted with flowers at the conclusion of a performance as the Countess in the *Marriage of Figaro* taking shape in her mind. After all, she had already mastered one of the arias!

"Well, my dear, if that is what you will like then we shall go," said Miss Tyne reassuringly. "Would you like to just drive about now and take some air. It is cold, but such a bright clear day."

"I should like it above all things!" declared Letty.

"You will accompany us, dear Miss Clark?"

Miss Clark shuddered delicately and declined, murmuring vaguely about letters to write. Letty and Miss Tyne rose to go and fetch their wraps and bonnets, and as they went down the hall Miss Clark heard Letty ask in a suspiciously innocent, childlike tone of voice.

"Do you think we might drive in the direction of the waterfront, Miss Tyne? I should love to see it."

A puzzled frown appeared between Miss Clark's brows for a moment, but then she shrugged it aside impatiently and made her way to the back drawing room where she had noticed a copy of the latest novel by Mr. Walter Scott, which she intended to spend the afternoon reading.

Chapter 18

❧

LETTY STARED INTO the full-length glass at her reflection and wished fiercely for one flashing instant that Harry could see her *now*. This longing was quickly, and sternly, suppressed. No more of that, she admonished herself. Romantic daydreams are childish, and from now on I must plan ahead in a mature way if I'm to take charge of my life! This resolution reaffirmed, she turned her attention again to her image in the glass.

The pale orange silk gown was vastly becoming to her, and in every way a far cry from the unsophisticated white slips she had worn for evenings in Vienna. Its neckline, though modest in comparison with the revealing costumes worn by ladies of elegance, was lower than any she had been allowed to wear before. It was edged in a ruffle of quilled lace and banded with a darker orange velvet, as were the short puffed sleeves. The gored, bell-shaped skirt was deeply vandyked in the same velvet in three flounces and stopped just short of the ankles. Altogether a gown to gladden the heart of any young girl.

Nevertheless, except for the small lapse of a moment before, Letty viewed herself dispassionately, unable to enter into the enthusiasm of the rest of the ladies assembled for this final fitting: Miss Tyne, chirping rhapsodically; Miss Clark, nodding and smiling; Mademoiselle Berthe, swelling and smirking with pride in her creation. Even the depressed-looking assistant seamstress, on her knees to adjust the hem, looked up with a shy smile of vicarious pleasure. But Letty's plans, worked out in careful detail this past week, caused a certain degree of detachment in her outlook. In the next week, if the opportunity presented itself, she would be far away from balls, and dancing, and the eligible young men whom this dress was created to impress.

Actually, she would have set her plans in motion earlier, but she had not had the heart to deprive dear Miss Tyne of this one ball to which she was looking forward with so much anticipation. Lady Mortimer's ball for the come-out of her eldest daughter was to be the most important social event of the pre-Christmas season, and for Miss Tyne it was to cap a week of visits, teas, musical evenings and dinner parties, attended for the purpose of introducing Miss Montressor to the *ton*. Miss Tyne had been poring happily over the invitations for future social engagements, which made a satisfyingly high pile on her escritoire.

Letty had watched her doing so guiltily, knowing she would be depriving the kind-hearted old lady of longed-for pleasures. But she dared not allow herself to dwell on this, for her mind was made up. As soon as possible after Lady Mortimer's ball, which was the one concession her conscience would allow her to make regarding Miss Tyne, she would go away.

She was confident she had only to apply to the manager of Covent Garden and her future would be assured, for opera and musical programs were enjoying a great vogue right now, and having attended two performances during the past week, she felt herself to be fully as qualified as the women she had heard singing there.

Harry had agreed amiably to these theatrical excursions, though he declined to make one of the party. He had even suggested other musical events she might want to attend and had she not been persuaded there was no way he could have guessed her plans, she would have suspected him of encouraging her for some sly ends of his own.

He called every day in Belgrave Square, always in good spirits, always solicitous of everyone's health and enjoyment, and always blandly noncommittal regarding his own activities. His visits occurred at varying times of the day, and sometimes Letty and Miss Tyne returned to find he had called during their absence and stayed to visit with Miss Clark. "Such condescension, Miss Tyne, such perfect manners. A credit to his relatives, I assure you," she had enthused.

She had repeated these praises to Lord Aubrey in Harry's hearing only two nights ago when they had all dined with him, and Lord Aubrey had been extremely gratified.

"I fear Miss Clark is well on the way to turning my head completely," murmured Harry into Letty's ear. She shot him a suspicious sideways glance, positive she had detected a note of smugness in his tone. But his eyes were twinkling so intimately into her own that for a brief moment the cold hollowness she felt inside was warmed and the corners of her mouth twitched into a responsive smile. But she called herself sternly to order and turned away to apply herself to her dressed lobster with more enthusiasm than she really felt.

"I'm sure she is far too late," she answered coolly, receiving in her turn a sharp glance from Harry, which she pretended not to see. Her heart thudded from her effrontery, fearing he would squash her before the company with one of his insulting epithets. But Harry, after studying her averted face intently for a moment, turned away to rejoin the general conversation, leaving her feeling somehow deflated. It seemed she was now so insignificant in his mind that he could not be bothered to reprimand her for her pertness. She felt again the icy hollow inside her, and she raised her chin proudly and stared about the table with a bright smile that never reached her eyes, as though daring anyone to think her other than perfectly contented with the present state of things.

"Letty, I do *beg* of you not to smile in that artificial way at Lady Mortimer's—really most unbecoming!" came Miss Clark's voice, returning Letty with a jerk to the present and the realisation that her remembrance of her reaction that night had unconsciously recreated the same smile on her face which, she was forced to agree with Miss Clark, was not an attractive smile.

On the night of the ball, however, her smile was all that it should be, for she had resolved to enjoy herself on this last lighthearted moment of her old life. It had also occurred to her that for the sake of her future as an entertainer, it would be as well for her to look upon everyone she met as a future member of her audience, who would remember having met her socially and having approved of her as a pretty-behaved, well-bred young lady.

"My dear, what a perfect squeeze! Lady Mortimer's parties are always so successful," whispered Miss Tyne happily as they progressed slowly up the broad, crowded staircase to the ballroom, which proved to be even more crowded than the hall and staircase when they finally attained it.

All eyes did not swivel to the door as Letty entered with Miss Tyne, all conversation did not stop, but Letty was aware of a gratifying number of interested glances and hoped they were interested enough to save her the mortification of spending the evening as an observer. Her *succès fou* in Vienna had spoiled her, she now realised. Arriving at a ball on the arm of the dashing Count Radoczy as the accepted "newest sensation" of Vienna was a very different matter from arriving on the arm of Miss Tyne in a roomful of strangers who had never heard of one.

But, she had underestimated Miss Tyne. No sooner had they made their way to an unoccupied sofa against the wall and seated themselves, then a veritable parade of

matrons towing sons of varying degrees of callowness
approached and asked to be allowed to present them to
Miss Montressor. Letty began to realise that all of these
ladies had been visited in the past week, each obviously
hand-picked by Miss Tyne as mothers of eligible sons!
Before the musicians began the notes for the first set,
Letty was promised for more dances than she could
remember, and though none of her partners was handsome enough to send her into a romantic dream, she
smiled upon them brilliantly in gratitude. Throwing
aside all thoughts of her future, she entered into the
spirit of the evening and allowed herself to enjoy being
part of the glittering, happy throng of dancers.

She had just been reverently handed back to the care
of Miss Tyne by the blushing scion of a noble family
whose fortune far outweighed his social poise, when the
first difficult moment of the evening occurred.

The young man, with only the least indication of his
habitual stutter, requested permission to call the following morning, when a familiar drawling voice interrupted
him.

"Well, Allardyce, I see you've finally succumbed to
the lure of the fair sex."

Letty spun about and there was Harry smiling lazily.
The young man rushed forward eagerly to grasp Harry's
hand. "Tyne! By all that's w-w-wonerful! Can't tell you
how glad—never b-b-belived any of that rot, y'know."

"Thank you, Allardyce," replied Harry simply, but it
was clear to all that he was touched by the younger
man's sincerity. Letty gathered from this exchange that
the transition from black sheep to prodigal son was now
an accepted fact amongst all those who mattered in
Society.

Harry greeted his aunt and then turned to Letty. "After dancing with royalty at Laxenburg, this must seem a
fairly tame affair to you. I trust you are managing to enjoy it?"

"Excessively," Letty replied with as much composure
as possible under the circumstances. She looked away

and fanned herself vigourously to conceal the breathlessness she was experiencing at sight of his extravagant dark good looks, set off to perfection by his white cravat and elegant black evening coat. "What has brought *you* here," she demanded when she had regained her poise, "I have always heard you say you disliked such affairs above everything."

"Why, naturally, I felt it my duty to look in on your first ball in London and make sure you were well supplied with partners."

Letty had the felicity of informing him smugly that she was very well supplied. "Fine! Since you're doing so well, I'll take myself off to the card-room—much more to my taste, you know. Perhaps I'll find you free later," he said, bowing, and strolled away.

Letty, steeling her heart against the painful thump of disappointment, turned to the young man who came to claim her hand at that moment and smiled upon him so dazzlingly that he became completely tongue-tied and led her to the floor without a word.

Though she refused to allow herself to search the crowd for a glimpse of Harry, she was aware that he was not in the room for at least the next hour. It was while she was being led out onto the floor by a wisp of a lad who made up in nose what he lacked in chin that she was subjected to her second unpleasant moment of the evening. A shout of loud, and odiously familiar, laughter caused her to freeze in midstep. Her partner bumped into her, but when she turned to apologise she saw that he was equally responsible since his head was directed over his shoulder toward the door. Resignedly she turned also, and there stood Lady Hester Luddington, who had succeeded in doing what no other woman had done that evening: every eye in the room was riveted on her and all conversation had stopped abruptly.

She was laughing up into Harry's face and clinging intimately to his arm. She was in a gown of sheer white silk, of a startling simplicity, being adorned only with a band of embroidered paillettes around the hem that weighed the delicate fabric into long, sculpted folds. The minute bodice allowed a lavish display of white bosom, upon which a large diamond depending from a string of pearls flashed and pulsed light with her every breath, absolutely mesmerizing the entire room, including Letty.

After a moment, however, she shook herself and tugged at the young man's arm. They proceeded to the floor and this movement seemed to break the spell, which, though it seemed much longer, had lasted only a few seconds in reality. The other guests resumed their former movements and conversations.

Letty fumed inwardly as the young man pushed her awkwardly around in the steps of the dance, aware of the cleverness of Lady Hester's strategy in haring back to London and immediately establishing her claim on Harry Tyne in case there were aspiring debutantes with plans that centered around becoming the future Lady Aubrey.

In the midst of these fulminations, Letty realised, devastated, that actually no one had a better right to follow Harry than Lady Hester. In fact, it was more probable that Harry himself had insisted upon her return at the urging of Lord Aubrey who was, as Letty well knew, anxious to see Harry married and settled down and who heartily approved of Harry's choice of a bride.

I will not think of this any more, she thought. It's nothing to do with me any longer, and soon I will never have to see them again, except perhaps across the footlights.

But the next dance being a waltz, Letty was forced to sit it out, since she had not been approved by the ladies of Almack's whose sanction was necessary before a young girl could waltz in public, and she was therefore unable to avoid the sight of Harry waltzing down the room with the ravishing Lady Hester. She turned away crossly and declared to Miss Tyne that she was tired to death and would like very much to be taken home.

Miss Tyne looked vastly relieved. "Dear child, of course we will leave at once. I admit I've had all I could do to keep from dozing off this past hour. It's the late hour, you see, I'm no longer used to it. And the heat, I suppose—and so many people—makes one sleepy—but so lovely—I can't think when I've enjoyed anything more. Such a success you've been too, dear Letty, I really must congratulate you—and the most enchanting gown at the ball, I assure you."

But Letty knew better. Compared to Lady Hester she felt positively dowdy. She stared gloomily out of the carriage windows and wished she had never agreed to come to this ball. She had thought to do a kindness to Miss Tyne in return for all the goodness shown her, and the result was that she had exposed herself needlessly to this torment.

Well, there would be no more! Tomorrow—or the following day—if the opportunity presented itself, she would leave. She had decided it would be better for her to depart during the daylight hours. Not only was it unthinkable that she would be allowed out of the house alone at night, it would also be difficult, as well as unsafe, to find her way in the dark.

The next afternoon, using the perfect excuse of exhaustion from the ball and a touch of the headache resulting from the late hour she had gone to bed, she begged to be excused from accompanying Miss Tyne on a round of calls. She had come down listlessly to breakfast, establishing the fact of indifferent health, and then allowed it to be seen that it was only with the greatest effort that she could entertain the several young men who arrived very early on the doorstep. When they were finally gone, she dragged herself up the stairs with the air of one who has spent her last strength and declared she would go to her bed. Both Miss Clark and Miss Tyne became quite alarmed, and Miss Tyne suggested they send for the doctor. Letty realised her performance had been too successful and toned it down somewhat. She managed to convince them that an afternoon in her bed would see her right again, and then Miss Clark said she would sit by the window while Letty slept in case she should become feverish, but that Miss Tyne must certainly go to her engagements.

"But you cannot mean that Miss Tyne should go alone," protested Letty hurriedly. "I assure you I would not be able to close my eyes with you sitting there watching me! I beg you will be kind enough to accompany Miss Tyne, who needs you much more than I do, I assure you!"

Having finished Mr. Scott's novel in any case, and the two weeks she had sworn she would not be in a moving vehicle having passed, Miss Clark allowed herself to be persuaded, and the two older ladies departed.

Letty lay there for a few moments, enjoying the crackle of the fire on the hearth and the pale lemony sunshine making a splash of white on her counterpane. Alexander, the canary, began an exuberant song, and Letty rose to dress herself in her warmest clothes, a dark green merino gown with a matching pelisse trimmed in swansdown. In her hatbox she folded extra undergarments, a morning gown and one of the white slips from Vienna with its matching white silk slippers and the wreath of silver leaves. Her throat tightened convulsively, but she swallowed determinedly and marched across the room with the hood for Alexander's cage and pulled it down over the bars. The ecstatic song ended abruptly in mid-note.

Chapter 19

❧

MISS TYNE ACCEPTED Miss Clark's arm as she descended from her carriage and the two ladies entered the house chattering amiably together of their outing. It had been an entirely satisfying afternoon for them both and they were very much in charity with one another. They had heard Letty's praises sung to the skies and indulged in some unmalicious gossip about the manners and morals of some of Lady Mortimer's guests of the evening before.

"I declare, Miss Clark, I really think I'll allow myself a glass of sherry before I go up to change for dinner. Will you join me?"

"With pleasure, dear Miss Tyne. I'll just step up and look in on Letty and lay off my bonnet and come right down."

Only a moment later she came rushing back in some agitation. "She is not in her bed, Miss Tyne! I wonder where she can have taken herself?"

"Not in her bed? Well, I—perhaps she is in the back drawing room."

They hurried together down the hall, but the back drawing room was empty. They stood for a moment in disbelief.

"Ring for Sills," suggested Miss Clark.

But Miss Tyne rushed out into the hall calling for Sills in a voice edged with panic. When he arrived she was too flustered to interrogate him, so Miss Clark took command. He replied gravely that Miss was sleeping in her room as she had been all afternoon. He looked slightly indignant when informed she was not there now. Other servants were summoned, but all professed to be unaware of Miss's whereabouts if she were not in her room. Her abigail stated that having been warned by Miss Clark not to disturb Miss, she had taken the opportunity to slip out for some personal shopping and since her return had been in the servant's hall having her tea.

Miss Tyne and Miss Clark stared at each other wordlessly for a moment, Miss Tyne white-faced and Miss Clark fighting to maintain her composure.

"It is possible she woke feeling very much better and decided to take a walk. We must not allow ourselves to fly up into the boughs, Miss Tyne, for that will not help the situation," said Miss Clark in her most governessy voice. But it had no effect on Miss Tyne.

"I must send for Harry!" she gasped in a shaking voice.

"I don't think it necessary to—"

"But he entrusted her to me! If anything has happened to her I shall feel entirely responsible. Sills, send around at once to Lord Aubrey's and ask Mr. Harry to come immediately! If he is away from home tell his man it is imperative that we find him at once!"

When Harry arrived, breathless, some twenty minutes later, it was clear he had not even waited for his carriage to be brought round, but had come on foot at all possible speed.

"What is going on?" he demanded as he entered the door and found the two frightened ladies clinging together in the front hall. "The boy said Letty had disappeared from her bed!"

"Oh, Harry, we would never have gone out, but truly she insisted—and she seemed so tired—all the dancing last night—she—"

"Nonsense! She is young and healthy and could dance three times as long and not feel it, and she left halfway through the evening. She could not have been so exhausted as all that!" snapped Harry.

"But she was, I assure you, Harry—even at breakfast she could hardly—am I not right, Miss Clark?" pleaded Miss Tyne.

"Well, she certainly seemed so," said Miss Clark musingly, "but now that I think about it, it does seem odd—well, I mean, in Vienna she was used to keeping very late hours and never seemed to suffer for it."

"Exactly! She's bamboozled the pair of you for some reason. Now, what can she be up to?" he said in a tone of annoyance. He paced across to the window and back, his brows contracted. "Have any young whelps been hanging about?"

"Why Harry! Certainly not! She only arrived last week and the first young men she met were at the ball last night. Several of them called this morning, but she was quite indifferent to them all, was she not, Miss Clark?"

"If I'm any judge, she was. There is no young man, Mr. Tyne," replied Miss Clark firmly.

"Is anything missing from her room? Clothes—or—I mean, has anyone checked?"

The two ladies looked at one another with wide-eyed dismay, then turned with one accord and hurried towards the stairs. But Harry was before them, springing up the stairs two at a time and flinging open Letty's door. He stood there for a moment, his gaze sweeping rapidly about the room. It was neat and empty, but never having been in it before it was impossible for him to judge if anything was missing.

Miss Clark arrived a moment later, while the panting Miss Tyne was still struggling up the stairs. She heard Miss Clark cry out, "Alexander! She's taken the bird and I didn't even notice before! She's gone away!" Miss Tyne burst into tears.

Thirty minutes later, having waited only for his horses

to be put to his carriage and brought around, Harry was driving rapidly away from Belgrave Square. In that time he had had time to calm the old ladies and put his mind to the problem. It had taken only a few moments' thought to decide where to begin his search. There were only two choices, and he was sure she'd never return to the indifferent relatives and the possibility of being forced into a marriage with another Mr. Sludge.

That left the nurse who lived on the barge. Harry was driving with all speed to the waterfront, grimly determined to search every barge tied up there until he found her, and when he did!—he ground his teeth in rage—little *idiot!* Going off without a word and frightening everyone to death! And to the waterfront, of all places in London where a young girl should never go unattended. And if the barge were not there!? Where would she go then, with dark falling? His heart leapt with fear as he thought of all the possible dangers she might encounter. He forced himself to concentrate on the probability that she had found her old nurse and was safe. Don't think of anything else now, he warned himself, first search the barges!

Easier said than done, he realised, when he reached his destination. He stared with dismay at the line of barges tied up to the river bank and seeming to stretch into infinity! A monumental task to search them all—no—an impossible task! It would take days, and there was no guarantee Letty's old nurse and her husband were here, in any case. Apart from that, he had never been told the name of the man Letty's nurse had married. An "accommodating sort of man," he heard Letty's voice saying on that dark night they had met, and then, "fancy going through one's whole life as Mrs. Sludge—which is why I'm running away to Nora." *Nora*, by God! he thought triumphantly. But then his shoulders sagged. What good would it do? There were likely to be at least twenty Noras amongst all these barges. Perhaps he'd been somewhat hasty in dashing off alone in this way. It would have been wiser to bring some of the servants to help in the search. But how the devil was he to guess there would be so many? *Damn* the girl, I'll ring such a peal over her head her ears will jangle for a week! he vowed. This renewed burst of anger dispelled the momentary discouragement and he moved decisively, jumping down from the carriage, tying up the horse, and striding off to the nearest barge. Surely that is where Letty would have enquired first.

The early dusk and the evening fog rising from the river gave the scene a cold desolation, broken here and there by small squares of yellow light from the windows of the cabins gleaming through the mists. Sure footed, he stepped across the gangplank and onto the barge to rap on the low door. It was opened by a small child who barely reached Harry's knees, dressed in a brief shirt and little else—a male child, thought Harry, suppressing a grin.

The bargeman and his wife and a startling number of children of all ages were crammed into the tiny cabin. They stared in surprise at the fashionably dressed toff stooping to peer into the room. A rush of warm, thick air, redolent of smoke and supper, gusted into Harry's face as he tipped his hat politely to the lady of the house—or barge—and stated his business.

"Oh—ah—t'lass, eh? She'm kin o' yourn?" asked the bargemen, eyeing Harry keenly from beneath his brows.

"You've seen her then?" Harry asked eagerly. The bargeman didn't answer but continued to regard him calmly. Harry realised the man was waiting for an answer to *his* question. "No, no relation to me, but my—er—ward. She has no relatives who will take responsibility for her so I have put her into the care of my aunt. So I will be obliged to you if you can direct me to Nora's barge."

"They Dartles be over Bristol way," replied the bargeman succinctly.

"Oh, my God! Then where did you send the girl?"

"Lookee yure, mister, us didn't send 'er noplace. Lass come down-along axing for Dartles, speakin' all finicky-like but not uperty, so I tells her they Dartles be over along Bristol that I knew certain sure. She give me thankee nicely and took 'erself off."

"But you should have stopped her! A young girl alone here after nightfall!" Harry protested, aghast.

"B' ain't my business to tell lass what to do. She be mortal sure o' herself. Went out-along bank like she'm knowed where she be goin', and that be last I seed o' 'er."

Harry knew it was pointless to continue, as there was nothing further to be gained from the bargeman. He apologised for interrupting the man's supper, thanked him politely and took his leave.

It was full dark now and his sense of urgency made his fingers clumsy as he untied the reins. He jerked them loose with an oath and sprang up to the seat, then drove off rapidly down the waterfront, peering intently up each street that opened onto the front. But there was little to be seen. Gas lighting had not extended into this part of London, and the narrow, twisting lanes were lit only by an occasional window or open doorway. Most of these cobblestoned lanes were too narrow to be nego-tiated by a carriage and even *he* would hesitate to enter them on foot. He fervently hoped Letty had been equally wary. When he came to a wider thoroughfare he drove rapidly up and then back to the front and along to the next. In this way he covered a number of streets, but without any sight of Letty, until it finally became ap-parent that this was a futile exercise. He pulled up and sat ruminating on what would be the best course of ac-tion. What would *Letty* have done when she learned her Nora was not here?

Where would she go? No!—the real question was where *could* she go? To the old Countess's niece or back to Aunt Hermione's? With a sudden decision he took up the reins and flicked them over the horse's backs. She'd go back to Belgrave Square, he thought.

He was over halfway back to his aunt's when he saw her, some way ahead just passing through a cone of light

cast by a gas lamp. If nothing else had identified the slim
figure, the shape of the birdcage weighing down one
shoulder would have sufficed. The other shoulder was
drooping with the weight of a hatbox, obviously containing a great deal more than a hat, but she marched
along determinedly, head up, looking neither to left nor
right. He checked the horses and sat staring after her for
a moment, the release of his pent-up fear for her safety
flooding through his whole body, a bubble of laughter
rising in his throat from sheer relief.

He was still smiling when he saw a hulking figure dart
out of the shadows and lay a large pawlike hand on
Letty's shoulder. Harry's heart leapt straight up into his
throat as every nerve-end jangled with horror. In the act
of rising to run to her rescue, he saw her swing around
without a second's hesitation; the hand holding her hatbox came around in the same movement and landed with
a sickening thud squarely on the bridge of the man's
nose. With a howl, the man staggered back and sat down
heavily, both hands holding his streaming nose. Letty advanced on him, the hatbox raised threateningly, and the
man scrambled to his feet and fled, casting a single terrified glance back over his shoulder.

The entire episode was over in less than a minute, so
quickly in fact, that Harry was still in the act of rising
when it was over. He sagged back into the seat limply,
his mind a chaotic jumble of reactions: a killing rage at
anyone who would dare touch her; anger at Letty herself for putting herself in such danger; relief that she was
safe; and undiluted admiration for her courage. Scruples
be damned, he thought fiercely, I must—but this thought
brought him back to his senses. It is too soon for that, he
admonished himself, much too soon. He sat up straight,
pulled down his waistcoat, flicked the reins over the
backs of the horses, and moved forward to catch her up.
She moved to one side of the road as she heard the carriage, but didn't look around or slow down.

"I take it you've decided to return home," he said conversationally as he came up beside her.

She whirled around and stared up at him. After a moment she replied, levelly, "For the night only."

He gazed down at her silently for a moment as he digested the implications of her answer. He felt unequal to dealing with it at the moment, so he ignored it.

"Have you decided what excuse you will make for your long, unexplained absence?" he enquired, with only the smallest tinge of irritation colouring his voice.

"Why, I had thought I would say I'd decided to take Alexander for some air and lost my way," she replied pertly.

"Get in!" he ordered abruptly.

She gazed up at him steadily for a long moment and then, without a word, walked over and handed up her box and the birdcage, before climbing in herself, ignoring his hand outstretched to help her. After a tense silence, he demanded "I would like to hear what maggots in your brain prompted this caper-witted trick!"

"If you are going to begin abusing me, I shall get down immediately. I would prefer to walk," she said firmly.

"I'm strongly of a mind to administer the beating you deserve for this idiocy, so I would advise you not to provoke me!" he warned.

"You do not frighten *me*," she returned, rounding on him. "If you touch me I shall scream—very loud! How dare you threaten me, anyway? I suppose I may go out if I choose without applying to you for permission. I assume I'm not being held *prisoner* at Miss Tyne's?"

"Since it seems not to have occurred to you, I will point out that you are her guest, and even you will be constrained to admit she has treated you as an honoured one. To repay her by causing her worry and suspense is a childish, bird-witted—"

"Don't call me bird-witted! I dislike it excessively and I will not have you calling me that ever again. And also, it seems not to have occurred to *you* that I might like to be consulted about my own future. No! You high-handedly decide I am to stay with your aunt, just as you decided I could be useful to you in Vienna and carted me off without so much as a 'by-your-leave!' You always treat me that way—as though I were a—a—*thing!* Never a word of respect or kindness—to say nothing of *gratitude!*"

"Ah-ha! Gratitude! So that's it! I had thought I was making up to you now for all you've done for me—but I see gowns and balls and new friends are not enough for—"

"A simple 'thank you' would have been sufficient," she replied with dignity, "though I doubt you will ever be capable of saying it. I must say I find it a serious defect in your character—it goes with excessive pride, I suspect. If the gowns and everything were meant as repayment of debt, I thank you, but I'm not a child who needs to be given treats if she's a good little girl, and I don't intend to allow you to treat me so anymore. I'm sorry if I caused your aunt distress, and Miss Clark, too, but I couldn't tell them my plans or they wouldn't have allowed me to leave."

"But why leave? Were you not surrounded by everything that love and care and money could provide? What is it you want? I should be happy to hear some reasonable explanation of why you found all this so disagreeable that you had to leave it!"

"I decided it was time for me to make my own way in life," she replied simply.

"Living on a barge with your old nurse is making your own way, I suppose?" he asked with terrible irony.

"I was only going to stay there till I could earn money. I was going to Covent Garden tomorrow morning to ask for an audition to sing. I hope I don't flatter myself too much when I think I sing at least as well as the ladies I heard there last week," she replied stiffly, her chin thrust up belligerently, daring him to deny it after the use he'd made of her talent in Vienna.

"Better in most cases—but the life would not suit you. You're much too innocent to take care of yourself in that crowd of thrusting egotists."

"I could learn! And anything is better than waiting around for you to marry me off!" she cried, stung into saying more than she meant to.

"Marry you off? *Now* what bee have you got in your bonnet, Miss Clunch?" he asked in what was, to her, his old belittling way.

Furious, she threw caution to the wind. "Oh, don't bother to deny it. Telling your aunt to dress me up and drag me about town like a prize mare at an auction, just to get me off your conscience so you can go your own way. I'm tired of feeling like an incubus that needs to be gotten rid of! I'm tired of people trying to marry me off! I don't need to be married off! So you go right ahead and marry your precious Lady Hester and don't feel any obligation concerning me. I wish you happy!"

"Marry Hester? Well, I thank you for your felicitations, but they are unnecessary, for I have no intentions of marrying Hester."

"—and if you ask me, I think—" she was rushing ahead unheeding for a moment before the import of his answer reached her brain. She stopped abruptly, closed her gaping mouth, then opened it again, "Then wh—" she began before closing her lips firmly over the question that rose irrepressibly and quivered on her tongue. She would not give him the satisfaction of thinking it mattered one whit to her *whom* he married. "I suppose you do not mean to keep me sitting here in the cold all night?" she finally asked icily, "I do not complain for myself, you understand, but I fear poor Alexander will take a chill. He is unused to the night air."

"Alexander may go to the devil! We will sit here until I am assured you have come to your senses, and I will require your promise that—"

"I'll promise you nothing! Why should I? All you want is for me to sit passively with my hands folded like a well-bred young English girl until your aunt can snare a husband for me. I'd rather snare my own husband, if you don't mind!"

"I don't mind in the least. Have you someone in

mind?" he returned politely. She turned angrily away
from him on the seat and stared fixedly into the dark.
"Now, listen to me Letty," he said in a more gentle
voice, "I am *not* going to marry Hester, and even if I
were, that would be no reason for me to try to marry
you off. Please stop enacting for me these Cheltenham
tragedies and be sensible."

She remained stubbornly staring away from him for a
moment before saying, in an unconvinced tone of voice,
"Well, I know your great-uncle is very anxious for you
to marry, for I heard him tell you so in Vienna, and I
heard him say what a f-fine wife she'd m-make," she
maintained, resolutely swallowing the lump rising in her
throat.

"Well, if you'd kept your ear pressed to the door
panel for a moment longer you'd have heard my answer
to that. Serves you right for eavesdropping. No, no—
don't bother to try the outraged innocence look on me,
for I remember that discussion with my great-uncle very
well, and you were definitely not in the room at the
time!"

She ignored this, hoping the darkness hid her blush of
shame, and said as scornfully as possible, "So I suppose
you've set him to comb the *ton* for a worthy bride for
the next Lord Aubrey!"

"I've no need for any assistance there, thank you. I've
chosen her already," he snapped.

"And of course she'll be the pick of the Season's crop
who'll swoon gratefully at your feet for the honour of
having been chosen! Really, you are the *most* arrogant—"

"And you're the most impertinent sauce-box—"

"Who is she?" she cried, beyond caution.

"*You*, you ninny!" he shouted, goaded beyond endur-
ance.

The words rang incomprehensibly in her ears, effectively silencing her for quite ten seconds before she
stuttered, "Y-y-you—b-but you don't—when did you—
you—?"

He looked into the beautiful face turned up to his in just the same way she'd looked the first night he saw her, and knew himself lost. He'd meant to go very slowly with her, to give her time to meet other men, but now the thought was unbearable.

"Quite early on, I think—I just didn't recognise it—didn't want to—the last thing I needed in my life was *that* sort of complication!"

"Well, you needn't make it sound so odious," she protested indignantly, "and I still don't know why you couldn't have said *something*—you were so—so—blighting all the time!"

"What would you have me do? I suppose you think it would have been wonderful for a man who earned his living at cards and was denied entree to every decent drawing room in London to make love to an innocent young girl with no family to protect her!"

"Oh Harry! What a—a—bird-wit you are! As though that would have mattered to me!"

"Exactly!" he said drily.

"When did you know—for sure?" She had to know the answer to that first and most important question of all lovers.

"After you eloped with that loose-screw, Radoczy."

"Oh pooh! I knew *long* before that," she said loftily. "But then why did you wait—after your great-uncle came and everything was settled—"

"Mostly thanks to you—what an unshakable little terrier you are when you get your teeth into something!"

She brushed this aside, gratitude being the last thing she was interested in now. "But *why* didn't you?"

"I discussed it with Great-uncle and he agreed with me that you were very young and had had no chance to enjoy life or meet other eligible men. We thought it only fair to give you some time in London Society as an unattached girl."

"But I never wanted to be unattached," she interrupted eagerly, "not since—since—very soon after we got to Vienna."

"Yes, I remember how quick you were to accept Radoczy's proposal," he replied, with a touch of bitterness.

"And what of you last night with Lady Hester! I'm sure I was not the only one at the ball who expected to learn of your engagement within the week!"

"Why must you continually be bringing up Hester? A person can't even propose to you without hearing of Lady Hester!" he said plaintively, as one sorely tried.

"You haven't made me a proposal," she pointed out primly, "and besides—you've never made the least push to engage my affections, so—"

His hand shot out and clamped around her wrist. "I cannot think where you learned such a missish way of speaking. Now stop it and kiss me," he demanded, pulling her across the seat to him.

"Well, you *haven't* proposed," she insisted, "and what is more, you haven't even told me you love me yet, and I—"

His mouth came down firmly over hers, and her protest, naturally, stopped. For some moments the silence was broken only by the soft moan she gave as she felt her lips melt beneath his, in a way quite unlike the experience with Count Radoczy!

Nevertheless, she finally pulled away from him, gasping, as though there had been no interruption, "—and I want you to say it."

He pulled her roughly back but she held her hands firmly against his chest. "Tell me!"

"You don't need to be told, Miss Malapert, you know well enough—" he murmured, his mouth reaching hungrily for hers.

"But I need to *hear* it," she insisted inexorably.

"Oh, for God's sake, Letty! You know I adore you! I love you! I *love* you! Now will you kiss me?" he shouted.

Letty sat in delighted amazement as the glorious words echoed about the streets, repeating and repeating them back to her. Before the last echo had died away she was obediently, enthusiastically, complying with his request.

Alexander removed his head from beneath his wing and chirruped grumpily at this disturbance, but was ignored. It became quiet again after a moment, so he rearranged himself and resumed his nap.

About the Author

THOUGH SHE WAS born in Ohio, Miss Darcy is very much at home in her special world, Regency England. So much so that readers of her novels find it hard not to believe that she was born and reared in the best Society of that day. Romantic, gay, intriguing, her books—from *Victoire* to *Eugenia*—are enchanting delights.

![Signet logo]

SIGNET Regency Romances You'll Enjoy